Fiction Catalog

MURDER AT THE WATERGATE

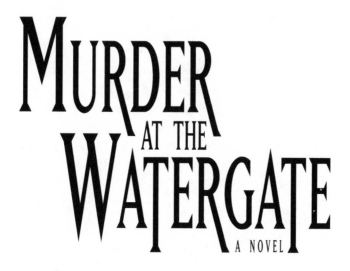

MURDER AT THE WATERGATE

A NOVEL

MARGARET TRUMAN

RANDOM HOUSE NEW YORK

LIBRARY OF CONGRESS CATALOGING–IN–PUBLICATION DATA

Truman, Margaret
Murder at the Watergate/by Margaret Truman.
p.   cm
ISBN 0-679-43535-2 (acid-free paper)
I. Title.
PS3570.R82M7547   1988   813'.54—dc21   98-3725

Random House website address: www.randomhouse.com

Printed in the United States of America on acid-free paper

24689753
First Edition
Book design by Caroline Cunningham

For my grandson,
Gates Bennett Daniel,
with love from Gammy

"We thank Mr. Nixon every day!"

—A longtime Watergate employee

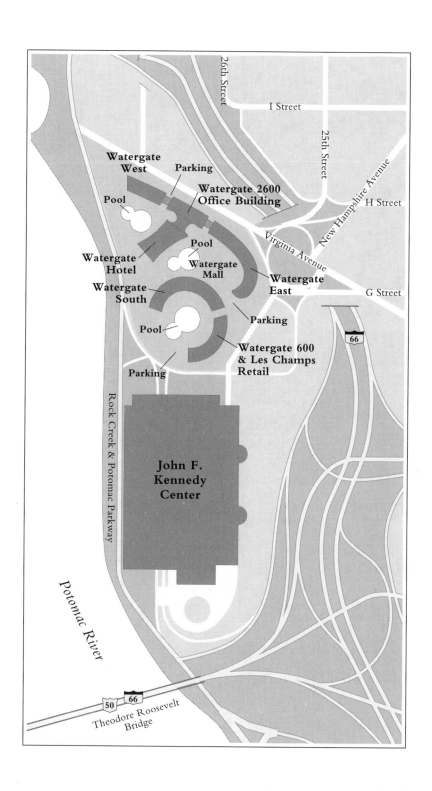

MURDER AT THE WATERGATE

CHAPTER 1

A Saturday

The South Building—the Watergate

"... and so Annabel and I decided it was time to make the move, although not, naturally, without months of debate."

Mackensie Smith, tenured professor of law at George Washington University, stood on the terrace of the three-bedroom co-op apartment he and his wife, Annabel, had recently purchased at the prestigious albeit infamous Watergate complex.

The terrace afforded a magnificent view of the Potomac River, ripples of water like crinkled aluminum foil, whipped up that evening by a brisk breeze. A few boats, manned by diehards refusing to acknowledge that summer was effectively over, added their V-shaped wakes to the scene as they headed downriver, the spires of Georgetown University behind them as their Gothic scrim.

"I know what really tipped the balance," said a guest at Mac and Annabel's housewarming party.

"What's that?" Mac really didn't want to hear but played the conversational game with his colleague from the law school, whose penchant for putting a negative spin on everything was as entrenched as his love of cognac and cigars. The latter vice had kept him out on the terrace for most of the party.

"You sold your house over on Twenty-fifth Street before your employer—*our* employer—could gobble it up."

The university had made a recent and, some said, aggressive move to buy up as much of surrounding Foggy Bottom as possible to accommodate its growing student population. GW was already the second largest landowner in Washington, trailing only the federal government, and its land-grabbing frenzy, as its detractors saw it, had dramatically begun to change the look and character of Foggy Bottom, home to the Kennedy Center, the State Department, the university, and the venerable Watergate complex.

"The Watergate is the last bastion of escape," Mac's colleague added. "Pretty soon they'll dig a moat around it and raise the drawbridges."

Mac grunted. He was not about to debate the issue. The fact was that he and Annabel had decided to sell their neat little row house on Twenty-fifth Street a year before GW launched its expansion project. And he hadn't exaggerated about months of debate before making the decision.

Why *had* they decided to give up the house for an apartment at the Watergate? Primarily, it had to do with wanting to get out from under the demands the house made on them. There was always something to be repaired, torn down, shored up, added to, or painted, and they simply did not have the time to keep pace with it. Mac had become increasingly busy. Not only did he have his classes to teach, he'd accepted an invitation by his good friend Joseph Aprile, vice president of the United States, to join a special commission to study relations between the United States and its important southern neighbor, Mexico. When Mac signed on to the commission, the position was presented as involving minimal time and work.

But it had turned out to be more than that, like being on everyone's mailing list once you've made a purchase from a catalog. In Washington, one commission invariably led to another, and so he'd ended up also as part of a group of American citizens and quasi-government officials who would be traveling to Mexico to join delegations from other countries to monitor the nation's upcoming elections, hosted by Mexico's Civic Alliance, and sponsored by the United Nations and the U.S. National Endowment for Democracy. Fortunately, Mac's dean at the law school saw the public relations value of having one of his esteemed professors engage in such important, visible acts of public service, and assured him he needn't worry about missing as many classes as necessary. "You make us all proud," said the dean, ever the sycophant.

Mac's schedule wasn't the only crowded one. Annabel's Georgetown gallery, which featured pre-Columbian art, had recently expanded into an adjacent empty store, and she'd been traveling more than usual, seeking new pieces for the added space.

"Isn't the view wonderful?" Annabel said, joining them on the terrace. The setting autumn sun caught her auburn hair, spinning it into a burnished copper work of art.

"Nice view," their guest said, "although I wouldn't have bought an apartment in the south building. Yes, I know, you paid a premium for the view of the river. And don't misunderstand. I appreciate a pretty sunset as much as the next guy. But you'll never be able to use this terrace in the afternoon in the summer, not with the sun setting on this side."

A jet on its final approach to National Airport came screaming up the river, the whine of its powerful engines rendering conversation difficult.

"That, too," said their nihilistic friend. "I would have bought something over on the east side. They say the apartments in the east building are bigger."

Mac and Annabel glanced at each other.

"I imagine the parking space downstairs set you back a pretty penny."

"It came with the apartment," Mac said.

"Lucky you. How much did it boost the price?"

None of your business, Mac thought. I'd like to boost you over the side. The parking space in the underground garage, the previous owner's property and included in the purchase price, had increased what they'd paid for the apartment by forty-five thousand dollars.

"I think Elfie is about to leave," Annabel said to Mac. "Come say good-bye."

They stepped through the open French doors into the spacious, and more positively charged, living room and went to where three people were in animated conversation.

"Mac, darling, I was afraid you'd fallen off the terrace," Elfie Dorrance said, placing long, delicate, bejeweled fingers on his arm.

"Not ready to take the leap yet," Mac said. "But I was thinking of doing a little pushing."

"Elfie was just telling us about the fund-raiser tonight for Joe Aprile." Herman Winkler was a career State Department employee in the Latin American division.

"Convenient for you two," Winkler's wife, Helen, said to the Smiths, "being so close to Joe Aprile's campaign headquarters."

"And close to Bernie, our dentist," Mac said. "Never have to worry about a midnight toothache."

"To say nothing of the hotel." Annabel smiled. "They'll send us room service any time we want it."

"Did they cater this little gathering?" Elfie asked.

"No," Mac said. "*We* catered it."

"You ought to go into the business."

Elfie Dorrance was sixty-four years old, a tall, physically fit woman with a perpetual tan whose ranking on Washington social and power lists never strayed far from the top. Married four times, three of the four to wealthy, politically consequential men, she often seemed to dominate the District's social scene, spearheading charity events for the opera, the symphony, the National Theater, a home for battered women, the Washington Canoe Club, and the tony St. Albans School, which was part of the National Cathedral. But perhaps most intriguing was her magnetic fund-raising for politicians with whom she chose to align herself, most recently Joseph Aprile, whose chances to garner the next Democratic presidential nomination were considered secure, or as secure as anything can be in politics.

Elfie's lifestyle reflected her money and position. Her Georgetown home, adjacent to the lovely grounds of Dumbarton Oaks, was the scene of some of the city's most lavish parties. Her approach to entertaining ran contrary to that of Washington's former hostess-with-the-mostest, Pamela Harriman, now deceased. Harriman believed that every social event should be driven by a "serious agenda." Elfie was more in tune with Sally Quinn's advice: "If you don't care about having fun, then have a meeting." Extravagant parties were also routinely held at her other homes, one in London, the other in San Miguel de Allende, nestled in the mountains of old, colonial Mexico.

Elfie Dorrance was many things, including an inveterate flirt.

"If I were to fall off the Washington Monument, Elfie Dorrance would be after you in a second," Annabel said to Mac on more than one occasion.

"She is interesting" was his usual reply.

"Beautiful and rich and cunning," Annabel said. "But I suspect she'll be married again before I ever take that fall, so I really don't worry about losing you."

"Thanks for the vote of confidence."

What Mac didn't say was that Dorrance's beauty, and charm, and money, and access to places and people unavailable to mere mortals, gave her the sort of allurement with which lesser females simply couldn't compete.

"Must run, God's work awaits me," Elfie said, laughing. "The catering staff at the hotel is top-notch, but you still have to oversee every detail. At least I do."

"Which is why your affairs—events—always come off without a hitch," Annabel said, wishing she hadn't used the original term. Elfie's wide smile, exposing as fine a set of teeth as one was likely to see in Washington, said she'd picked up on Annabel's inadvertent indiscretion.

"I love the fact you're living here," she said. "Having a Watergate address simply suits the two of you. The apartment is lovely. Your decorator did a superb job."

"You're looking at the decorator," Mac said, indicating Annabel. Their only help had been suggestions from friend and art connoisseur Bill Wooby, of the Washington Design Center.

"Wonderful to see you, Elfie," Mac said. "Thanks for gracing our little housewarming."

"And I'll be seeing you in a few hours at the hotel. I thank you in advance for gracing *my* little drumbeater for the next president of the United States."

Annabel walked Elfie to the elevator. When she returned, she went directly to the kitchen to answer the ringing phone.

"Annabel. It's Carole."

"Hi. How are you?"

"Fine. How's the party going?"

"Good. About to break up. Elfie Dorrance just left. All set for the big evening?"

The wife of the vice president, Carole Aprile, said she could do without it. "Fund-raisers always set me on edge. Not a good thing for a politician's wife to admit."

Annabel laughed. She and Carole Aprile had been college roommates, and had kept in touch through the years. Becoming the second lady of the land had cut seriously into the time the two friends could spend together in Washington, but they kept in frequent touch by phone, and enjoyed what opportunities they could to see each other.

"I'm dying for you to see the apartment, Carole. We're still adjusting to posthouse life, but it's shaping up nicely. The one having the biggest problem is Rufus."

Now, a giggle from Carole. "And how is your Great Blue Dane, the world's biggest dog?"

"Still sniffing out his new surroundings. At least he hasn't decided yet to stake out his territory with a lift of the leg. It's actually harder on Mac. We used to just let him out into that postage-stamp backyard we had on Twenty-fifth Street. Now—"

"Mac?"

"No, Carole, Rufus." Both women giggled. "Mac walked him sometimes but that backyard was a godsend. Now he has to be walked all the time. But Mac puts a positive spin on it, says it gets him out a little more."

"I won't keep you, Annabel. Love to Mac. See you tonight?"

"Wouldn't miss it."

Mac and Annabel had been enthusiastic boosters of Joe Aprile when he was chosen as running mate to the now sitting president. It was a second term for both men, which meant the president could not run again, leaving the field open for his capable and popular vice president. The Smiths' support, modest financially, intensely ideological, had far more to do with their belief in the administration than their personal friendship with Joe and Carole. The administration had taken the country in the right direction in general, they felt, and they supported it without hesitation or reservation. That their good friend might one day sit in the Oval Office was a heady contemplation.

The last of the guests departed, leaving Mac and Annabel alone on the terrace. Hand in hand, they looked out over the darkening Potomac.

"Successful party," he said.

"We always have successful parties," said Annabel. "We're the perfect host and hostess."

"I wouldn't argue with you, although I'd hate to do it for a living. I don't know how Elfie does it, a party every night, sometimes three a day."

"It's in her genes. She has party DNA. She thrives on it."

"Well, I don't. I think I'll take Rufus for a walk, then get dressed for the gala."

"It's not a gala, Mac, just five hundred rich people wanting to press Joe's flesh and shove money into his pockets."

"You have a wonderful way of summing things up. Joe wants me to meet him at his office before the party. How convenient, a one-minute walk, underground if it rains. We'll catch up in their suite."

"Right."

Mac returned to the living room, where Rufus was napping noisily in front of a couch. "Come on, big guy, let's take a walk and have a talk. But no politics. And no comments about not being able to use the terrace in summer, or jet noise. Not if you ever want to eat again."

CHAPTER 2

The Fairfax Room–the Watergate Hotel

The Secret Service had designated the Fairfax Room, one of the hotel's fourteen private conference rooms, as its command post for the evening. Because it was adjacent to the ballroom, the larger space created by rolling back partitions between the Monticello, Continental, Chesapeake, and Mount Vernon rooms, it was a perfect location for an ops center, and had been used as such for many events.

In charge of the detail that evening was veteran Michael Swales, who'd been providing security for presidents and vice presidents for fourteen years. He'd seen the nation's leaders in every aspect of their lives, including moments of intense private vulnerability. He had tales to tell but never did, unlike some of his colleagues, who, when off-duty, couldn't resist swapping stories about the families they served, confident their words would remain between them.

Swales had just returned to the Fairfax from a walk-through when a voice said into his ever-present earpiece, "We've got an alert on Straight Arrow."

"Explain," Swales said into his tiny lapel microphone.

"Intelligence report from the Company. Out of Mexico City. Pigeon says there's a plot to attack Straight Arrow."

Maybe the CIA was onto something, Swales thought. You couldn't always depend on "the Company's" intelligence but you couldn't ignore them, either.

"Tonight?"

"Not clear. It just came in."

"More details?"

"Negative. Kick security up a notch. That's from the boss."

"Roger. Add personnel?"

"Being dispatched now. Ten minutes."

"Okay. Straight Arrow's heading for his office in the six hundred, then to his suite. I'll send some additional bodies up. Have the new troops report to me in Fairfax."

"Shall do."

"Always some nut out there," Swales's second-in-command said. And indeed there always seemed to be, in one place or another, some plot or other, some storm brewing.

"Mexico City," Swales muttered. "The veep doesn't have a lot of fans there these days."

His colleague smiled. "And they let you know how they feel. Pitura said this morning that the two most popular Mexican sports, after bullfighting, are kidnapping and assassination."

Swales, an inveterate animal lover who owned three dogs, all strays rescued from the city's mean streets, said, "There are hobbies a lot more civilized. Any loose ends?"

"No."

"There's Mexicans on the kitchen and serving staffs."

"All cleared. Police checks on everybody. You know how this place operates, Michael. They run a tight ship."

"Check the route in again from the entrance to the ballroom," Swales said.

"Okay. Think he'll make it?"

"Who? Make what?"

"Straight Arrow. Think he'll be president?"

"Probably." And he muttered to himself, "As long as we keep him alive."

CHAPTER 3

The West Building—the Watergate

Chris Hedras was groggy, felt like roadkill.

He'd been up all night with strategy planners for the Aprile for President committee, and had continued working throughout the morning and early afternoon. Finally, a chance for some sleep, if only a few hours.

Although Joe Aprile had not officially declared himself a candidate, only the most naive of Washingtonians didn't know that he intended to seek the nomination. It was never too early to put a campaign into motion, even for an undeclared candidate.

The topic of fund-raising had dominated most of last night's skull session. Hedras, thirty-five years old and arguably the handsomest member of the president's inner circle—*Washingtonian Magazine* had recently crowned him that—stood in his bathroom and brought his face closer to the mirror. The dark circles under his eyes were real, as though ink had penetrated the skin from beneath. He knew when he'd accepted the president's call to become deputy chief of staff that it would be an exhausting four years, assuming he lasted that long.

It hadn't been an easy decision for him to make. He'd carved a nice niche for himself in Boston's Democratic machine, parlaying a sterling academic record at Harvard, natural charm and good looks, and his father's few remaining contacts into positions of leadership, to the extent of even running for office himself one day, perhaps.

It was when he accepted the post of state chair for the president's second run for the White House that the name, face, and potential of Christopher Hedras became known outside of Massachusetts. Although no one expected the president, a Democrat, to lose in liberal Massachusetts, the margin of his victory stunned even the most jaded of political pundits. Chris Hedras was a rising star, the sort of young man this president liked to have around.

"Deputy chief of staff? The White House?" Hedras's girlfriend of the moment exclaimed after he'd told her of the call from Washington. They'd met for drinks at Brandy Pete's before heading for dinner at a friend's house.

"*A* deputy chief of staff," Hedras corrected. "Not *the* deputy chief. Not yet, at least."

"You're going to accept?"

"Sure. And if you treat me right, I'll invite you to stay over in the Lincoln Bedroom. I always wanted to make it in a place like that. You know, the middle of Grand Central Station, first class on a plane, the White House."

She laughed, but knew he wasn't saying it in jest. With all his education and privileged upbringing, there was a Rabelaisian streak in him that sometimes caused her discomfort. But not that night. The sexual aggressiveness he demonstrated later, back at his Cambridge apartment, was welcome, and encouraged.

She was one of but many young Boston women in Hedras's life who, once he left for Washington, became just vague, pleasant memories, replaced by Washington's glut of single women. Finding suitable female companionship was easy for Chris Hedras. It was carving out time for them that posed his biggest problem. Despite knowing what he was in for when he agreed to come to Washington, he'd never dreamed the work would be quite this relentless, this all-consuming.

He groaned as he raised his hands high above his head and stretched. He didn't need a lot of sleep, but two hours didn't do it. "You need your beauty sleep, baby," he said to his mirror image, again scrutinizing the effects a chronic lack of sleep was having on his square, planed face, topped by a shaggy helmet of black curls. Working for any president was a young man's game, young woman's, too, unless you were a senior advisor type, who caught plenty of sleep in airplanes while traveling the world giving advice to leaders who didn't want it, and cozying up to those to whom you wouldn't give the time of day if your job, and the nation's well-being, didn't demand it.

He tossed his blue terry-cloth robe onto a stool and was about to step into the shower when there was a knock on the bathroom door.

"In a minute," he said loudly.

The door opened and a fine, aquiline nose led a pretty face through the gap.

"I'm leaving."

"Yeah," Hedras said, not attempting to shield his nudity from her. Why bother? They'd been naked in bed for the past three hours, one of which he was awake for and remembered.

"You'll call me?"

"Yeah, only not soon. Craziness for the next couple of weeks. I'll call you at the office."

She formed a kiss on her lips and made a loud smacking sound.

"Take care, Cindy. And tell that guy from Agriculture to stop hitting on you or I'll punch him out. Stay away from farmers—they're always looking for more support."

She groaned and closed the bathroom door. A moment later he heard the door to his apartment open, and shut.

Cindy was a junior partner at a DC law firm. She and Chris had met only a week ago, but it hadn't taken even that long for them to fall into bed. Hedras appreciated women like Cindy. She was as caught up in the whirl of the nation's capital as he was, didn't make demands, and was willing to engage in a relationship dictated by respective schedules and needs. No time for developing a relationship even approaching meaningful. You caught your intimacy in short bursts and when you could, like grabbing a catnap between meetings.

A half hour later, he stood at his living room window and looked down at Virginia Avenue. Across the street was the Howard Johnson's Premier Hotel, where lookouts for the Watergate burglars had hunkered down in Room 723 to peer out at the 2600 office building. Located adjacent to Hedras's apartment building, it had been home to the Democratic National Committee and target of the Liddy-Hunt-McCord break-in team that broke in, bungled, and was discovered, providing reason after the cover-up for President Nixon to resign.

It had been over twenty-five years since that fiasco took place, but it still resonated. Room 723 had been turned into a mini break-in museum, with a brass plaque, newspaper stories framed on the walls, and bookings at premium prices to voyeurs wanting to see what the lookouts had seen. The Watergate Hotel had celebrated the twenty-fifth anniversary of the break-in by offering "Break-In" packages, replete with a complimentary copy of *All the President's Men,* the Woodward and Bernstein version of the event. Tourists still stood outside the 2600 building and gaped, took pictures, asked, "Is this where the break-in happened?"

One thing was certain. President Richard Nixon and his Watergate "plumbers" had put the Watergate complex on the map. Interest was so intense that the hotel's management had its name and logo removed for a period of time from everything that couldn't be nailed down. And as one longtime employee was fond of saying, "We thank Mr. Nixon every day!"

Hedras surveyed clothing in his closet. Suit, or sport jacket and tie? The former, he decided. People would be dressed to the nines if they intended to go from the fund-raiser to the eight-thirty Placido Domingo concert at the Kennedy Center, a few minutes' walk from the hotel. The party for Aprile had been scheduled so as not to conflict with the great tenor's performance.

Hedras chose a dark blue suit with muted stripes, pristine white shirt, blue tie with tiny red birds on it, and highly polished black loafers. He left the apartment and rode the elevator down to the lobby.

"Evening, Mr. Hedras," Bob, the desk clerk, said.

"Hi, Bob. Anything for me?"

Bob turned and checked the wall of boxes in which mail for the building's tenants was sorted. "No, sir."

Hedras could have taken the elevator to the basement and walked underground through the parking garages to the hotel, but the weather was nice. He preferred to get a little air before being cooped up yet again with movers and shakers trying to corner him to get their messages across to the veep. That's what he disliked most about the job of helping guide Aprile's run for the White House, having to suffer all the rich fools who thought

that in addition to money, they had the answers to every domestic dilemma and international crisis, and who weren't reti-
cent about making their views known. That's what their checks
bought, somebody's ear. For Chris Hedras, the debates that had
been going on for years about reforming the way campaigns
raised money was a waste of time, energy—and, yes, money. It
was politics; you needed money to run, and those giving it to
you damn well would have their moment in court. Those who
were out moaned about the unfairness of the system. Those who
were in weren't about to change what got them there. If avoiding hypocrisy were high on his agenda, Washington, DC, was the
last place he would work.

It wasn't. There were more urgent things to worry about.

He stopped for a moment in the Watergate's circular driveway
at the main entrance to chat with the doorman, who'd been
with the hotel for more than twenty years, then went through
the doors and paused in the lobby.

"Good evening, Mr. Hedras," the guest relations manager said
from behind her desk.

"Good evening."

"Big night," she said.

"It's supposed to be."

They stopped talking as Placido Domingo, surrounded by an
entourage, came in from the other direction. Two black stretch
limousines waited outside, engines purring, doors open.

"I wish I could sing like him," Hedras said.

She laughed. "He just bought an apartment here. He's the
new artistic director of the Washington Opera. He's so sexy."

"Oh, yeah? What about me?"

"What about you?"

"Don't you think I'm sexy?"

She waved her hand in a way that said she'd heard that kind
of talk from him too many times before. He grinned, walked in

the direction of the small reception desk, took a quick right before reaching the Potomac Lounge, and went down a carpeted, circular staircase to the next level, where the public rooms were located. He was stopped at the foot of the stairs by two Secret Service agents.

"Hello, John," Hedras said.

"Mr. Hedras, how are you this evening?"

"Great. Everything buckled down?"

"Yes, sir. Always is."

Hedras looked to his left, where a contingent of other agents had fanned out. This was the second entrance to the hotel, the one used by dignitaries and celebrities to avoid the busy main lobby.

"Excuse me," Hedras said, continuing down a long carpeted hallway leading to the public rooms, including the 6,500-square-foot ballroom with huge windows overlooking the Potomac. Agents were posted at regular intervals along his route. There was something satisfying about being recognized by them and not being challenged. The black-and-gold pin in his lapel was his grail; with it he could approach even the president. That little piece of metal made you feel powerful, made you feel good. On the other hand, he occasionally felt a twinge of resentment at the Secret Service agents guarding the president and vice president. If they wanted to, for any reason deemed necessary for security, they could stop him, detain him, even whisk him away, little black-and-gold pin or no pin. Of course, they wouldn't do that, considering his position as one of the president's men, now on loan to the campaign of the man likely to be next to occupy the "People's House."

"Chris," a young woman said. She was a member of the campaign's meeting-planning committee, and had been working 'round-the-clock with the hotel's catering people to set up the event.

"Hey, Janet. How's everything?"

Her long, dramatic sigh said it all. "I'll be glad when this one is over and we're all rich."

Hedras passed her and went to the ballroom entrance, where dozens of hotel employees were putting finishing touches on tables. Although it would not be a sit-down dinner, plenty of tables had been provided for those wanting to get off their feet, or wishing to confer with others more comfortably.

Elfie Dorrance was on the other side of the room speaking with characteristic animation to the Watergate's sales and catering manager. When she spotted Hedras, she abruptly ended her conversation and came to him in her trademark self-assured, regal manner; Elfie Dorrance was as graceful as she was handsome.

"Christopher, darling, I wondered where you were. You're generally early."

"I was up all night, caught a few hours' sleep."

"Come with me," she said, touching his arm and leading him from the ballroom to a room off the hallway called the Crescent Bar, which at one time was open to the public but was now reserved for the cocktail portion of weddings and other social events.

"Off limits, Mr. Hedras," a Secret Service agent on duty said.

"Just a few minutes," Hedras said. "We need a quiet place."

The agent stepped back to allow them to enter. Elfie led Hedras to a remote spot in the room, looked around unnecessarily to be sure they were alone, and said, "Thank you for straightening out the mess with Manuel."

Hedras's voice was lower. "It wasn't easy, Elfie. He can be intractable when it comes to people like Manuel."

"I know, and if Joe doesn't get off that stance it could kill his chances next November. Does he realize, Chris, that one out of every sixteen Americans is of Mexican descent?"

"Of course. Look, we both know what has to be done. But you're pushing him too hard and fast, Elfie. You know what he's like. He's easygoing until he gets a piece of gravel in his craw, like the stuff going on in—and coming out of—Mexico. Then he plants his feet, draws a damn line in the sand, and it takes tanks to move him."

She broke into a large, engaging smile. "Or some gentle persuasion. All I'm saying, Chris, is that pulling further away from the president's position on Mexico is eventually going to become public, set him at odds with the administration and, I might add, with our friends to the south. I couldn't believe it when he argued against inviting Manuel for this evening."

"He's sensitive to any contributor whose name ends in a vowel. All this talk on the Hill about investigating the president's so-called Mexico connection in the last election has him on edge. Sometimes I think he might fall off."

"This is different, Chris. Manuel Zegreda is an upstanding, successful American businessman of Mexican descent. And a citizen, I might add, who heads up an American subsidiary of a Mexican conglomerate. If he wants to give money to a presidential campaign, he's entitled to do that. It's legal."

"You know it goes deeper than that with Joe," Hedras said, glancing toward the door where Janet, of the meeting-planning committee, was waving for him to join her.

"Let's talk this out another time," he said. "The important thing is that Zegreda got his invitation and will be here. Are you staying in town for a while?"

"No. Off to London in the morning, then to San Miguel. I'll be there through the elections." She touched his tie. "Why don't you come down, relax with me a few days?"

"Relax with *you*? The last time you relaxed was when they put you out for your appendectomy. Soon, though. We'll grab some time when you're back. By the way, the president made it

official this afternoon. The veep will represent the country at the presidential inauguration in Mexico City."

"Good. You look splendid, Chris. New suit?"

"Yes. I won't bother to say you look splendid because you always do."

She kissed him on the cheek and they left the Crescent Bar, she returning to the ballroom, he to give Janet some advice on how to handle the crisis of the moment.

Mexico. Maybe he *could* wangle a trip there in advance of Aprile's official visit. A couple of days in the sun at Elfie's hillside mansion would do wonders for mind and body. He winced against a headache that had developed, decided he'd get to bed as early as possible, and alone, and headed for the elevators.

CHAPTER 4

The 600 Office Building–the Watergate

The pert, plump Mexican girl answered the phone: "*Buenas noches.* Mexican-American Trade Alliance."

It was good the office hadn't upgraded its technology to include videophones. The sour expression on her face in response to the caller's stern tone would not have been appreciated.

"He's in a meeting, Senor Zegreda. He said he is not to be disturbed."

Another series of winces as Manuel Zegreda told her why he thought she should get her boss out of the meeting.

"But, Senor Zegreda, I—"

The click of the phone caused her to hold the instrument away from her and look at it as though it had just performed a social indecency.

The door behind her opened.

"Who was that?" Valle asked. The managing director of the alliance was a stout man who wore suspenders to avoid creating a bulging belt line. Venustiano Valle's shirt was yellow, his tie brown, the suspenders black. His hair was coal black with the consistency of a shoe brush, growing unnaturally low on his forehead.

"Senor Zegreda," she said. "He wanted me to interrupt the meeting but—"

"Get him back. Where is he?"

"At his office. He said he would be there for another hour. Then he goes to the party for Senor Aprile."

"Get him back. Now!" Valle slammed the door.

Fifteen minutes later, after having spoken with Manuel Zegreda, Valle went into the hallway, turned right, and stopped at an adjacent office whose small, gold-on-wood sign also read MEXICAN–AMERICAN TRADE ALLIANCE. He rang the bell, waited impatiently until the door opened, entered, passed a section of the suite devoted to high-tech communications equipment, and went directly to a small room to the rear where a young man sat behind a desk, his sad, brooding expression straight off the pages of a men's magazine fashion spread. He looked up, leaned back in his swivel chair, and put his hands behind his head.

"Have you heard from Mexico City yet?" Valle asked, taking the only other chair in the room.

"No," the younger man said. "You know them. They never respond when they say they will."

"Zegreda is impatient."

The comment brought a trace of a smile to the younger man's face. "That is hardly news," he said.

Valle did not smile. He said in Spanish, "I don't like these gaps in communication. I don't like not knowing what they are doing. That is the way problems arise."

"I know, I know, but I can do nothing. Mexico City is aware

of the situation. I have called them four times since noon today, and sent E-mail. Each time they say the information will be coming. If you would like, I will try again."

"No, don't bother." Valle went to the window that overlooked the Kennedy Center, where cars had begun to arrive for that evening's concert by Domingo. He said without turning, "Zegreda is attending the fund-raising affair tonight. Vice President Aprile did not want him there, but our friend convinced him. The vice president is a fool, Jose. He should take lessons from the president, a man for whom pragmatism has always worked."

When Jose Chapas did not respond, Valle turned and looked at his younger colleague as a professor might at a student who'd woefully missed the point of the lesson. "Where will you be in the next hour?"

"Here."

"And what does your Senorita Flores say about you working late?"

"Laura? She works late herself."

Chapas had recently begun seeing Laura Flores, an attractive young Mexican woman working in Washington. Valle knew Laura's family back in Mexico City, particularly her father, a wealthy businessman. He knew the family well enough to be aware of Senor Flores's disappointment in his daughter, a headstrong young woman always, it seemed, leading a protest while a student in Mexico, and now stridently proclaiming her views— decidedly socialist, Valle was convinced—in Washington.

"I am going home," Valle said. "You will let me know the minute you hear. The car phone. My private number. You can always reach me."

"Of course."

Valle returned to his office, packed his briefcase, put on his suit jacket, raincoat and hat, and stopped at the reception desk to say good night to Rosa, who browsed the lavish photographs in the latest copy of *Artes de Mexico.*

"I am sorry if I was short before," he said, smiling. "The pressure. Sometimes it sets us on edge."

"No need to apologize. I know how things are these days."

"You hear from your family?"

"*Sí.* They are fine. My brother starts the university."

"UNAM?"

"*Sí.* He wanted a private university but the fees—"

"Yes, that would be expensive."

UNAM, the acronym for Mexico's state-run university, the National Autonomous University of Mexico, had been for years a hotbed of Marxist learning, particularly in its department of economics. But as the nation began to embrace free market theories—and practices—in the 1990s, enrollment at private universities, which taught more pragmatic, marketable economic theories and skills—and despite their high tuition and fees—increased by almost 200 percent, while UNAM's student population went up only a small fraction of that. Mexico's fledgling leaders sensed the direction their country was taking and were preparing for it. They'd seen too many help-wanted ads carrying the tag line: "UNAM Graduates, Please Abstain."

"If I can do anything," Valle said.

Send money, Rosa thought. *"Gracias,"* she said.

"Good night."

"Good night."

Valle retrieved his car from the parking garage beneath the office building and drove in the direction of his house in the vibrant, multicultural section of Washington called Adams-Morgan.

He and his family had moved there a year ago, after he'd been tapped to replace the previous managing director of the

Mexican–American Trade Alliance, who'd died of cancer. Although the position represented an expression of trust by his Mexico City superiors, he was reluctant to leave what had been a comfortable existence. He'd been in the right political position in 1982 to enjoy the fruits of the government takeover of the Mexican Central Bank, as disastrous as it might have been for the economy. His demonstrated loyalty to the ruling Institutional Revolutionary Party, the PRI, Mexico's "rotating dictatorship," had been rewarded through a succession of lucrative jobs at the bank, affording Valle and his family an upper-middle-class lifestyle. He'd tried to dissuade his bosses from sending him to Washington, but they'd prevailed; Mexico's economic stake in the next U.S. presidential election was enormous. A man of Venustiano Valle's knowledge and experience was needed to guide the fortunes of the trade alliance. Valle was aware it was calculated flattery, but he also knew that to refuse the post could mean a diminution of his authority at home.

"Give it two years," he was told. "Successfully carry out the alliance's mission and you will be rewarded."

One relatively uneventful year had now passed.

The second year was shaping up to be considerably less quiescent.

Chapter 5

The Ballroom—the Watergate Hotel

The Watergate Hotel's catering and sales manager seemed to some to be surprisingly young to hold such an important position, dealing day and night with Washington's most powerful personalities, many of them excessively demanding and rude. But in the two years she'd been there, she'd established herself as one of the city's most efficient and skilled purveyors of hospitality. Her energy was without bounds; she was in perpetual motion, the teasing of her sun-washed blond hair with her fingers the only sign of reacting to the job's inherent stresses. She consulted a clipboard as she gave the serving staff last-minute instructions.

"Okay, everyone should have their assignments down. The key with this group is to keep the drinks flowing and the hors d'oeuvres coming. Some of the guests will consider it dinner before heading for Kennedy Center. Vice President Aprile is scheduled to arrive about halfway through. Stay out of the way of the Secret Service. Back off when the VP arrives."

She looked at a young waitress, smiled, and said, "And no pained expressions when you're serving a smoker. We've set the tables with ashtrays in one corner, and hopefully they'll gravitate to it. But they're free to smoke anywhere, so don't go making editorial comments with your face. Got it?"

The waitress nodded.

"The baby lamb chops, crispy crab balls, and sesame chicken strips are likely to go the fastest. I've instructed the kitchen to stay ahead with those. Make sure everyone has access to the platters you're carrying, but don't intrude upon conversations. A few could determine the fate of the world. And others could fix your fate. For God's sake, don't butt heads with Mrs. Dorrance. Where she's concerned, the customer is *always* right. Any questions?"

"Should we continue to serve while the vice president is speaking?" a waiter asked.

"Sure, but keep it low-key. No noise. Don't push the platters on anybody, just be there if one of them decides he needs more substance than he's getting from the speech. Let's go."

Elfie Dorrance had taken a suite in the hotel for the evening. After making sure every subtle aspect of the affair was in order, she went to her suite, where her personal assistant, Sara, a middle-aged woman who'd been a costume designer on Broadway before falling under Elfie's spell, helped her dress. Sara was a square, plain, and pleasant woman who considered serving Elfie just an extension of her show biz past. Elfie's personal hairdresser was also there, and made last-minute adjustments to her already exquisitely arranged hair. While the hairdresser practiced her art, Sara handed Elfie the phone.

"Jason, darling, how nice to hear from you. How did you track me down?"

The caller, Jason Pauling, whose ability at self-promotion was as keenly honed as his ability to recognize young artists destined for success, was calling from his apartment on Dupont Circle.

"You make it sound as though you're a CIA spook," he said, laughing. "You always take a suite at the hotel when you're putting on one of those grotesque fund-raising events. Take their money, for God's sake, but don't touch the hand that gives it to you. They're all dirty."

"I might say the same where some of your so-called patrons of the arts are involved. Why are you calling? Is there something I can do for you? I don't have much time. I'm due downstairs."

"My dear Elfie, why do you always assume I call you when I want something from you? Of course I want something from you. When are you going to San Miguel?"

"In a few days. London first."

"Wonderful. What I would love you to do for me while you're in jolly old Mexico—I don't know why they call the British jolly; they're *soooo* serious—while you're in San Miguel, try and talk sense into that pompous ass of an artist, Salas. He's a talented slob, but he thinks he deserves prices that even Picasso wouldn't have asked at this stage of his career. I want him in the gallery, but I'll be damned if I'll represent him at those prices. And the commission he's offering me. Outrageous. I just thought you might have a word with him, tell him there's no one in the world better qualified to take him to new heights than yours truly."

"Jason, what I'll do is go to San Miguel, buy up every last one of Salas's works, and offer them to you for double what he's asking. And you know I'll strike a harder bargain than he will. Besides, your commissions have always been too high, absolutely obscene. I really must run. Nice hearing from you. We must stay in touch."

"You look lovely," Sara said after her mistress had been dressed and had chosen jewelry for the evening. She meant it; she was as much in awe of Elfie as she had been of the Broadway stars she'd served.

"Thank you." Elfie looked at herself in the mirror, turning her head left and right to view her image from every angle, and said—was it to herself in the mirror, or to her assistant?—"Do I look ambassadorial?"

When her assistant didn't respond, she turned and faced her. "To be specific, do I look like the next ambassador to Mexico?"

The assistant broke into a grin. "You look as though you could be ambassador to any nation in the world, Mrs. Dorrance."

"You're such a dear, even though I know you don't always mean what you say."

Sara was stung by the comment but the smile remained on her round face.

"Thanks for the help," Elfie said. "I'll be back here late, provided I can round up some of the A-list once the party is over. I hope they aren't all music lovers heading for the Domingo concert. Of course they aren't. Money and the arts so seldom seem to go together. Nothing like a little personal massaging to get them to realize there's more in their checking accounts than they claim. Order room service. Caviar, salmon. Some of those heavenly phyllo rolls with artichoke and goat cheese. Oh, and plenty of champagne. People are always more generous when they're celebrating something."

CHAPTER 6

Dulles Airport, Washington, DC

Morin Garza waited until the other passengers had deplaned, then slowly, wearily stood, collected his small carry-on bag from where he'd kept it beneath the seat in front of him, and headed for the 737's exit.

"Thank you for flying United," the flight attendant said.

"*Sí*. Yes. Thank you," he said, avoiding her eyes.

He stepped into the spacious terminal, stopped, and took in the hundreds of men and women going to and from flights. Had things been different, he would have gotten on the next plane back to Chicago, to Dallas, then the car to El Paso, retracing his steps of that day, possibly even crossing the border and going home.

But home to what? To whom?

It had been a month since he had left his wife and children in the middle of the night, looking back only once at his lovely Cecilia and the young son she held in her arms. They, too, would leave, in the early morning. But not to where he was going.

Their house was located in a Mexico City suburb that had sprung up on the southern edge of the sprawling city, built around Perisur, one of dozens of American-style shopping malls offering Mexicans a feast of American goods without their having to cross to *el otro lado,* the other side of the border. The house, small by American standards, but modern and nicely equipped and furnished, represented a dream for Morin Garza and his family. He'd worked hard to achieve enough status and income to afford it, starting as an organizer for the union. The Shoe Shiners' Union was one of many labor groups belonging to the state-controlled Federation of Organizations of Non-Salaried Workers. Getting the city's six thousand *boleros*—shoe shiners—to join the union wasn't difficult. You needed a union permit in order to shine shoes on the streets of the city, and the intersection to which you were assigned depended upon how much you kicked back to your union boss. That's where the real money was for Garza and others in his position. That's where the money came from to buy the new house in the clean, new suburb near the mall, where his wife and children could spend the day enjoying American fast food and shopping for American sneakers, CDs of American pop stars, and designer jeans.

Garza had done his various jobs well, and had caught the eye of the federation's president, who brought him into the larger, umbrella organization, where his authority was expanded, and by extension his ability to demand expressions of gratitude from a wider variety of union members—streetcar washers, photographers belonging to the Union of Five-Minute Photographers, or the larger Union of Photographers of Church, Social and Official Ceremonies, and the more than three thousand members of the Mexican Union of Mariachis. No longer was Morin

Garza responsible for recruiting new members. That took care of itself—if you wanted to work.

Now he found himself involved in the more important and germane task of ensuring that each member of every union paid appropriate homage to the PRI. The Institutional Revolutionary Party, whose political grip on Mexico went back to 1929, had outlasted other one-party states—the Fascists, the Nazis, and the Bolsheviks—with ease and impunity, controlling everything and everybody, including millions of union members. To belong to a union was to belong to the PRI; the shoe shiners wore blue uniforms provided by the union but sporting the PRI logo.

"Sir?"

"What?" Garza spun around at the sound of the voice.

"Can I help you with anything?" the uniformed airline employee asked.

"No. *Gracias.* No."

He had stopped, daydreaming. He looked left and right and behind as he walked hurriedly across the terminal, through the doors and to the sidewalk, where taxis and buses and cars jockeyed for position. You couldn't be too careful, even this far away from the trouble.

He scanned the handwritten signs held up by limousine drivers. For a moment, the name didn't register. ORTIZ. That was it. The name they would use.

Unlike other limo drivers, this one did not wear the requisite white shirt and black tie, nor was his car long and black. He was an American man in his thirties, with thin, golden hair the consistency of silk, a pale complexion, and watery blue eyes. He wore a tan raincoat over a suit; his vehicle was a nondescript green sedan.

"Mr. Ortiz?" he said.

"*Sí.*"

"Please."

Garza climbed into the rear. The driver came around after closing the door, deftly navigated a break in the traffic flow, and headed for Washington.

An hour later, the green car turned off New Hampshire Avenue and down into the entrance to the underground parking lot beneath the Watergate's 600 Office Building, across from the Kennedy Center, where Placido Domingo was sipping hot tea with honey in preparation for his concert.

The driver parked near a door leading into the office building, turned, said, "Wait here. Someone will be down to get you." He walked away, disappearing in the direction of the adjoining garage beneath the east building.

Morin Garza clutched his small black carry-on bag on his lap, drew a deep breath, closed his eyes, and thought of Cecilia.

Chapter 7

The 600 Office Building—the Watergate

The Aprile for President campaign headquarters in 600 New Hampshire Avenue, one of two office buildings in the Watergate complex, had been open for more than a month. It was two floors above the Mexican-American Trade Alliance.

As preparations for Christmas had been starting earlier each year, the same phenomenon had been occurring with politics, particularly on the national level. Of course, as some had observed, each new campaign began on the same day that the previous campaign ended, or earlier. Already, two other Democratic presidential aspirants, one a liberal senator from Wisconsin, the other a fence-straddling member of the House from California, had begun traveling the country making speeches to influential groups of Democrats, initiating the tortuous process of raising money, and had started their sniping at VP Aprile's stance on issues. More accurately, their attacks were on the administration itself, with Aprile suffering the fallout, as if he had engineered every issue and problem.

Claire Coyne, recently hired as press secretary for the campaign, huddled with an assistant in one of six offices comprising the suite. The remaining five offices were occupied by other staffers, each convinced that his or her role in Aprile's drive for the White House was the crucial one, that his or her insight into the electorate's psyche was the most pertinent and most valuable; failure to heed their admonitions was to ensure defeat. Embrace them and victory was in hand. They didn't express this in so many words, certainly not to Joe Aprile, but they believed it in their hearts, which was less important than the cognitive reasoning of more senior staff members, whose pacemakers were the polls.

Chris Hedras conferred with the campaign's finance chairman, Philip Hentoff, a New York investment banker, who looked older than he really was thanks to prematurely graying hair and a perpetual expression of disagreement. He'd been wooed into a leave of absence from his firm to handle things financial for the Aprile campaign, having heard the siren call of power and responded to it. He already had money. Power was the logical next acquisition in his hierarchy of needs, as psychologist Abraham Maslow might have explained.

The largest of the offices was the campaign's boiler room, where a dozen phones stood at attention on two sturdy folding tables. This was where calls soliciting money for Aprile's coffers were routinely made: "We know you've supported the administration in the past and wouldn't want to see the country be derailed by a new administration. Joe Aprile knows you, knows what you need. It's imperative he be the next president, but he needs your financial support. He's counting on you and other Americans with your values and vision to put it on the line. And believe me, he won't forget that you stood up for him and his vision of a strong and prosperous America."

Aprile had put out the word that he was not about to become ensnared in the sort of imbroglios that had dogged previous administrations. There would be no fund-raising calls from federal offices, especially the White House. Members of the administration, and certainly those working directly for the vice president, made the daily trek from the White House to the Watergate to make solicitations. "The vice president is obsessed with this," members of Aprile's staff were lectured on a daily basis. "Break the rule, even once, and you're gone."

Mac Smith sat in another office with a policy advisor and two of the campaign's speechwriters. He listened quietly as the writers argued over a line Aprile was to use in his remarks that evening. It seemed to Mac that the differences between the two versions were so minor it wasn't worth debate. Pride of authorship was, at best, quaint where the ghostwriting of political speeches was concerned. Still, Mackensie Smith, who considered himself politically astute, at least to the extent that few things surprised him, was aware that the wrong word in a speech, or even the right word interpreted the wrong way, could have serious negative impact in the media the following day. He stayed out of it.

The writers were still arguing over the line when the vice president arrived, flanked by his usual contingent of Secret Service agents. With him was his appointments secretary, an advisor on domestic policy, and a deputy chief of staff to the president who'd been promoted after Chris Hedras relinquished his official White House duties to take hands-on control of the Aprile campaign.

Wresting Hedras from the president's staff had not been easy. Negotiations had gone on for months, with the president adamantly refusing to lend Hedras to his veep's run for the

White House. But he eventually acquiesced when Aprile made a personal plea to his boss. Joseph Aprile liked Hedras. More important, he agreed with many of the young Bostonian's views on how to get elected. You stayed above the fray and applied a tolerable amount of near-demagoguery, meanwhile acting presidential, assuring those already in your camp that you wouldn't change positions on them, while indicating you might be willing to shift perspective for those who hadn't yet made up their minds. And you raised and spent money, plenty of it, hammering away on television, your face and message always there, establishing a share of the market for the product—a person named Joseph Aprile. Like laundry detergent, your brand had to promise to do a better job than the competition's. Hedras had had mixed emotions about this switch in duties. On the one hand, he was comfortable with most of the president's policies, finding them easy to defend when that was necessary. He was not as sanguine in his acceptance of some of Joe Aprile's political positions.

On the other hand, he'd begun to wilt somewhat under increasing criticism of him by other members of the president's inner circle, who painted him as arrogant, bordering on fascist. If they wanted something to reach the president's ear, Hedras was the conduit. He reveled in such power. But a call for investigations by key Republican members of Congress into alleged campaign finance abuses during the administration's last election had cast an unpleasant pall over Hedras's daily activities. It seemed that the sort of intrigues that had plagued politics for years were about to raise their ugly heads again, same script, different players. China. Now Mexico. Tomorrow, who knew? Maybe Germany, or Argentina, or some Arab country plainly, if covertly, seeking to buy influence in the American governing process.

Hedras was well aware, too, that this was a lame-duck president who would be in a position to delegate power for only another year. The future was, very likely, Joe Aprile. Successfully running Aprile's campaign meant Hedras would be able to call his shots in a new administration, a zestful contemplation for a thirty-five-year-old whose requisite energy for handling such jobs would one day wane, but certainly not for another four years. He'd learned back in Boston the need to suck it up, to always keep something in reserve when the main tank threatened to run dry. Most important, his earlier political experience had instilled in him one inviolate rule: The only person you could trust was yourself. Slaps on the back lasted only as long as you had something to give. When you no longer did, those slaps quickly turned to daggers.

Aprile came directly to the office in which the speechwriters continued their bickering. "You have my remarks?" he said, extending his hand.

The writers started making their respective cases but Aprile shut them off, waving that same hand and saying, "Give me the version I saw this afternoon."

"But Mr. Vice President, I really think—"

The victorious writer handed her version of the speech to Aprile. The other writer shrugged, leaned back in his chair, and looked at Mac, his brow knitted into a frown. Mac managed a small smile. His friend Joe not only had the reputation of being a stiff, staunch square shooter, he was decisive, a trait Mac always admired in people provided they were decisive about something with which he agreed.

"Hello, Mac," Aprile said, taking a chair one of the writers had vacated. "How was your party?"

The veep, as usual, looked fit and ready for whatever might come. Mac sometimes thought Aprile was the right man in the wrong job, too decent to spend his life in the often bitter, disingenuous world of politics. More suited to be a high school guidance counselor. But Aprile's long and successful political career testified to his political skill and backbone. You didn't aspire to the White House unless you were a warrior, no matter how genteel you appeared on the surface.

Aprile wore his customary conservatively cut dark suit, white shirt, and unremarkable tie. Although he ordered his suits custom-made from London's tony Savile Row tailor Anderson & Sheppard, they looked as though they might have come off a local department store's rack. But that was part of Joe Aprile's appeal to the masses; he didn't wear his wealth and expensive taste on his sleeve. He appeared to be the quintessential common man—which he certainly wasn't—a serious, thoughtful expression on his long, Lincolnesque face, clear, understanding green eyes, his ready smile not masking another agenda, soft brown hair cut by a local barber, not a tonsorial artiste, aka stylist. (In reality, the Watergate Hotel's resident hairstylist, Zahira, regularly traveled to Aprile's office to trim him.)

Joseph Aprile was, as Mac Smith realized long ago, the perfect political package, born to the calling and comfortable with it. "Went well, Mr. Vice President. Annabel took a page from Pat Buckley. Kept it simple, made sure it was right."

"Chicken pot pie?" Aprile asked, laughing. The wife of conservative columnist and commentator William F. Buckley was known as much for her pot pies, meticulously prepared, as for her omnipresence in fund-raising.

"No, that would have been a little too elaborate for us. We stuck to finger food. Nice crowd. Elfie made sure of that."

"Good old Elfie, everywhere at once. I think there must be a half dozen Elfie Dorrance impersonators around Washington, like society orchestra leaders who book six jobs the same night and seem to be at every one of them."

"She is dynamic, that's for certain," Mac said. "Nice to have someone like her on your side when you're running for president."

They were interrupted by Chris Hedras, who handed Aprile a sheet of paper. "These are the people I think you ought to acknowledge tonight."

Aprile shook his head as he perused the list. "Everybody in the room is on it," he said.

"I did it in classic journalistic form," Hedras said. "The inverted triangle. If you're going to lop off names, do it from the bottom up."

Aprile said nothing as he put the list in a file folder.

"A couple of minutes alone?" Hedras said.

"Sure."

Mac and the others in the room stood on cue and left. Mac went to a window in the phone room and absently looked through it. He wasn't quite sure why he was there, included in the vice president's official circle. Actually, he knew the answer. Like every leader, Joe Aprile needed to include a few people around him with whom he was at ease and who did not play a direct role. Mac had committed himself to being at Joe Aprile's side whenever summoned, no questions asked, willing to listen and, when asked, to give an opinion without worrying about its political ramifications. Joe Aprile was a friend. But Mac was also quick to admit, at least to himself, that he enjoyed a certain psychic pleasure in being close to so powerful a man, to being an invited member of his kitchen cabinet, and being allowed to share some of his more intense concerns. Like Joseph Aprile, Mackensie Smith was, among many things, human.

During the twenty minutes Joe Aprile conferred in private with Chris Hedras, Mac passed the time chatting with the loser in the speechwriter debate, who still seemed anxious to convince Mac he'd been right.

When the door opened and Aprile stepped through it, followed by Hedras, it was obvious that it had not been a pleasant conversation. Additional anger lines had been added to the vice president's handsome face. Hedras didn't look especially cheerful, either.

"See you later," Aprile said to no one in particular as he prepared to leave the offices, surrounded again by staff and protectors. He turned to Smith: "Coming with us?"

"You bet."

Mac accompanied the vice president to a suite on an upper floor, a staging area to be used before Aprile's entrance into the ballroom. Annabel would be linking up with Carole Aprile in an adjacent suite where wives readied themselves. When that plan had been announced, Annabel had commented that it sounded like an anachronistic dinner party where the men retired to a separate room for brandy and cigars while the ladies stayed at the table to discuss domestic help.

"A civilized practice that ought to be resurrected," Mac had replied.

"Like foot binding and bloodletting," Annabel said, kissing him on the cheek.

Mac thought of again being with Annabel in a few minutes. Although they'd been together just an hour ago, the contemplation of seeing her always elevated his spirits.

Chapter 8

The Ballroom–the Watergate Hotel

Invited guests had started to arrive. A Secret Service checkpoint had been established just inside the doors leading into the hotel from the lower-level entrance. A second checkpoint at the top of the winding staircase that linked the banquet-room level with the lobby floor above was also in place. There had been a debate whether to use metal detection equipment for the affair, but the decision was made that it wasn't necessary. The area had been "swept" three times in the previous two days, including a last-minute examination late that afternoon. Every access to the route the veep would take on his way to the ballroom was secure.

But now that an alert had been issued, Mike Swales wished he had those metal detectors. No time to order and set them up now. Protecting the vice president would be strictly a human endeavor.

Swales intensified his visual scrutiny of the area. He was known within the Secret Service as a belt-and-suspenders sort of agent, always looking for that extra security edge even if it meant overdoing it. Better safe than sorry. If he had his way, the president and vice president would spend their days in offices encased in bulletproof canisters. If nothing else, that would ensure that there would be no more JFK or RFK assassinations, no crackpot coming up to Reagan on a sidewalk and putting a bullet in him. No chance of something like that happening on Mike Swales's watch.

But this was a democracy, the most perfect form of government on earth—and the hardest to make work.

Because Aprile was already in the hotel, there wasn't any need to arrange for security outside the entrance doors, except for making certain that anyone pulling up in a car for valet parking had been invited—and could prove it. Aprile and his party would leave the suite and be escorted to an elevator that gave the lower floors access to the Watergate's modern health club, complete with Olympic-size swimming pool, sauna room, exercise area, and massage facilities. Downstairs, the elevator opened onto the banquet-room level in a reception area reached through two sets of sliding glass doors from the outside. Stairs down to a door leading to an underground passage to the Kennedy Center were secured by agents placed there by Swales.

The additional agents arrived at the Fairfax Room and were dispatched by Swales to where he wanted security beefed up. If he'd had his way, the hallway to the right of the reception area leading to the Watergate Hotel's acclaimed restaurant, Aquarelle, would have been shut down, too. But there was a limit to how much a commercial establishment could be put out of business to satisfy security needs. Patrons of the restaurant were met at the bottom of the circular staircase from the lobby by three agents, who guided them in the direction of the restaurant and away from the fund-raiser.

Because he'd secured so many events at the Watergate, Swales knew the layout by heart. A hundred feet of green carpet with red roses spanned the distance from the second set of sliding glass doors to the Crescent Bar, another thirty-five feet from there to the entrance to the ballroom.

When the vice president and his entourage walked from the health club elevator to the ballroom, they would pass one of multiple doors to the vast kitchen that served both special events like this one, as well as the Aquarelle's Euro-American cuisine created by German-born chef Robert Wiedmaier, who'd come to the Watergate from the competitive Four Seasons Hotel.

Ever since Sirhan Sirhan gunned down Robert Kennedy in the kitchen of the Ambassador Hotel in Los Angeles, being even in the proximity of a kitchen set Swales on edge. Some agents felt that way about the street, or stairs, or getting in and out of cars. Kitchens were Mike Swales's thing. The only one he trusted was in his home.

The door to the kitchen opened, and a waiter in a black tux emerged carrying a pile of napkins. Swales eyed him. Definitely Hispanic. Mexican? Cognitively, he knew he couldn't assume that every Hispanic was a potential assassin that night. But the CIA report had come out of Mexico City. Probably nothing to it as far as this particular evening was concerned. There were always cells of kooks planning to assassinate one leader or another, religious zealots, social misfits, righting perceived wrongs, ridding the world of their own personal devils.

He looked into the ballroom and saw Mrs. Dorrance conversing with hotel staff. She was insisting that the liquor bottles behind the multiple bars be rearranged to feature a certain brand of single-barrel bourbon produced by a major campaign donor.

Quite a gal, Swales thought. Picture always smiling out at you from the *Post*'s Style section. He'd met her a number of times, usually in conjunction with events like this, but once when she raised a lot of money for a social agency championed by his wife. A piece of work. How many husbands? How many millions?

"Mike, Straight Arrow's getting ready to come down," an agent told him.

"Okay," Swales said, casting another glance at the kitchen door. "It's showtime. Let's rock 'n' roll."

CHAPTER 9

Underground Garage–the 600 Building–the Watergate

Fifteen minutes had passed since the driver of the green sedan had left Morin Garza alone in the car in the garage beneath the 600 office building of the Watergate complex. A stream of cars had entered since his arrival, people attending the Placido Domingo concert at what they called the Kennedy Center for the Performing Arts, across the street. Then, the cars stopped coming. It was Saturday night; the offices were dark except for the Aprile for President campaign headquarters and a few foreign embassy offices. New Hampshire Avenue, at least that section of it that ran past the Watergate complex, was considered one of the safest streets in the city. Security was extensive and tight at the white-marble Saudi Arabian embassy on the other side of the avenue, a welcome additional source of safety for Watergate residents and Kennedy Center visitors. Too, the Watergate's three apartment buildings, two office buildings, and the hotel all had their own highly trained and ready security forces.

A safe place.

The metal door from the office building opened noisily. Garza, who'd almost dozed off, was startled into wakefulness. Lighting was dim, but sufficient for him to see two men come through the door and approach the car. He clasped his small overnight bag tighter to him. One man stood on the driver's side, the other came to where Garza sat. He opened the door. Garza saw that he was Hispanic. The other man was the one who'd picked him up at Dulles.

"*Buenas noches,* Senor Garza."

"*Buenas noches.*"

"Come, come. They are waiting for you."

Garza got out of the car. The Anglo joined them. "Welcome to Washington," he said.

The sound of their footsteps on the concrete floor was as resounding to Garza as the orchestra's overture to the Domingo concert across the street was to the ears of the standing-room-only audience. All of Washington, DC, was an opera that night, tales of love and lust, treachery and betrayal, power, passion, and death being played out in every corner of the city, including the prestigious, magnetic, curious complex known as the Watergate.

The curtain was about to go up for everyone.

Chapter 10

Suite 1216—The Watergate Hotel

By the time Chris Hedras took the call from Elfie Dorrance that it was time for Aprile to make his appearance in the ballroom, the vice president had relaxed. He'd left the campaign office with jaw clenched and eyes narrowed. Now Mac saw that his friend's previous tension had abated. Not that he was ever one to be called gregarious—jokes about Aprile's reserved, poker-faced demeanor were abundant in Washington. Many of his supporters said, "It's about time we had a straight arrow in the White House." He now mixed easily with two dozen associates and friends in a presidential suite. It was one of a dozen such suites, each located on a different floor. Originally built as apartments by an Italian construction firm, with major funding from the Vatican, the Watergate Hotel's suites were all oversize, with closets, bathrooms, and kitchens more appropriate to an apartment than a hotel room. Suite 1216 had been taken off the availability list three days earlier to allow the Secret Service to secure it for the veep's pre-party gathering. Brochettes of smoked duck breast, Belgian endive with Boursin cheese and toasted almonds, salmon mousse on pumpernickel bread, and assorted other hors d'oeuvres, and drinks, were served from the full kitchen by staff borrowed from the White House.

"Time to head downstairs," Hedras said.

Aprile said, "Shame to break this up."

"We could just stay here," Carole Aprile said to Annabel. She wasn't her usual radiant self, Annabel decided. Her college chum, now the nation's second lady, was known as a vivacious, ceaselessly cheerful woman with a glass-half-full personality, fond of bright colors, gospel music, and fattening cookies. But this night, although she seemed on the surface to be happy and involved, Annabel sensed an underlying solemnness that simply couldn't be explained, considering the time, place, and circumstances. Annabel wished they could find a few minutes alone.

"Not a chance," Joe Aprile said. "If I have to suffer through another fund-raiser, so do you."

"Team Aprile," Annabel said. "That's sweet."

"Don't encourage him." Carole smiled.

"Got the jokes down?" the veep's policy advisor asked, laughing.

"Did you hear the one about the vice president who got to his own fund-raiser on time?" Hedras said.

"Coming back here?" an aide asked.

"No," Carole answered. "Straight home. But the place is yours for the evening. You'll have to manage without the Secret Service."

Agents lined the hallway between the suite and the elevators. Spirits were high in the vice president's group.

"We get right in the car when it's over?" Aprile asked Hedras.

"Yes, sir, although you'll have to stay around to shake as many hands as possible, photos, the usual. Elfie has the really heavy hitters prepped. She'll keep the glad-handers to a minimum."

Aprile laughed. "Elfie Dorrance is incapable of keeping *anything* to a minimum," he said. "She thrives on conspicuous overabundance."

Mac and Annabel were directly behind the nation's second couple. Carole Aprile turned as they neared the elevators, said, "It's the shaking hands that gets to me. I was thinking a minute ago that anyone with a germ phobia could never run for office."

"That rules out Donald Trump," Mac said.

"For more reasons than that," a man behind them offered.

The protocol for the entrance had been explained in the suite. Everyone except the VP, his wife, Hedras, and three top policy advisors would ride the large guest elevators to the lobby level, then be escorted by Secret Service down the winding staircase to where the Apriles and their party would arrive by the health club elevator. The Apriles would then lead the procession down the hallway to the ballroom. Aprile's introduction would be handled by the vice chairman of the Democratic National Party, the chairman having declined the honor in order not to offend other Democrats who might contest the nomination.

Downstairs, agent Mike Swales stood with two colleagues next to the health club elevator and received a step-by-step progress report through his earpiece.

"They're getting off the main elevators. Straight Arrow and group heading for this one."

A minute later Mac, Annabel, and others descended the staircase and were lined up to one side of the elevator door.

"Straight Arrow on his way."

The door slid open. Joe Aprile allowed Carole to exit first, then followed her.

"This way, sir," Swales said, indicating the hallway leading to the public rooms.

Flanked by agents, the veep and his party followed Agent Swales's lead in the direction of the laughter, the drone of conversation, and the faint strains of a piano.

Elfie Dorrance stood at the entrance to the ballroom. As Aprile approached, she extended her arms in a grand gesture of welcome, perfect white teeth made more so against the tan of her face, head slightly cocked as if to say, "You made it, you devil." Behind her, the doorway was chockablock with guests craning to witness the veep's arrival. Agents smoothly moved them back to create a clear passage for Aprile to reach a podium with THE WATERGATE prominently printed across it. Two large American flags hung limply behind it.

As the arriving party came almost abreast of the kitchen door, Swales saw that it was opened slightly to allow two kitchen workers to peer out.

"Get that closed," he said to a young agent who hadn't noticed. The agent said something to the workers and pushed his hand against the door, closing it.

Elfie took one of Carole Aprile's hands in both of hers and offered her cheek to the vice president, which he kissed lightly. The pianist cued other members of his band and they launched into a spirited "When the Saints Go Marching In."

Guests closest to Aprile clamored for his attention and recognition. The vice president was pretty good about sticking to the script written by his Secret Service detail, but he had his moments. This was one of them. Instead of going directly to the podium, he detoured into the crowd, reaching over people to grasp the outstretched hands of others, smiling, tossing out stock greetings—"Good to see you again." "Thanks for coming." "Hey, you look great."

Mac and Annabel stood side by side just inside the ballroom's entrance, taking in the scene, their faces creased with smiles. What a remarkable spectacle this political system of ours is, she was thinking. It was natural to become skeptical of it, to find it hypocritical and distasteful, yet it was exhilarating when you were caught up in it.

"Mackensie, Annabel, this way," Elfie Dorrance said, guiding them to a spot behind the podium where Aprile was to deliver his remarks. Although they'd both known Elfie before Mac had been drawn into Joe Aprile's inner circle, and before Annabel had reestablished her close friendship with her former college roommate, they'd never been treated with the deference they now enjoyed. Elfie possessed many strengths, including a keenly honed sense of who was close to power and, more important, who could influence the powerful. That sort of behavior might be construed as disingenuous when played out by others. But somehow, it wasn't when practiced by Elfie. It *was* Elfie Dorrance, to the well-bred bone, and she had enough power of her own to pull it off with aplomb.

The DNC's vice chairman, after having greeted Aprile and his wife and leading them to the podium, made a few amplified attempts at bringing order to the room. "Ladies and gentlemen," he said, "the longer you keep talking—and drinking, I might add—the longer it will be before you hear from the next president of the United States, Joe Aprile." He glanced at Aprile for approval, received a pale smile in return.

The room eventually lapsed into a modicum of attentiveness, allowing the DNC spokesman to make his introductory remarks. Then, to boisterous applause, whistles, and shouts of encouragement, Aprile stepped to the podium, pulled his notes from his inside suit jacket pocket, and launched into what would become a boilerplate speech for the coming year.

He'd been speaking for five minutes. Mac Smith was pleased to see how relaxed his friend seemed to be. On other speaking

occasions at which Mac was present, the VP was capable of losing energy and focus, and of sounding, well, somewhat disinter-
ested. Not tonight. He was on a roll, and the gathering loved it.

"The direction this great country of ours takes in the coming
years will demand leadership characterized by integrity, commitment to values and human rights, and creating an open and
equal economic playing field on which everyone is free to compete. In addition, tomorrow's leaders will be called upon to
wield a strong hand with nations whose chosen course is in conflict with America's aspirations. . . ."

"Don't start," Hedras mumbled to himself, recognizing that
Aprile was about to deviate from the prepared text. He looked
to where businessman Manuel Zegreda stood with other
Mexican–American business leaders. Zegreda, slender and aris-
tocratic in carriage, had a drink in hand, one eyebrow raised in
editorial comment, lips set in a way that you could read as dis-
dainful or approving. It was said Zegreda looked like the recently
deceased Mexican movie star Luis Aguilar Manzo, which Hedras
accepted although he'd never seen a picture of the actor. Maybe
it was the debonair mustache, Hedras decided. Didn't all Mexican actors have mustaches?

". . . and we are part of the global economy, and that same level
playing field I spoke of must apply internationally, too. I sometimes wonder whether—"

Secret Service agent Mike Swales pressed his fingertips against
his earpiece to make sure he'd heard right. He immediately
stepped to Aprile's side at the podium and whispered something
into the veep's ear. Aprile's face mirrored his sudden confusion.

"Now, sir," Swales said.

"Thank you for coming," Aprile said into the microphone.
"Thank you very much."

Two agents flanked Carole Aprile. One said, "We have to
leave, Mrs. Aprile."

"But—"

"*Now,* ma'am."

Carole looked to Annabel, whose raised hands asked the obvious question. The agents led Carole to where her husband was being escorted from the ballroom. Agents formed a tight wall around them.

"Out of the way," Swales barked as he briskly managed the Apriles' escape from the ballroom, down the carpeted hall, to the reception area, through sliding doors, through the second set of doors, and to the waiting black bulletproof limousine flying the flag of the vice president of the United States of America.

CHAPTER 11

Underground Garage–the 600 Building–the Watergate

While the vice president and his wife made their way rapidly through the Watergate Hotel's lower entrance, a dozen people looked down at the lifeless body of Morin Garza. A security guard had discovered it on his rounds. The single bullet hole in the back of Garza's head had opened a spigot through which his blood drained freely, creating a crimson circle that had soaked into the porous concrete.

"Who is he?"

"Don't know. No ID. No wallet. Nothing."

"Robbery?"

A shrug.

"Latino. What do you figure?"

"Central American, maybe. Who knows?"

"Whoever did it got up real close."

"The VP's upstairs."

"Gone. Secret Service got him out of there."

"Any of these cars belong to the deceased?"

"Don't know. Checking them."

"I heard there was some concern about a Mexican tonight. The VP. An assassination attempt. Maybe this was the guy."

"If he was," said a detective from the MPD who'd just arrived, "he sure got it wrong."

CHAPTER 12

Sunday Morning

The State Department

"His name is Morin Garza. Forty-two years old. Married, two children. Lived in Mexico City. Was a union organizer for the Federation of Organizations of Non-Salaried Workers. Started with the Shoe Shiners' Union, worked himself up. Last job was in the political wing of the union. Then again, the whole union is a political wing of the PRI."

The briefing took place at eleven o'clock in a conference room on the seventh floor of the State Department, between Twenty-first and Twenty-third streets at C Street, NW, Foggy Bottom, one floor below the diplomatic reception rooms, where visiting heads of state were lavishly feted.

Gathered around a long teak table were seven members of State's Latin American division. They'd been summoned to the meeting by phone the night before by the chief of the Mexican desk within that division, Craig Verplank, who gave the briefing.

"Garza was turned by a CIA source six months ago. He started feeding information to us, which according to our sources was of minimal value. Still, he was considered worthwhile enough to be given protection. As far as we know, he—"

Verplank was interrupted by Herman Winkler: "How did we nail down identification on him so soon? He was killed only a little over twelve hours ago. As I understand it, there was no ID on his person. No wallet. Nothing."

"He was expected."

"Expected?"

"Yes. About a month ago, his handlers got wind he'd been identified by PRI officials as being untrustworthy. They got him out of Mexico to El Paso, closeted him there until they decided what to do with him. He knew a lot. Nothing especially important involving national security. More political. Corruption within the PRI, kickbacks, coercion, that sort of thing."

"You said he was expected, Craig," another at the table said. "Please explain."

Verplank sighed. It was always a problem deciding how much to share with colleagues. Need-to-know dictated the decision, but within that time-honored parameter was considerable latitude.

The men he'd called to the meeting on that bright, sunny Sunday morning had all been involved, to a greater or lesser extent, with Mexico. But missing were his two top Mexico analysts, Ward Kramer and Richard de LaHoya, who were in Mexico conferring with embassy officials about the upcoming national elections, to take place in two weeks. Verplank had been on the phone with them numerous times throughout the night;

they'd been the ones who'd filled him in on Morin Garza's background, their source CIA operatives based at the American embassy in Mexico City.

Verplank was a hard worker, pragmatic, a good soldier. Colleagues joked that his idea of a vacation was to return late from lunch. Short, stocky, with a cratered bald head and heavy beard shadow, he did not fill the stereotypical description of someone involved with international diplomacy, which could be said of most employees at State. The diplomats were a different breed. Verplank, and others in similar positions, were there to soak up information, keep close tabs on what was going on in the countries for which they were responsible, crush facts and figures, run them through the computers, digest rumors, analyze speculation, make sense of it all—and pass on that knowledge to the diplomats and other higher-ups.

It wasn't often Verplank was asked for his opinions, which was fine with him, although he certainly had plenty of them, which he shared with his wife and a few close friends.

He didn't understand the administration's soft policy on Mexico, not with its decades-old pattern of corruption, and especially since the country was serving happily as a profitable pipeline into the United States for South American drugs. Of course, he was well aware that behind that gentle policy was commerce and trade. NAFTA had been rammed through Congress, for better or for worse depending upon who you were, and this administration seemed content with the status quo where Mexico was concerned despite ... *despite* all the facts and figures the Mexico desk had gathered, chewed on, spit out, and ingested again like cows. Verplank knew them by heart; he'd lived with them for eleven years.

Seventy-five percent of all cocaine entering the United States came across the Mexican–U.S. border, supplanting Florida as the route of choice for Colombian drug barons.

Billions of dollars in drug money were being laundered through myriad Mexican political leaders, officials, families, and hangers-on, making them rich. A recent listing by *Forbes* magazine of the world's wealthiest individuals had thirteen Mexicans on it; Mexico now ranked only behind the United States, Germany, and Japan as having the most billionaires.

Certain drug lords in Mexico had recently gone on a killing spree, eliminating anyone posing a threat to their empires. These were equal opportunity murders: members of the clergy, reluctant politicians, rogue members of the police and other law enforcement agencies who didn't cooperate, and citizens who just happened to be in the wrong place at the wrong time, all were fair game.

Mexico, Verplank knew, had become what was being called a narco democracy. As far as he was concerned, the country's leadership and its drug kingpins were interchangeable. It wasn't even debatable. The facts said it all, and Craig Verplank believed in facts. If he were calling the shots—and of course, he wasn't—Mexico would be called to account, to purge its political system of the pervasive influence of drug money before benefiting from any future American largesse, and until what Mexico's leading political analyst, Jesus Silva Herzog, had written was no longer true: "Politics is the easiest and most profitable profession in Mexico."

He answered the question. "Garza was brought here to testify."

A burst of questions from everyone at the table: "Testify?" "Where?" "Congress?" "A committee?" "A hearing?"

"TMI. The Mexico Initiative."

"That private think tank?"

"Yes."

"Why would someone like this Garza character be brought to Washington to talk to them?"

Verplank said he didn't know the details, just that he'd been told on the phone last night by LaHoya and Kramer that Garza was coming to Washington to brief The Mexico Initiative on corruption in Mexico.

The youngest member at the table said, "If that's so, plenty of Mexicans would have wanted him dead."

"My thinking exactly."

"He had nothing on him. Am I right?" another man asked.

"That's the information we have."

"Then it could have been a robbery gone awry."

"Possible," said Verplank.

"Who's funding that think tank?" Verplank was asked.

"People who want to change our direction with Mexico," Verplank said.

"People with *money* who want us to change direction."

A nod from Verplank.

Verplank wanted to end the meeting, hadn't wanted to call it in the first place. But protocol dictated that he brief senior members of the staff. Besides, he knew that if he didn't, speculation would percolate and boil over, like an unwatched pot.

"Nothing in the paper this morning about this," a man at the end of the table offered. "Just a DC murder. At the Watergate. Why was he there?"

"At the Watergate?"

"Yes."

"Maybe he was staying there."

Verplank said, "I think we might as well wrap this up. Naturally, this stays in the room with us. When and if I receive further information, there'll be another briefing."

As they filed from the room to return to their homes and an afternoon of golf, or tennis, or baseball watching on TV, the youngest staff member took Verplank aside.

"Craig," he said, "I heard recently that the Initiative isn't as private an organization as it wants us to believe."

"Oh? Where did you hear that?"

"A friend over in the House, a staffer on the Western Hemisphere Subcommittee, International Relations."

"What does your friend have to say?"

"Sort of vague but—"

Verplank grimaced. "Is anything not vague these days when it comes to Mexico?"

"Yeah, I know. He told me The Mexico Initiative is developing a case for reversing favored nation status for Mexico, and for killing those other proposals coming out of the White House."

"That's news? They've been stating that as their purpose all along."

"But what they're *not* saying is that they're being supported, at least in part, by political interests."

"Interesting. What political interests?"

"He didn't know. But I read into it he meant Congress. Or somewhere in government."

"I'll give that some thought," Verplank said. "Sorry to have fouled up your morning."

"No problem," the young man said, grinning. "My wife's mother is visiting. Any excuse to get out of the house is welcome."

Verplank watched his young colleague walk away, leaving him alone in the room. He went to the window and spent a few contemplative minutes watching the activities on the Mall. Good Sunday weather always coaxed everyone out of their homes and apartments. Frisbees flew, lovers walked hand in hand, and a game of touch football was being enthusiastically played in the shadow of the Washington Monument. Verplank's wife's mother, too, was visiting. But unlike his young colleague, he was anxious to get home and spend time with her. She was getting old; how many more years could he enjoy her company?

He locked the room, stopped by his office to pick up a few things, then rode the elevator down to the lobby, where he was greeted by the security guards.

"Catch the game this afternoon?" he was asked.

"I don't think so," Verplank said. "I have visitors, not baseball fans."

"Well, enjoy what's left of the weekend, Mr. Verplank."

Although he made it a point to try and never bring work home with him, the conversation about the true nature of The Mexico Initiative would dominate his thinking for the rest of the day and evening. Until that moment, Verplank had been confident that he, and only he in the Latin American division, had been briefed on what was really behind that allegedly private think tank. But that was obviously no longer true.

Make phone calls when he got home? Or could it wait until Monday morning when he could confer in person?

He returned to his office, called his wife to say he'd be there in an hour, and placed a second call.

CHAPTER 13

Metropolitan Police Headquarters

Indiana Avenue was quiet on this Sunday morning, with the exception of activity in and around MPD headquarters. It had been a relatively peaceful night in the nation's capital. The blotter showed two murders, a rape, three muggings, assorted domestic disputes, a few prostitution arrests, and the murder of an unidentified Hispanic male in the underground garage of the Watergate complex.

The two homicide detectives assigned to the Garza killing were working together as a team for the first time. Joe Peterson, his blotchy Irish face deeply scarred by severe teenage acne, had recently lost his partner of long standing to retirement. Wendell Jenkins, whose regular partner had injured himself while fixing the roof of his house and was on disability leave, was a young man with pitch-black skin and a weight problem.

At eleven that morning, Peterson and Jenkins sat in the homicide day room and sipped tepid coffee. Peterson held four Polaroid pictures of the deceased taken at the Watergate crime scene. One showed his full face. The second was of a tattoo on his right forearm. The third photo was of a three-inch-long scar on the left side of his neck. The fourth picture was of his right ear, one of the body's most distinguishing features.

"What do you figure him for?" Peterson asked his partner.

"I peg him as Mexican."

"A Juan Doe."

"Yeah."

"Robbery?"

"Or a hit. Man, that was a clean shot to the back of the head. Perfect spot. And close. Singed his hair."

"You know what doesn't speak to me, Wendell?"

"What's that?"

"Why the guy was where he was."

"The Watergate? Maybe he was heading for the thing at the Kennedy Center."

"Nah. He had no car. They've all been accounted for."

"What gets me was that his body was right outside the door leading up into the office building. Was he trying to get in there? You have to have a key for that."

"Maybe he did."

"And what? The shooter stole the key, too?"

"Sure. Maybe he figures to come back and use it, rip off the offices upstairs."

Jenkins said, "Doesn't figure. If I had a bet on the line, I say he was whacked."

Peterson pondered what his partner had said. "A Mexican mob hit?"

"Our Latino friends from the south are getting more active

here in DC every day, Joe. Vicious bunch, huh? Bad as the Jamaicans and Russians."

"I've got a Mexican family on the block. Nice people. Quiet, you know? When they moved in I figured all-night parties with those—whatta you call them?—those bands."

"Mariachis."

"With the big hats."

"Yeah. They don't?"

"What?"

"Your neighbors. Wear big hats and sing all night?"

"No. Like I said, real quiet."

"Uh-huh."

"Forensics will ID him. All those gold fillings, the scar. You notice his hands?"

"Small."

"Very. How come the shooter didn't take the two rings off him?"

"In a rush."

"Probably. I'm outta here," Peterson said. "My daughter's coming over with the grandkid. Cute little guy. Only a year old but smart."

Jenkins grinned. "I've got two married kids but no grandchildren. My wife is getting impatient. Wants to be a young grandmother in the worst way."

They signed out and went to where their cars were parked.

"Enjoy, man," Jenkins said. "See you Tuesday."

"Yup. Glad tomorrow's off. You know what?"

"What?"

"I think it *was* a hit. Take it easy."

Chapter 14

Four Days Later

London

The ladies were to meet for lunch in the salmon-pink River Restaurant of the Savoy hotel, overlooking the Thames. Previous luncheon gatherings had been in that same hotel's Savoy Grill, but it was the ladies' consensus that the grill's food and service had slipped of late, and so they changed venues to the larger, more genteel River Room.

Elfie was, as usual, late.

"I don't care what he claimed, Constance, I never trusted him," Phyllis Vine said of Elfie Dorrance's second husband, Dieter Krueger, a German industrialist who'd prospered during the war as a supplier of die-cast metals to the Nazi military effort. Ms. Vine was a big woman in all ways, whose square jaw moved curiously sideways when she spoke, accentuated by too much, and too red, lipstick.

"Elfie obviously believed him when he said he was never a Nazi sympathizer," said Constance Dailey, a tiny, sparrowlike woman whose pretty face had a gray cast that almost matched her suit. "Good Lord, Phyllis, I mean, after all, she did marry him."

Phyllis's nose moved. "He claimed his company—which I understand was very successful before the war broke out—was conscripted along with other German manufacturers with products useful to the paperhanger's military machine. Typical story, I'm afraid. No German knew what was going on, of course."

"Of course."

"What Elfie ever saw in him is beyond me," Phyllis said.

Constance guffawed. "Deutsche marks, Phyllis, and plenty of them."

"Yes, quite. She was terribly young, wasn't she, when she married him? He was twice her age, at least."

"At least. She'd had that failed first marriage, which I understand was sordid but mercifully brief. Has she told you about it?"

"Well—just the bare bones. Where is she? Perhaps we should order. The usual?"

"I suppose so."

"We really shouldn't question Elfie's motives, should we? I mean, she isn't here to defend herself—the way he died was so shocking—it must have been—oh, there's Elfie now. I will say one thing about her, Constance, she's aged gracefully."

"Elfie, darling, we were worried about you."

"And dissecting me, I trust," Elfie said, sliding into the chair held out by a waiter.

"Oh, don't be silly," her companions said, almost in unison. "The usual?"

"Yes," Elfie said. "I'm afraid I'm a bit rushed today. I'm having tea this afternoon with Laughton Starkgrave."

"Oh? Brown's?"

"Home. Waiter, we're ready to order."

— — —

Elfie's multiple marriages provided plenty of grist for natter, as gossip was known to the British, and Elfie knew it. She wasn't bothered by it; it was her opinion that being discussed was infinitely better than being ignored.

Truth was that Dieter Krueger had not been a Nazi sympathizer. Like other business owners with a product useful or convertible to Hitler's war effort, you went along or . . .

He'd considered at one time injecting deliberate glitches into his production lines to hamper output. But pragmatism overruled that, and he rode out the war meeting his quotas and waiting for the inevitable collapse of the Third Reich, which came to seem more certain with each passing month.

When the war ended, Krueger Industries was a sturdy, viable company, poised to expand to other European nations in desperate need of rebuilding. Krueger took advantage of it, beginning with Great Britain, then France, the Netherlands, and into Scandinavia. By the time he met the vivacious and charming Mrs. Dorrance-Robinson at a London party, he was a multimillionaire, a widower, and a prize catch among Europe's eligible bachelors. That he was twice Elfie's age—he fifty-nine, she thirty—only added to the newsworthy aspects of the relationship.

There were those who preferred to view the marriage of Elfie Dorrance to Dieter Krueger as a classic pretty young thing snaring the wealthier older man. There was a modicum of truth to that; Elfie would never have married Krueger if he hadn't been wealthy. But she was hardly an impoverished waif, or a predatory gold digger. She brought to the marriage a trust fund, albeit a modest one, established by her deceased father, Malcolm Dorrance, who'd done well as a New England real estate developer. Created and funded when Elfie was in her teens—her formal given name was Elfreda, after her paternal grandmother—the terms of the trust stipulated that as long as Malcolm Dorrance was alive, the trust's funds were unavailable to his only daughter if she married someone of whom he disapproved. That certainly applied to Elfie's first marriage at the age of twenty-three to Wayne Robinson, an aspiring alleged artist who swept Elfie off her feet and whisked her away to Paris, where they immersed themselves in the West Bank's bohemian life. It lasted a year.

Elfie knew when she married Robinson that he was a drug user and heavy drinker. But she had neither the wisdom at that age, nor the inclination, to look ahead at what it might mean in terms of his treatment of her. His physical abuse and multiple infidelities led to their separation and divorce.

A month after the papers had been finalized, Elfie's father died of a stroke. Elfie and her trust fund had been liberated, and she took full advantage of both.

Elfie and Dieter Krueger took up residence in his handsome home in Munich. But she hated Germany and its granitic culture, its harsh, impenetrable language, and Third Reich ghosts. Because her husband spent considerable time in Great Britain tending to business, she easily persuaded him to find a house there: "All those expensive bills from the Savoy and the Ritz," she told him. "It would simply be good business to have a permanent place in London."

The house, in the elegant Belgravia section of the city, on Eaton Mews, was a three-story white stucco home of terrace design. It was love at first sight. Its Belgravia address certainly was appealing. Developed in 1825 on 150 acres taken from the Grosvenor estate, and encompassing Belgrave Square, Belgravia was, from its beginnings, a desirable area of the city in which to live. From the moment they took possession of the house on Eaton Mews, and the interior designers had worked their magic, Elfie considered it home, her only home. Her trips to Munich became increasingly infrequent; she and Dieter spent much of their marriage apart, he devoted to addressing the myriad demands of his business, and Elfie remaining in London to nurture her flourishing social status.

Although she regularly assured Dieter that she missed him during their long separations, she was aware that his absences were in certain ways beneficial. Krueger was handsome and socially adept. With exceptions. He was also a German; how many guests at their dinner parties laughed at his witty, worldly remarks while remembering the V2s raining down on their city, thousands killed, babies rushed from hospital delivery rooms to basement shelters, rationing and deprivation and fear and loathing of the crazed nation on the other side of the channel?

Elfie had awoken that morning in the five-foot-wide Victorian brass bed she'd shared with Dieter and two subsequent husbands—and others. She'd arrived in London the night before, her circadian rhythms out of sync and destined to remain so for at least a few days.

Her housekeeper, Julie, served her toast and tea in the sun-flooded sitting room at the rear of the house, overlooking a lovely garden surrounded by a beech hedge dressed in its autumnal reds and golds. She handled correspondence for the remainder of the morning, showered and dressed, met her friends, Constance and Phyllis, for lunch, then returned to the house to await the arrival of Laughton Starkgrave, a member of the House of Lords and briefly a British ambassador to the United States during the Nixon administration. He arrived precisely at three-thirty and was ushered to the library by Julie.

"You look in fine fettle," he said after taking one of two Queen Anne armchairs. They were separated by a fine, small table set with early Staffordshire china. A fire spat in the marble fireplace behind them. Observing their meeting from the walls was a collection of sepia prints of members of William I's court.

"Feeling fine, Laughton. Being in London lifts the spirits. Anything new and exciting?"

"Personally or politically?"

"Start with the personal."

"Not much to comment on there. I've sold the Cotswolds house—getting too old to make that trip often enough to justify holding on to it—the prime minister continues to lead the Laborites but acts like a Tory—better that, I suppose, than acting out his liberal inclinations—no Iron Man, he—but that isn't personal, is it?—feeling quite well aside from the hearing loss and . . ."

Elfie had become sufficiently Anglophilic to understand most of Lord Starkgrave's mumbled comments, words being swallowed or lost in a rumble of amused chuckles at what he was saying.

"What's the hot debate these days in the House of Lords?"

"Rather dull, actually."

Always dull, Elfie thought.

" . . . and we've imported the debate about doctor-assisted suicide from you people in the States. They'd bloody well better make up their minds soon if I'm to take advantage of it. . . ." A loud laugh this time, setting the pouchy cheeks of his bland, bloodless face into motion.

Starkgrave had not aged gracefully. When ambassador to the States, he'd cut a dashing figure in diplomatic circles, promising to become overweight but successfully containing it, bright-eyed, and very much on top of things. In his dotage, he'd allowed nature to override his resolutions and had become flabby and even somewhat slovenly, seemingly no longer concerned with his physical appearance or the clothing he chose to accompany it. His blue tie was stained, his fingernails less than pristine. Perhaps if his wife had lived things might have been different.

One thing hadn't changed about Starkgrave, however, and Elfie knew it only too well. He may have reached a point in his life where his outward appearance was that of a cartoonish character, the tottering old man dozing in his club chair while younger members waited for him to die and vacate it, but his mind was as sharp as it had ever been, and his contacts within his government—other governments, too—were vast and secure.

Julie served their tea, and thin sandwiches of cucumber, salmon, and cheese. Starkgrave sipped noisily, sitting back and resting his cup, held in both hands, on his belly.

"Enough about me, Elfie," he said. "Let us hear about you and your latest Washington escapades. Your friend, Mr. Aprile, appears to be unbeatable next time round."

"No one is unbeatable, Laughton. He's certainly the front-runner, but you know how fickle politics can be."

"Quite. Yes, yes, know it well. He seems like a decent chap, although looks can be deceiving. Is he? A decent chap?"

"Yes. A good man. I'm very fond of him, although he does have certain views that can be—how shall I say it?—can be disconcerting at times."

Laughton nodded. Julie reappeared with a three-tiered silver tray of scones, clotted cream, jelly, and assorted miniature pastries. Starkgrave filled his small plate. Elfie declined with a wave of her hand.

"You were saying?" Starkgrave said through a cream puff.

"I was saying that the vice president holds certain views that make me uncomfortable."

"Oh? Domestic or foreign?"

"A little of both, although one looms largest in my mind."

"Lovely pastries. From the Ritz?"

"Pâtisserie Valerie."

"None better. Which of your friend's views bothers you most?"

"Mexico."

"Yes?"

"He's making the Mexican government's slow progress on corruption, especially where it concerns drugs, his cause célèbre."

"Quite at odds with your president."

"Glaringly so. Of course, he's managed to keep his disagreement with the administration's Mexico policy—which has worked so well—pretty well under wraps, at least until now. But lately I fear his rigid views on the subject will soon become more public."

Starkgrave chewed his cheek and dabbed at his mouth with the linen napkin he'd spread across his stomach. "Awkward situation, I'd say," he said. "We can't very well have a country's two top leaders bickering over foreign policy, can we?"

" 'Awkward' is a gentle way of putting it, Laughton. You do know of my love for Mexico and its people."

He maneuvered himself into a less slouched position. "Of course I do. Spending enough time there, I trust."

"There's never enough time. I'm leaving for Mexico from here in a few days. Now that British Air is running direct flights from Heathrow to Mexico City, it's almost easier going from London than the States."

"Yes, quite. The last time we had the pleasure of tea, Elfie, we discussed your thinly veiled aspirations to be ambassador."

"I remember that conversation."

"It was at that party given by your ambassador, Brown."

"Yes."

"Still angling for that post?"

"Angling?" A soft laugh. "I don't angle, Laughton. I curve. But yes, that is my goal."

"If Aprile is elected next November, your chances are good."

"What I'd like to do is improve the odds."

"Always a prudent approach to anything we covet. But it seems to me that Vice President Aprile's breach with his administration on Mexico could toss the proverbial monkey wrench into things, including your things." His raised eyebrows asked whether he was correct.

Her nod silently affirmed.

"I think you'd make a splendid ambassador to Mexico, certainly better than that insufferable man they sent to us. You speak the language fluently, already own a home there, have a unique understanding of the people with whom you'd be interacting."

"Can I hire you to make my case before Congress?"

"What would you like me to do, Elfie?"

"I'm not quite sure. Nothing specific. By the way, I'll be seeing Senor Hurtado tomorrow. A social visit."

"Give him my best. Having you do it will spare me the unpleasant chore of needing to spend time with him myself. Surely, Mexico could have come up with a better candidate for ambassador to the Court of Saint James."

"Laughton, would you be good enough to speak to a few people, indicate to them, casually and subtly of course, that you think I would be an effective ambassador to Mexico? Sort of begin to grease the skids, as it were. That would be especially helpful if such sentiment were to meander its way back to Washington."

His smile was wise. "It would be my pleasure, Elfie. You and— you've been so helpful to me over these many years."

"No need to ignore my husbands, Laughton. They were helpful, too."

"But not nearly as winning. Especially the German chap. Never did feel especially comfortable around him. The war and all, I suppose. I really must go. Tea was excellent, and the pastries."

He struggled to his feet, using the chair's arms to help him up. "When do you leave?"

"Day after tomorrow."

"We'll chat again before then. Oh—what was that messy situation I read about in the press, your friend the vice president being spirited out of the Watergate because of a threat on his life?"

"Nothing, really. They found a man murdered in one of the underground parking garages and thought he might be part of some assassination attempt."

"Was it?"

"No. An unfortunate coincidence of timing. Thank you for coming, Laughton. It's always such a pleasure seeing you."

Were a survey taken of the hundreds of people who'd been close to Elfie Dorrance over the years, it's doubtful that any of them would have used terms such as morose, melancholy, introspective, or sorrowful to describe her. And for good reason. She was perpetually upbeat, positive, the wide smile always there, the animated conversation, the enthusiastic outreach to everyone around her. But like many such people, there were private moments for reflection, not all of them uplifting.

She sat in the library, twilight diminishing the outside light through the mullioned windows, while the housekeeper cleared the tea service.

"Would you like something, ma'am?" she asked.

"Thank you, Julie, no," Elfie said. "I think I'll just sit here a bit."

— — —

She thought less about her marriages than did her friends. The past was just that, and the present and future were consuming enough to avoid squandering emotions on what had been. But when she did find her thoughts drifting back to the men in her life, particularly her husbands, it was always the ends of those marriages that provided the most interest, that were the most memorable.

Wayne Robinson, her first, had been the obvious mistake of impetuous, rebellious, and, yes, romantic youth. She thought of their final night together when she announced she was returning to the United States and would divorce him. At first, he'd laughed, told her to hurry up and do it because he couldn't stand the sight of her. But as the evening wore on—she packed, he drank and smoked marijuana—he became abusive, struck her repeatedly, then tried to strangle her. Fortunately, his drunken state allowed her to fight him off and to leave the apartment for a hotel, then a plane the following morning to New York. Remembering his blows as she sat in the library in Belgravia caused her to wince, as though being struck again.

But it was Laughton Starkgrave's mention of Dieter that caused her greatest preoccupation that waning London afternoon.

By 1969, theirs was a marriage in name only. He spent little time in London. When he did, they occupied separate rooms in the house. Few knew of their situation, although the long absences naturally caused speculation.

Dieter had grown chronically depressed during their last year together. His company was under intense competitive pressure and was losing heavily. Too, a recurring series of brutal, lingering headaches had prompted him to seek medical advice in Munich. The news wasn't good. It was an inoperable brain tumor; he was given six months to live.

He shared his illness and prognosis with few people, and certainly not with Elfie, most pointedly not with her. In April of that year, he traveled to London and stayed at the house. A succession of small dinner parties was carried off with the usual equanimity, although Dieter often excused himself because of the headaches.

One morning, as he and Elfie had breakfast, he told her he

was going to New York to seek American refinancing for his firm. He suggested that she accompany him.

She readily agreed, suggesting that they travel by steamship, make a holiday out of it. The thought of days at sea wasn't appealing to Dieter, but he didn't argue. Elfie had read recently that Cunard's magnificent new ship, the *Queen Elizabeth II,* would be making its maiden voyage from Southampton to New York on May 2. It wasn't easy obtaining reservations, but she'd made friends with two of Cunard's board members, who happily accommodated her.

"Are you feeling ill?" she asked Dieter as they waited to board the newest and grandest ship ever to ply the waters of the North Atlantic. He looked sick, was listless and distracted.

"Yes," he said. "Just tired. A few days of sea air will make all the difference."

As they left Southampton and began the crossing, with a stop in Le Havre before heading for New York, Elfie found herself wanting the cold distance between them to thaw, at least for the days they'd be at sea. The first night out, as she sat up late in their stateroom after a lavish dinner and round of dancing and watched him sleep, a profound sadness came over her. This was a good and decent man. She was lucky to have found him, and she silently wished that by the time they returned from New York, they might pour a new foundation upon which to base a more congenial relationship. It was not to be.

After one relatively smooth day, the weather turned violent. Forty-five-foot waves buffeted the huge ship, sending any furniture not nailed down across rooms, and tossing elderly passengers against walls. The captain repeatedly announced that no one was to venture outside to the decks until they'd ridden out the storm.

At noon, Elfie made her way to the elegant Queen's Grill for lunch. It was half empty; many passengers had opted to remain in their cabins rather than risk injury. Dieter had gone to the ship's library but said he would meet her in the dining room. He never arrived.

By two that afternoon, the ship's crew had been alerted, and a discreet search was under way, without success.

Elfie stayed in the stateroom throughout the day and into the early evening, receiving periodic calls to report that Dieter had not been found. By this time, the assumption was that he'd disobeyed the captain's orders, had ventured to an outside deck, perhaps lost his balance when close to a railing, and gone over. What other explanation could there be?

Elfie spent the evening in the captain's private quarters being comforted by his wife, and other senior members of the ship's staff, including a chaplain. At midnight, she excused herself and went to her stateroom with the hope of sleeping, if only for a few hours. She opened a built-in dresser drawer in which she'd put her nightclothes. Resting on top of a favorite lacy pink negligee was an envelope with her name written on it in Dieter's hand. She removed it from the drawer, sat on the bed, opened it, and read its contents:

My dearest Elfie—

When you discover this, I shall be at peace deep in the waters of the Atlantic. I have not been truthful with you, although my motivations were pure. I was informed the day before we left that there would be no financing of Krueger Industries in the United States. The future of the company is grim, and I see no practical way to reverse its downward course. Perhaps if I were in better health, I would have the energy and faith in the future to keep fighting. But that is not the case. I have a terminal illness, a brain tumor, that would have taken my life soon. I choose to hasten that inevitable demise, and have chosen to do it from the deck of this magnificent ship.

Fortunately, I had the foresight to purchase large amounts of life insurance before my illness manifested itself. The proceeds of those policies, coupled with what you shall gain from the eventual sale of the company, will provide you with ample funds for the rest of your life. I am proud of having done this for you.

There is nothing more to say, except that I trust you will understand my decision. I realize having me take my own life might prove somewhat embarrassing for you if it becomes known, and I apologize for any discomfort it creates for *mein Liebchen*. Know that I love you, Elfie, and always have.

Your lover, husband and friend, Dieter

By morning, the storm had abated and the decks were awash with brilliant sunshine. Elfie exited to the boat deck, stood at the railing, and looked to the limitless horizon. Had his death been quick, or had he struggled once in the water? Was it cold enough to numb him? Was his last thought of her? Would his insurance policies be invalidated by suicide?

She pulled the note from the pocket of her coat, tore it into a dozen pieces, and released them into the wind, watching them flutter toward her husband's final resting place until they were no longer visible.

The arrival of the *QE2* in New York Harbor was greeted with dozens of fireboats spraying water into the air from their fire pumps. Two U.S. Navy ships rode proudly on her port and starboard sides. The trip from Le Havre to New York's Ambrose Light Tower had taken four days, sixteen hours, and thirty-five minutes, the average speed 28.02 knots.

Journalists covering the maiden voyage now had a second story to pursue. Reporters on the ship had used its communications technology to inform their colleagues in New York of the tragic death of German industrialist Dieter Krueger, and that his wife, the socially prominent Elfie Dorrance-Krueger, was aboard.

"What would have possessed your husband to venture out on deck in a bad storm?" she was asked.

"Dieter was an adventurer," she replied. "He thrived on challenge, on facing danger. I wish he hadn't done what he did, but wishing will never bring him back. He's at peace somewhere in that vast ocean, and I have his memory to sustain me for the rest of my life. Excuse me. There's a memorial service to be planned and so many other matters to attend to. Thank you so very much for your courtesies."

— — —

And in the weeks to come, she made careful lists of those who sent condolences and those who didn't.

Chapter 15

The Next Day

The State Department

Mac Smith left the building with his friend from State's Latin American division, Herman Winkler, after he and four others designated to travel to Mexico as election observers had been briefed by the Mexican desk's chief, Craig Verplank. Winkler had sat in on the meeting as an observer.

"Lunch plans?" Winkler asked.

"No. I thought I might swing past Annabel's gallery to see if she's hungry. She won't be."

"Then have lunch with me."

They walked to the Foggy Bottom Cafe in the River Inn, on Twenty-fifth Street, steps from where Mac and Annabel had lived until moving to the Watergate. After ordering chicken Caesar salads and a bottle of sparkling water, they settled into the sort of comfortable conversation friends of long duration are capable of having—who'll play in the World Series, the improving state of the District, whether the coming winter would be more severe than the one past, and their wives. It was over espresso that their topics turned to more substantive matters—aside from their wives, of course.

"Anything new on the murder at Watergate?" Mac asked.

Winkler sat back and glanced left and right.

Mac said, "I take it there is, and it's not for public consumption."

Winkler now leaned forward, elbows on the table. "I don't have this officially, Mac—I mean, no one's sent around a memo. But the gentleman who was killed was here on what might be termed government business."

"Whose government?"

"Ours. No, correction. Quasi-government business."

"I stopped using 'quasi' years ago, Herman. Things either are or they aren't."

Winkler laughed, said, "Everything in DC is quasi to me. At any rate, his name was Garza. A union organizer in Mexico City. He'd ended up on the wrong side of the PRI and had to be gotten out of the country."

"What did he do to get on the wrong side?"

"Started telling tales out of school about corruption, kickbacks, business as usual there. He was in Washington to talk to people at a think tank."

"What think tank?"

"The new one with Mexico as its only agenda. The Mexico Initiative. Haven't heard of it?"

"No. Then again, I haven't heard of most of the associations in DC. Name a cause or interest, there's a group here to lobby for it. What's *their* story?"

"Oh, gathering information, I suppose. They'd like to see the president's soft-glove approach to Mexico changed."

"Sounds like Joe Aprile would enjoy hearing what they have to say."

"I was thinking the same thing. A friendly wager, Mac, on when Aprile and the president have their public falling out?"

"Won't happen. Aprile is a loyal lieutenant. He won't challenge the president's policies until he's sitting in the Oval Office himself."

"Maybe not the best strategy. Remember Humphrey and Johnson, Vietnam. Didn't serve Hubert very well to defend Johnson's stance."

"You've heard something that says the VP won't wait until he's elected before going to the mat with the president?"

"Nothing specific. I'm in the mood for key lime pie."

"By all means. It's good here."

Outside, in the beginnings of a light drizzle, Winkler asked when Smith was leaving for Mexico.

"Nine days. Annabel's coming with me, at our expense, of course."

"Another scandal averted."

Mac nodded. "Should be an interesting trip for more reasons than the elections."

"How so?"

"The day after the election, Annabel and I are heading for San Miguel de Allende."

"Second honeymoon?"

"It would be our first. No. Annabel's been there a few times in the past buying art and artifacts for the gallery. She says it's beautiful, very quaint, artistic."

"Sounds lovely."

"Yeah, I'm looking forward to it." He looked up into the gray sky. "We'd better get moving before it opens up. Good to see you, Herman. Best to Helen."

"Same to Annabel, Mac. What I told you inside . . . between us?"

You didn't say anything, thought Mac. "Of course," he said.

Mac turned up the collar of his suit jacket against a real rain that had suddenly begun to fall. He didn't have far to go to reach the Watergate, was there in minutes, riding the narrow escalator down from Virginia Avenue to the Watergate Mall, a self-contained shopping area in the middle of the complex, and surrounded by its buildings. The rain had sent people scattering from where they'd sat beneath white umbrellas at white metal tables sipping coffee taken out from the large Safeway or smaller deli, or having an alfresco lunch from Chen's Chinese fast food.

Watergate's own mall was lagniappe appreciated by everyone living there, the Smiths no exception. Mac stopped in at Watergate Valet to pick up shirts he'd left a few days ago; bought a bottle of red wine in the wine and beverage store where the Watergate's own brands of bourbon, scotch, and gin were prominently displayed; said hello to his barber; perused the enticing signs in the window of the travel agency; purchased a small bouquet of flowers for Annabel; and unsuccessfully fought the temptation to make a final stop at the city's famed Tivoli Watergate Pastry Shop to buy two small pieces of homemade honey-and-orange chocolate in case a sweet tooth need came on after dinner.

Rufus lumbered to his feet to greet Mac. After the ritual scratches behind the ears and the dispensing of a treat, Mac put the flowers in a vase with water, hung his shirts in the closet, and was about to settle in the third bedroom, which served as an office-study, when the phone rang. He picked it up in the kitchen.

"Smith."

"Mac. Chris Hedras."

"Yes, Chris. How are you this wet day?"

"Is it raining? I haven't been out. Mac, the vice president is going to initiate a series of breakfast meetings, informal get-togethers to discuss policy issues. He asked me to call to see if you could attend."

"I'm not much on policy, but I'm flattered to be asked. Where and when?"

"Tomorrow morning will be the first. I've booked the private room in Aquarelle, in the hotel. He wants to get as far away from anywhere official as possible. Bob Dole held his campaign breakfast meetings there."

Didn't do him much good, Mac thought. The former Republican senator from Kansas, and presidential candidate, was a neighbor in the Watergate's south building.

"I can make it," Mac said. "What time?"

"Seven?"

"Early to bed, then. How are things going?"

"Pretty good. Bring you up to date in the morning."

That morning's meeting at State had resulted in the participants walking away with briefcases filled with background information, mission goals, and protocols. Nothing like a quiet, rainy afternoon to wade through such material, Mac thought, picking up his briefcase from where he'd dropped it in the kitchen and carrying it to the office.

He settled in his chair and turned on a small color TV set on the desk. It was perpetually set to CNN, although he usually found himself switching back and forth between that all-news channel and C-SPAN, particularly if Congress was in session. The House of Representatives was carried gavel-to-gavel by C-SPAN 1, the Senate on C-SPAN 2. A regular CNN program devoted to politics had just begun. The co-anchor's lead item played in the background as Smith started to empty his briefcase.

But the words coming from the tiny speaker quickly drew his attention to the screen.

... allegations of illegal fund-raising in the last Scott-Aprile campaign have been floating around Washington for months now, and there's been a growing movement on the part of Republicans in Congress to launch a formal investigation into those allegations. . . . Earlier today, Indiana Congressman Don Curtain announced he would seek House approval for an investigation by his Government Reform and Oversight Committee into ties between the Democratic National Committee and foreign contributors to the president's campaign, notably from Mexico. With us now is Congressman Philip Broadbent, Democrat from Wisconsin, a member of that committee and a staunch supporter on the Hill of the administration's foreign policies. Thank you for being here.

BROADBENT: My pleasure.

ANCHOR: Congressman, you heard your Republican colleague Don Curtain call today for an investigation into allegations of Mexican money having been illegally funneled into the Scott-Aprile campaign. Your reaction?

BROADBENT: I was disappointed in hearing it. It's just an example of the Republican-controlled Congress playing politics. The reality is that nothing will be accomplished by another partisan political witch-hunt costing the American taxpayers millions of dollars, without any substantive result.

ANCHOR: Congressman Curtain also said that his committee's investigators have uncovered sufficient evidence to warrant a call for a special prosecutor.

BROADBENT: All innuendo and veiled threats without specifying what this so-called evidence is. It amounts to a slur campaign against this sitting president, and the vice president's run for the presidency next year.

ANCHOR: Democrats don't have the votes in the House to derail an investigation. What can you do?

BROADBENT: Let the American people know just how unnecessary and costly an investigation will be, the partisan reasons behind it, and trust they'll let their elected officials know they're against it.

ANCHOR: Two names of prominent Mexican-American businessmen were mentioned during Congressman Curtain's press conference. Are you familiar with them and their alleged ties to the White House?

BROADBENT: I know both. They're fine, upstanding gentlemen who have been supportive of the Democratic Party, legally, I hasten to add. The Republicans want to sabotage the strong economic ties this administration has forged with Mexico, and they don't care who is smeared in the process. I think this represents a low point in this Congress.

ANCHOR: Thank you, Congressman Philip Broadbent, Democrat of Wisconsin.

BROADBENT: Thank you!

That night, Mac mixed perfect Manhattans for them—five ounces of blended whiskey, an ounce each of sweet and dry vermouth, carefully measured, and a dash of bitters for each drink. The elegantly shaped cocktail glasses had spent a half hour in the freezer before use. Mac mixed the drinks in a mixing glass filled with ice, held a coiled-spring strainer over the top, and poured to the rim of each glass. A lemon twist completed the creation; he hadn't used cherries as a garnish in years.

"Perfection as usual," Annabel proclaimed after tasting.

"Accolades accepted," Mac said.

After a dinner of pasta, salad, and crunchy French bread, he and Annabel sat on the terrace and looked out over the river to the lights of Georgetown, and the Key Bridge to Rosslyn, Virginia. The rain had stopped earlier in the evening, giving way to a warm, humid breeze. An almost full moon came and went behind fast-moving black clouds.

As usual, the day's news had dictated much of the subject matter for their dinner table conversation, which continued outside.

"You didn't speak with anyone in Joe's office about it?" she asked.

"No. I considered calling Chris Hedras but decided not to. I assume it will come up at breakfast in the morning."

"God, it's a brutal business, isn't it?" she said, wrapping her arms about herself.

"What is? Running an art gallery?"

"Running for president. It's like facing a firing squad. You stand there open and exposed while they line up to take their shots."

"Not for the faint of heart. Or faint of wallet."

"Not for anyone with any sort of heart. Mac, do you think there's any truth to what Curtain is charging?"

"I wouldn't know. The president's the consummate politician, which translates into knowing how to rake in the money from a great many disparate sources, including foreign interests. He probably doesn't know where half the contributions to his campaign come from."

"And Joe?"

"I don't think he'd accept money unless it was aboveboard, and he's able to keep track of it himself. The problem is, if the president did look the other way when Mexican money was raised, maybe even encouraged it, Joe Aprile gets painted with the same brush. It's worse for him. The president risks only being treated with less kindness in the history books. Joe Aprile risks losing his run for the White House. Pretty high stakes, wouldn't you say?"

"Joe could distance himself from the scenario, couldn't he? I mean, if there's any validity to the claims, he'd have to."

"From what I can discern, he might already be considering it. I had lunch today with Herman Winkler."

"Oh? How is Herman?"

"Good. Sends his best. I had a sense from him that a public split on Mexico between the president and vice president might not be too far off."

"That would make things interesting."

"Too interesting. Feel like dessert?"

"What are you offering?"

"Honey-orange chocolate from downstairs."

"You devil."

"Two small pieces. Not big enough to contain any calories."

"You always say broken cookies don't have calories."

"They don't. Come on, share my vice."

"Only if you promise it isn't your only vice tonight."

She winked, ran her hand provocatively along his thigh, and followed him into their new home.

CHAPTER 16

That Same Evening

The Watergate–East Building–South Wing

"The trade alliance party in seven-ten, please."

"Go right on up."

The clerk behind the desk in the Watergate's east apartment building pushed a buzzer, unlocking the glass door leading from the lobby to the elevators. Laura Flores checked her appearance in one of the lobby's mirrored columns, and liked what she saw. Twenty-eight, five-five, and trim, she'd chosen to wear this evening a black silk pants suit recently purchased at Rizick Brothers, a favorite of workers at the city's myriad foreign embassies. It had stretched Laura's budget, but she'd lately been invited to a number of evening parties that called for a fancier wardrobe than she was used to wearing.

But few would notice her suit. It was her hair that always attracted attention, thick and shiny and blue-black, healthy hair in which she took pride.

She thanked the clerk and stepped into a waiting elevator, pushed the button for the seventh floor, and drew a deep breath.

It had been a cyclonic week at the offices of The Mexico Initiative, located in a commercial building on M Street, NW. News of Morin Garza's murder in the Watergate parking garage had brought normal activity to a halt, spawning a series of phone calls, feverish meetings, and intense speculations.

Laura, whose title was research director, had spent that afternoon meeting with the Initiative's president, Ramon Kelly.

Kelly's father, a young, childless widower, had traveled to Mexico in the late fifties, following the death of his American wife, to take a job with a multinational oil consortium under contract to develop Mexico's burgeoning petroleum industry in the state of Chiapas. While there he met and married Consuelo Martinez. They had one child, Ramon, who lived with his parents in that southern Mexican state until going to the United States at the age of eighteen to attend the University of Chicago on a scholarship. In those eighteen years in Mexico, he'd seen enough poverty and despair to last a lifetime, the vivid, lingering visions of it determining his life's work. He earned a master's in social work, and launched a professional career involving a number of nonprofit organizations dedicated to bettering the lot of Mexico's impoverished campesinos, its peasant farmers, and other indigenous groups.

Chiapas, home to more than eight hundred thousand Indians of Mayan descent, was the worst of all, Kelly well knew. Rebellious since the nineteenth century, Chiapas had never shaken the yoke of its landowners despite the advances of the 1994 revolution by what was called the Zapatista Army of National Liberation, two thousand strong, with the revolutionary Emiliano

Zapata as its symbolic idol. They'd timed their march into San Cristobal and three other towns to coincide with NAFTA going into effect on January 1, their goal to embarrass the ruling Partido Revolucionario Institucional, the PRI, that had governed Mexico with an iron hand for more than seventy years. Many died in the effort. The PRI's leadership promised numerous reforms in Chiapas, none of which had taken place.

For Ramon Kelly, the situation in Chiapas was indicative of the cruelty of the country's leadership against its dirt-poor population. One of Mexico's richest states in natural resources—supplying 60 percent of the nation's hydroelectric power, 47 percent of its natural gas, and 22 percent of its oil—Chiapas's citizens ranked along with the states of Oaxaca and Guerrero as its poorest. A third of households were without electricity; half the population did not have access to clean drinking water.

Kelly had been recruited a year ago to head the start-up Mexico Initiative. His first official act was to hire Laura Flores as his research chief.

Their backgrounds were decidedly different. She was the youngest of three daughters of a prominent and well-to-do Mexico City family. Her father managed one of four television stations in Mexico City owned by Televisa, the omnipotent communications empire whose creator was considered the wealthiest businessman in Latin America. He'd given more than fifty million dollars to the PRI for the next election, and had been rewarded with government licenses to operate sixty-two new stations throughout Mexico. Already, his channels in Mexico City boasted a 97 percent share of the audience. Their programming reflected the PRI's bidding. They were one and the same.

Laura and her sisters attended private universities in Mexico before she enrolled at New York University over her father's vehement objections, a man she loved deeply but whose philosophies ran counter to her developing social convictions. Although she never openly expressed such sentiments to him, she freely discussed them in the city's cantinas, sipping Herradura tequila, smoking pot, and with her contumacious friends condemning the government.

She'd intended to return home after receiving her graduate degree in sociology from NYU, but she met Ramon Kelly. They became good friends, and occasional lovers. When Kelly moved to Washington to launch the Initiative, Laura had just started a job as a translator at the UN. She didn't hesitate to throw that job aside and head south. The Mexico Initiative, as Kelly described it, would be well funded and had the potential to make a real difference in U.S. policy toward Mexico.

"We have powerful people behind us," Kelly told her on the phone the night he offered the job.

"Who?"

"When you get here, Laura. Not on the phone."

"But—"

"We'll have plenty of time to discuss it after you're here. In the meantime, pack your things and get moving. We have a lot of work to do."

— — —

"Ah, Senorita Flores, welcome, welcome."

Jose Chapas led her to the living room of the three-bedroom duplex, where two dozen people milled about, drinks in hand, served by a white-jacketed bartender in the kitchen. "A drink?" he asked.

Laura knew that there wouldn't be any tequila or margaritas at the party. Those were reserved for gringos in the city's prodigal Mexican restaurants. Washington's Mexican population preferred top-shelf whiskey, fine cognacs, and vintage wines.

"White wine, please."

Chapas worked at the Mexican-American Trade Alliance as special assistant to its managing director, Venustiano Valle. That's what he'd told her when they met a month ago in the Cha-Cha Lounge on trendy U Street, where they fell into easy conversation, sipping wine and taking their turn at the hookah pipe, its smoke cooled as it passed through an urn of water. Laura thought it might be illegal; Jose assured her it was just smoke, no illegal substances involved. He laughed when she inhaled and started coughing.

"I don't smoke," she said.

"All Mexicans smoke," he said.

Which was almost true, with exceptions—like herself.

They dated occasionally after that initial meeting, a few dinners, a movie, and a night of dancing at Polly Esther's that culminated in his apartment in Crystal City, across the Potomac in nearby Virginia.

Laura liked Jose Chapas, although she suspected that his feelings for her were progressing beyond just having fun together. Too, there was an awkward aspect to going out with him, enough so that she hadn't told Ramon Kelly she was seeing him.

The MATA, its stated purpose to foster trade between the two countries, had a less lofty mission in the eyes of some, including Ramon Kelly. Lobbying without license to change U.S. policy toward Mexico? A covert extension of the army's "Second Section," its intelligence service? The PRI's eyes and ears on Washington?

No matter. Laura Flores enjoyed her time with Chapas. And, there was something to learn. Although he was closed-mouthed about his job and the organization, he occasionally said something that Laura filed away and added to her expanding folders of research on all things having to do with Mexico's relationship with the United States. She was, and had always been, an inveterate note maker.

"Thank you," she said when he handed her the wine. "This is a lovely apartment."

"My pleasure. We maintain it for out-of-town guests, to entertain, that sort of thing. I'm glad you could make it tonight."

"I looked forward to it. It's the first time I've been at an Alliance party."

"And I hope it won't be the last. Come, I'll introduce you around."

"Ah-ha," Venustiano Valle said to her, "I finally get to meet the reason my young friend here arrives at the office with tired eyes."

Laura laughed gently. "That is a reputation I do not wish to have."

"He jokes," Chapas said. "He is always joking."

That comment prompted Valle to tell a long, convoluted joke in Spanish. He fumbled the punch line, but Jose and Laura laughed anyway.

"That's Manuel Zegreda," Laura said to Jose after they'd moved on for further introductions, indicating a tall, impeccably dressed man in the opposite corner.

"*Sí*. You haven't met him?"

"No."

"Well, now you shall."

"*Mucho gusto,*" Zegreda said, taking her hand.

"The pleasure is mine," Laura said, aware that Zegreda was taking in every inch of her.

"*Tienes un rostro tan atractivo.*"

She answered his comment about how attractive she was in English. "That's very kind, Senor Zegreda. Will you be going back to Mexico for the elections?"

"Oh, yes. You?"

"I'm planning to," she said. "I haven't seen my family in too long."

"And where does your family live?"

"Mexico City."

"Flores? Your father, is he with Televisa?"

That Zegreda knew her father would not be unusual. Both were successful businessmen. On the other hand, the mention of him caused Laura to stiffen, not because she'd been estranged from her father since coming to New York, but because it said politics to her, Mexican politics, with all its baseness and oppression, the PRI, to whom her father owed much of his business success. Zegreda, she knew, was a potent force in the ruling party, not a politician but a man whose wealth and behind-the-scenes manipulations were well known in both countries.

"Yes, he is," Laura said.

"I know him well. A fine man. His expertise is of great benefit to the station."

"Thank you." To Chapas: "Would you get me another wine, please?"

"Of course. White again? Or red? Whiskey?"

"No, wine. White."

She hadn't wanted another glass of wine. She'd said it in order to divert the conversation. It hadn't worked. Now, without Chapas at her side, she was alone with the multimillionaire, who continued to undress her with his eyes.

"And what do you do here in Washington, Senorita Flores?"

"I work for—for a private agency."

"Ah. Do I know it?"

"I don't know."

He waited a beat, then smiled. "And unless you tell me which agency it is, I shall never know."

"The Mexico Initiative."

"Yes, I know it. Very new."

"A year."

"And what do you do there?"

"Research. I'm the research director."

"An important job. What sort of research do you do?"

"Economic, mostly. Social issues."

She sensed that Zegreda knew precisely the mission of The Mexico Initiative and was toying with her. Chapas arrived with her glass before Zegreda could ask more. And she was spared further when a man and woman joined them and began asking questions of Zegreda about his businesses. Laura and Chapas drifted away toward the kitchen, where a young man stood alone, arms folded, back leaning against a wall, boredom on his face.

"Harry, I would like you to meet Laura Flores."

She extended her hand, which he took half-heartedly.

"Standing guard over the bar, I see," Chapas said, lightly slapping his friend on the arm.

"A trick I learned long ago," Harry said. Although he was a big man, well over six feet tall and appearing to be sturdily built beneath the gray suit he wore, his voice was surprisingly high, bordering on effeminate.

"Excuse me," Chapas said, disappearing.

"You're here with Jose?" Harry asked.

"Yes. Well, actually no. He invited me, but couldn't bring me because he had duties here."

Harry's small smile exposed teeth prematurely yellowed for his age, which Laura pegged at thirty. "Jose always has duties some place," he said. "He works hard."

"I know."

"Do you—work hard?"

The question took her aback for a moment. She laughed and said, "Yes, I do, but not always."

"You leave time for play?"

"A little. What do you do, Harry?"

"Dabble."

101

"Dabble? What does that mean?"

Another smile. "Investments, odd jobs. I prefer to not be tied down to any one thing."

"Sounds intriguing."

"Your job—when you aren't playing?"

"Research. For a private agency."

Chapas returned, said, "Laura, you'll have to excuse me. Something has come up at the office. I must go there immediately."

Her disappointment showed on her face.

"But I leave you in good hands. Harry is a gentleman, among many other admirable things."

"The last of a breed," Harry said, bowing slightly.

Laura laughed.

"Call you later in the week," Jose said, kissing her on both cheeks. He said to Harry, "Take good care of my lovely friend. I hold you accountable." With that, he was off.

"Another wine?" Harry asked.

"I haven't finished this one."

"That's warm by now. I'll get you a fresh one."

With Chapas's sudden departure, Laura decided not to stay much longer. But Harry took her in tow and introduced her to younger Mexicans who worked at the embassy. The conversation became spirited; there was much laughter. Laura found herself relaxing. Zegreda wished her a pleasant evening on his way out. So did Jose's boss at the Alliance, Valle, who said, playfully, "And no more keeping my young friend out late at night, young lady."

"I promise," Laura said, adopting a solemn expression and crossing her heart, then giggling.

Before she knew it, it was midnight.

"I must go," she announced to the few people still in the apartment, Harry and three others.

"You can't leave yet," Harry said.

"But we can," said the others, getting to their feet and heading for the door.

"More wine?" Harry asked when they were alone.

"Oh, no. I've had much too much to drink as it is. I'm going home."

"I'll drive you," Harry said.

"That isn't necessary."

"It would be my pleasure. But only if you let me show you a special place here in the building."

"Special place?"

"Yes. A special place with a special view."

"Sounds . . . interesting. Where is this special place?"

"Come," he said, taking her hand and pulling her up from her chair. "You'll love it."

He led her from the apartment and to the elevators. They rode to the top floor, exited, and proceeded down the carpeted hallway to a door. Harry inserted a key and opened it, stepped back to allow her to go first.

"Where are we going?" Laura asked.

His answer was to close the door behind them and to gently guide her from behind up a short set of metal stairs, illuminated by a single bulb. At the top was another door. They stepped through it to the building's roof. Immediately in front of them was a long brick wall to keep visitors from going to the roof's edge and looking out.

"What is this?" Laura asked.

"The Watergate roof gardens. Apartment owners can buy a space up here and use it for gardening, as a patio, whatever. One woman has created a sculpture studio."

"Interesting," Laura said.

"I'll show you the one belonging to the apartment."

"Do you live here in the Watergate?" she asked.

"Yes. In another building."

He used a second key to open an iron gate leading to a large space in which there were a half dozen outdoor chairs, a table with umbrella, and a number of potted plants in oversize red earthenware urns. Harry went immediately to a low railing at the patio's edge. He turned, motioned for her to join him.

"Pretty night from up here," he said, allowing his arm to casually drape over her shoulders. "Know what that is down there?" He pointed.

"What? Oh, the statue of Juárez."

"Yes."

"I have been there. On holidays, our people living here come to pay respects."

"Tell me about him."

"About Benito Juárez? What is there to tell? He did good things for our people, made free education mandatory, encouraged industry. I have been to his museum in Oaxaca."

"Have you? It's funny."

"What is funny?"

"Having a statue of a Mexican hero on Virginia Avenue, right outside the Watergate."

"It isn't funny. The city has statues of many great foreign heroes."

"I think it's funny."

A breeze came up, causing her to shudder. It caught his yellow-white, corn-silk hair and sent it flying.

She looked at him and laughed. "Your hair. It's a mess." The moon was like a spotlight on his pale, ghostly face.

She turned away, leaned on the railing, and drew a deep breath.

He rammed his right hand into the back of her neck, and in one continuous motion took a step behind, jammed his left hand between her legs from the rear, and catapulted her over the railing. He waited, not looking down, until he heard the dull thud of her body making impact. Then, slowly, methodically, he wiped her wineglass he'd carried to the roof with a handkerchief and placed it on the slate ground, took a marijuana cigarette from his pocket, lighted it, drew a series of deep drags, and dropped it next to the glass.

A film of perspiration had developed on his forehead. He patted it dry with a handkerchief, replaced the handkerchief in his jacket pocket, placed the roof and patio keys next to the glass and joint at his feet, and left the building, pausing by the statue of Juárez on Virginia Avenue to light a cigarette.

"Buenas noches," he said to Juárez, and walked away at a leisurely pace, humming, in the direction of the apartment he was using in the Watergate's south building.

CHAPTER 17

The Early Hours—the Next Morning
Metropolitan Police Headquarters

Homicide detectives Peterson and Jenkins had just entered headquarters on Indiana Avenue after having investigated a savage murder in the southeast quadrant of the District. An estranged husband, with an order of protection against him, had killed his wife with a hammer, then to make sure she was dead stabbed her multiple times with a kitchen knife. They thought they could write their reports, hang around until it was time to call it a night, and head home.

But their boss, Homicide Chief Pete LaRocca, called them into his office. Joe Peterson started to recount the murder they'd responded to when LaRocca said, "Just write it up. Let's talk about the jumper tonight."

"We caught it on the radio," said Wendell Jenkins. "The Watergate again."

"That's two there," LaRocca said.

"The Mexican in the garage. Who went off the roof tonight?" Peterson asked.

"Female, age twenty-eight. Name's Laura Flores."

"Flores?"

"Yeah."

"Mexican?"

"Yeah. Coincidence?"

Shrugs from Peterson and Jenkins.

"Who caught it?"

"Monroe and Silverstein."

"So?"

"So, I thought since we're dealing with coincidence, you and them might put your heads together, see if there's more of a link than where they were born."

Peterson screwed up his face to indicate he didn't understand. "Different MO," he said. "One guy gets it in the back of his head, the lady believes she can fly. What's the connection?"

"Mexico. The Watergate. That's enough to at least *not* rule out a connection."

"Was the guy in the garage hit ever ID'd?"

"Out of our hands," said LaRocca. "Somebody over at State jumped in because of the guy's nationality. I hear he was a union organizer back in Mexico. Scuttlebutt."

Jenkins laughed. "Those union guys lead dangerous lives."

"Newspaper guys, too, at least in Mexico," LaRocca said. "They just whacked another one for writing unkind things about the druggies."

"Maybe we should import them," Peterson said.

"Import who?" LaRocca asked.

"Mexican hit men. You know, bring 'em in to thin out our reporters. There's too many of them anyway, and they're not worth a damn."

"Any question whether this Flores woman jumped?" Jenkins asked.

"Always a question," LaRocca replied. "They found an empty wineglass, a half-smoked joint, and keys to the roof gardens where she jumped. Monroe and Silverstein are questioning people in the building. Seems there's an apartment there rented by some Mexican-American trade group. Doorman says the jumper was at that party. They're at the building now. Get over and lend a hand, compare notes."

Peterson and Jenkins looked at each other. As Jenkins was fond of saying, "Sometimes you eat the bear, sometimes the bear eats you."

"Let's go," said Peterson, standing, "and see how the rich and famous live."

CHAPTER 18

Later That Morning

The Aquarelle Restaurant—the Watergate Hotel

Mac Smith sat at a table for sixteen in the private room that was part of the acclaimed restaurant. Glass partitions had been closed to seal it off from the larger space, but it still afforded sweeping views of the Potomac. The room was decorated in a light lemon color, the carpeting patterned and harmonious. The armchairs were large and comfortable, framed in heavy wood, the cushions an amalgamation of earth tones. On Sundays, an elaborate brunch was served there. This morning, at seven, the political menu was less caloric but meatier.

Only seven of the sixteen chairs were occupied. Conspicuously absent was the vice president. His chief domestic policy advisor, Alex Jankowski, chaired the gathering. He waited until two waiters had finished delivering pitchers of freshly squeezed orange juice, pots of coffee and tea, and trays of bagels and pastries before saying, "The vice president was detained this morning. He'll try to swing by before we're through. I speak for him when I say how much your being here at this early hour is appreciated."

Mac glanced about the table. Chris Hedras, the VP's campaign helmsman, was also missing.

Jankowski continued: "I conferred earlier this morning with the VP. We agree that the top item on the agenda, at least for this meeting, is the administration's eroding union support."

The program having been established, the six men and one woman weighed in with their thoughts on why organized labor, historically staunchly Democratic, had lately—if years could be termed "lately"—been withholding its support for the administration and, by extension, Joseph Aprile. Mac mostly listened, although he did offer a few comments about how the perception of the administration's labor policies didn't necessarily coincide with the reality of them.

"It keeps coming back to NAFTA," said Susan Kaplan, a former official in the Labor Department, now a signatory to the Aprile campaign. "When Congress slapped down fast-track trade negotiating authority, it took the heat off the unions. But President Scott's attempts to resurrect it has pushed their paranoia buttons all over again."

"But Joe Aprile is against fast-track," someone said.

"True," said another participant. "But he's hardly in a position to take on the president over it."

That led to a debate on just how far the VP could distance himself from the administration on certain issues, particularly international trade.

Jankowski offered his take: "As long as the news out of Mexico continues to be bad, the more imperative it is, I believe, that Aprile begin somehow to put forth an alternative approach to the president's trade agenda. Look."

He laid a batch of newspaper clippings on the table.

"The *Times, Post, L.A. Times, Wall Street Journal,* a dozen others with stories about corruption in Mexico, virtually all involving the drug trade."

He picked up the pile.

" 'Mexico Editor Hurt in Ambush; His Bodyguard and Gunman Die.' This editor wrote editorials critical of the drug runners. The founder of *La Prensa* was murdered for the same reason a few months back. Here's another: 'Crime Against Tourists Rises in Mexico City.' Know what the figures say? Crime was up thirty-five percent in 1995, thirty-three percent in ninety-six, and climbing. How's this? The army had to go in and take over a police barracks because it was a hotbed. The army is becoming the country's only law enforcement agency, and it's rife with drug payoffs. 'Drug Ties Taint Two Mexican Governors.' 'Drug Connection Links Mexican Military to Abductions.' 'Ex-Officer Says He Took Bags of Cash to Mexico Anti-Drug Chief.' 'Drug Trade Feeds off Payoffs at Mexico Line.' 'Drug Gang in Mexico Outguns Police with High-tech Devices.' "

As Jankowski read the headlines, his voice became more strident. Finally, he tossed the clips back on the table. "Seventy-five percent of all cocaine entering this country comes through Mexico and right up our kids' noses. Mexican drug overlords earn as much as thirty billion a year. They pay off everybody, top government officials, police, the military—"

He sat back and threw up his hands. "As long as this is the case in Mexico, voters here will be taking a harder look at anyone running for president who turns his back on it in the interest of trade—dollars—money."

Aprile's liaison with Congress, Tom Costain, said, "I agree with Alex. But it's not just what the press is reporting about Mexico. The Republicans in Congress pressing for a hearing into the president's fund-raising are damned serious about it.

Congressman Curtain is vicious. He hates this president, will do anything short of assassination to bring him down. My prediction is that there will be hearings and that they'll drag on well into next year, maybe even up to the election. What comes out won't be pretty, and it'll stick to Joe Aprile like Krazy Glue."

"More coffee?"

"We need more."

Jankowski held up an empty pot to a waiter who stood just outside the sliding glass partition. The conversation took a time-out from politics until a new ration of coffee had been served.

"Horrible, what happened to that young woman here at the Watergate this morning," Susan Kaplan said, refilling her juice glass.

"What was that?" Mac asked, assuming she meant at the hotel.

"You didn't hear?"

"I left the apartment in a rush," Mac said.

"She jumped from the roof of the east building."

"Jumped? A suicide?"

"Seems that way," Costain said. "Just a quick item on the radio this morning."

"Seems like this esteemed address is taking its lumps," Smith said. "Two violent deaths within a week. Who was she?"

"I hadn't heard it, either," Jankowski said.

Others shrugged in response to Mac's question.

The second round of coffee served, they got back to the issue at hand, the vice president's Mexico dilemma, and were ten minutes into the second act when Chris Hedras arrived, out of breath and carrying an armload of folders, magazines, and newspapers.

"Sorry I'm late," he said, dropping the pile on an empty chair and taking the adjacent one. "What did I miss?"

"The raspberry Danish," Jankowski said. "We finished them."

"Now I know who my friends are."

Jankowski brought Hedras up to date on what had been discussed.

"Don't let me interrupt," Hedras said. "I'm listening."

"Will the veep be here?" Susan Kaplan asked.

"No," Hedras answered.

"All right," Jankowski said, "let's hear from each of you on this problem of the unions backing away from their support."

The breakfast meeting lasted until a few minutes before nine. Its participants gathered their belongings, walked through the restaurant's main room, where hotel guests enjoyed breakfast, and down the corridor to the anteroom leading to the hotel's lower entrance. As Mac was about to break away from the group and go up the stairs to the lobby, Hedras intercepted him.

"A word, Mac?"

"Sure. It was a good meeting, some false starts but productive, I think, at least for our initial get-together."

"Glad to hear it. Mac, the vice president wondered if you could meet with him later today."

"Hmmm. I have a few things on the docket, but nothing that can't be rescheduled. What's it about?"

"He'll fill you in. He asks that we keep it between us."

"Not a problem. Where and when?"

"His office at the White House. Two o'clock."

"I'll be there."

"Great. Your name will be at the gate. Have them call me. I'll come out and get you."

Smith watched Hedras scurry away, legs moving fast, body bent forward to pick up added momentum. What a delirious life it must be for someone like Hedras, he thought. Look up "rat race" in the dictionary and the illustration is someone running for president of the United States, and those around him running even faster.

He picked up a newspaper in the lobby and sat at the empty

Potomac Lounge's bar. The attractive, young Asiatic bartender came from behind the back bar and asked if she could get him anything.

"No, thanks." He considered having another cup of coffee, but decided to wait until he got home. Mackensie Smith was a self-acknowledged coffee snob; even the Watergate's coffee was not up to his standards. "A club soda, please. Wedge of lime. I'm thirsty."

He scanned the paper and sipped his drink, enjoying the half-hour respite. As he turned the pages, he wondered about the purpose of the afternoon's meeting. Probably had to do with his upcoming trip to Mexico, he decided.

He skimmed the sports pages—the Orioles were in a tight race for the pennant; George Foreman had come out of his most recent retirement and knocked out another journeyman heavy-weight; and the Redskins had signed a free-agent lineman with mediocre credentials to a two-year contract worth seven mil-lion. Smith shook his head. He was about to leave when a small item inside the first section caught his eye. It was about the young woman who'd fallen to her death the night before from the east building. It reported only that the event had happened, that her name was Laura Flores, and that she was Mexican and worked in Washington. The police were investigating.

"Mexican," Mac muttered to himself as he stood and placed money on the bar. The man shot to death in the parking garage had been Mexican. Joe Aprile's campaign for the presidency seemed increasingly to hinge upon his posture toward Mexico. The Mexican national elections were coming up, and he and Annabel would be there.

Funny, he thought, as he left the hotel through its main en-trance and headed for his apartment in the south building, how once you became interested in something, it seemed to be everywhere. Consider buying a certain model car and that's all you seem to see on the streets. Enjoy a play by an unknown play-wright and his name suddenly appears in every newspaper and magazine.

"Mexico," Smith said aloud.

A nation of masks, as Nobel prize–winning Mexican poet Octavio Paz had described it.

"We lie out of pleasure and fantasy," Paz had written, "just like all imaginative people, but also to hide and protect ourselves from strangers. Lying has a decisive importance in our daily lives, in politics, in love, in friendship. By lying, we not only pretend to deceive others, but also ourselves. . . . That is why denouncing it is futile."

Mac took Rufus for a walk after returning home. They circled the Watergate complex, the dog stopping every few feet to smell the grass and bushes, Mac's thoughts going nowhere in particular. It was when they reached the statue of Benito Juárez on Virginia Avenue, and Mac saw police yellow crime scene tape securing a small area on the ground next to the east building, that his mind focused. He looked up to the roof. Now all he could think of was the young woman falling from it. What thoughts were racing through her mind as she fell? Did she scream? Were her arms and legs extended, or was she curled into a fetal position? Did she hit headfirst, or on her legs, ramming them up into her body?

He closed his eyes for a moment. When he opened them, he found himself suddenly desiccated. Sadly, he said to his dog, "Let's get home, Rufe—where it's safe."

CHAPTER 19

That Same Morning
Metropolitan Police Headquarters

Peterson and Jenkins had spent six hours with fellow detectives Monroe and Silverstein questioning people in the south wing of the Watergate's east apartment building. It hadn't been productive.

The lobby clerk confirmed "the young lady" had gone up to the party at approximately eight-thirty. He hadn't seen her again.

"How long did the party last?" Peterson asked.

The clerk gave a shrug. "Had to be before midnight 'cause that's when I went off. They were all down by then."

"How do you know all of them were down?" Jenkins asked. "Did you count them when they went up?"

"No, but—"

"But you figure most of them had come down by then," Peterson offered.

"Right."

"Who replaced you?"

He gave a name and a phone number.

Neighbors of the apartment in which the party took place had nothing to offer, except that things had gotten noisy at one point.

"I don't like having an apartment used only for parties," an elderly woman said. "People should live in apartments. Nice people. Families. Married people."

"Yes, ma'am."

None of the neighbors had seen anyone from the party.

Before leaving the building, Peterson got a call from Chief LaRocca: "Grab some breakfast, then get over to the Mexican-American Trade Alliance, talk to whoever was at the party from there. I just called. They're in on Saturday. Get a list of other guests. Check in when you're through. It's in the Watergate six-hundred office building, on New Hampshire." He gave Peterson several names.

Peterson and Jenkins went to a McDonald's and settled in a booth with coffee, juice, and breakfast sandwiches. Jenkins ordered two sandwiches and ate them quickly.

"So how come Monroe and Silverstein get pulled off?"

Peterson's laugh was wearied. "Looks like we're the designated Mexican team, Wendell. Better enroll in Berlitz."

Wendell Jenkins leaned back and worked his neck against a stiffness. He squeezed his eyes shut, opened them, and said, "This doesn't square with me, Joe. The jumper didn't live in that building but she ends up with a set of keys that open the doors to the roof. She goes up there by herself, smokes a joint, drinks wine, then jumps? Who gave her the keys?"

"Maybe she'd been there before, knew where they were hanging."

"Could be. The lobby clerk says there were a couple of dozen people went up to the party. Wish they'd had to sign in, sign out."

"It'd help. You want something else, Wendell?"

The heavy black detective grinned. "I could eat a couple more but I won't. Gotta keep up with the diet. Or keep down with it."

As they were about to get into their car, Peterson asked, "How can you be on a diet and wolf down two of those sandwiches?"

"Usually, I'd have four. See, I'm doing great. I cut the calories in half. Come on, let's get this over with."

—　　—　　—

The Mexican-American Trade Alliance's managing director, Venustiano Valle, showed the detectives into a small, cluttered conference room where Rosa, the receptionist, served them strong coffee. Windows at one end of the room looked out over New Hampshire Avenue and the Kennedy Center. Another wall was covered by a relief map of Mexico. Crooked photographs of PRI politicians, and industry leaders, hung haphazardly on the wall opposite, making for odd symbolism, Jenkins thought.

"A great tragedy," Valle said after taking a chair across the oval table from them.

They'd decided that Jenkins would ask the questions while Peterson took notes.

"Tell me about this apartment in the east building," Jenkins said.

Valle extended his hands; the corners of his fleshy lips curved downward. "A corporate apartment," he said. "For visiting dignitaries, and occasional social occasions."

"This is a corporation?"

"No. We are an association."

"Lobbyists."

"Yes."

"Registered?"

"Yes."

"How long have you had the apartment?"

"Less than a year."

"Must be pretty expensive."

"Not as expensive as using hotels."

"I suppose not. What was the purpose of this party last night?"

Another gesture for understanding, and a guttural laugh. "Since when do Mexicans need a reason for a party?"

Jenkins and Peterson gave him a hard stare.

The smile disappeared. "We wished to thank some of our friends who have recently been helpful in our work. That is all. To thank them."

"You have a list of who was at the party?"

Valle frowned. "Perhaps not a formal list. I could ask Rosa to bring what we have."

"Yeah, do that."

A few minutes after Valle called, Rosa entered the room carrying a piece of paper on which names were handwritten.

"Give it to them," Valle said.

Peterson scanned the names, looked up, and asked, "Are these the ones who were invited, or the ones who actually showed up?"

Valle looked to Rosa.

"The ones who received invitations," she said.

"Written invitations?" Jenkins asked.

"No," said Valle. "They were called."

"Uh-huh. Mr. Valle, did you spend time with Ms. Flores at the party?"

"Yes. We joked." To Rosa: "Thank you. That will be all."

"About what?"

"My young assistant. He and Ms. Flores had seen each other a few times."

"Dated?"

"Dated? Oh, yes, dated. I joked that she kept him out late."

"She was in a good mood?"

"She seemed to be. Well . . . "

Peterson looked up from his notepad. "Well, *what?*"

"I sensed a certain sadness in her. *Tristeza.*"

"What was she sad about?"

"I do not know."

"Was she still there when you left the apartment?"

"Yes. I left early."

"This assistant of yours. What's his name?"

"Chapas. Jose Chapas."

"Is he here?"

"Yes. Would you like me to get him?"

"When we're done with you."

— — —

Fifteen minutes later, Valle escorted the melancholic Jose Chapas into the conference room. Peterson and Jenkins noted that he seemed anxious, had difficulty meeting their eyes.

"Thanks for coming in," Peterson said. "Only take a few minutes."

"About Laura," Chapas said, head lowered, focus on the floor.

"That's right," Jenkins said. "We understand you and she were dating."

Chapas looked up. "Dating? Like a boyfriend and girlfriend? No. We were friends, that's all."

"That's not what we hear," Peterson said, a deliberate edge to his voice.

Chapas looked down again, not responding.

"Did you bring Ms. Flores to the party?" Jenkins asked.

"No." His voice picked up animation. "I was at the party working. She came alone."

Peterson said, "I see she isn't on this invitation list, Mr. Chapas. You invite her?"

"No. I mean, I asked her to come, to stop by. Not a formal invitation. I was there working."

"So you said. You spent time with her at the party?"

"Of course. Not much. I had to leave suddenly to go to the office. An emergency."

"This office?"

"Yes."

"What time did you leave?"

"I'm not sure. Maybe ten. A little earlier."

"Was Ms. Flores in good spirits at the party?"

Jenkins's question caused Chapas to straighten up, sit back, and consider his answer. "It is interesting you ask that," he said.

"Why?"

"Because I hadn't thought of it before now. She was—she was sad, I would say. Distracted. No, not happy at all."

"Why?"

"She didn't say."

"But you knew her pretty well. What about before the party? When you were on a date."

"Nothing. Always happy. But not that night. I—"

"Yeah?"

"I don't feel well. Are we finished?"

"For the moment."

Chapas stood. "I want you to know that I liked Laura a lot. I respected her, too."

"Love her?"

"Please, could I be excused?"

"Sure. We'll get back to you."

After Chapas had left the room, Jenkins turned to his partner and said, "He and his boss both say she was sad. His boss says he joked with her. How the hell does he know she was sad? How come they both came to that conclusion, used the same word, 'sad'?"

"I'd say they got together on it. This kid Chapas can be cracked."

"I had the same feeling. I think his relationship with the girl was more than he's admitting to."

"Definitely worth another visit."

"Definitely."

Peterson stood, yawned, and headed for the door. "Let's get back and fill in LaRocca. Christ, I'm beat. *Cansado.* That's Spanish for 'tired,' I think. I remember it from high school."

When they reached the lobby, Peterson paused to peruse the building's directory.

"Joe Aprile's campaign headquarters is here."

"Maybe there'll be another break-in," Jenkins said, his laugh bordering on a giggle.

"Yeah," Peterson said. "Wouldn't that be a hoot?"

Chapter 20

Two O'Clock That Afternoon
The White House

Mac Smith was escorted into the West Wing by a young female marine and asked to wait for Chris Hedras, who arrived ten minutes later.

"Sorry I'm late," he said. "Keeping to a timetable around here isn't always easy, weekends included."

"Not a problem," Smith said. "I hear the president isn't the most punctual of people."

Hedras said without smiling, "Drives the veep nuts. He considers himself late if he isn't early. Come on. He's waiting for you."

"I assumed we'd meet in the old Executive Building," Smith said as they walked. The vice president's official office was there, not in the White House.

"The vice president has been spending more time these days over here, Mac. Getting the feel for it, maybe, for when he moves in."

Hedras led them to a cozy pocket dining room on the first floor with windows looking out over a rose garden considerably smaller than the famed one. The table could accommodate six; three places were set with starched white linen, weighty silverware, and etched glasses.

"We're eating?" Smith asked.

"Yes. Lunch. The vice president doesn't get around to lunch until about this time."

Mac was glad he'd had only fruit a few hours ago.

Joe Aprile came through the door followed by two staffers. "Mac, hello. Thanks for coming."

"My pleasure."

Aprile said to the young people with him, "Have the Norwegians in place at three for the photos."

"They want to meet with you before that," one said.

"Five minutes, no more."

"Yes, sir."

The door closed, leaving Smith, Aprile, and Hedras alone in the room. The vice president sat at the table and gestured for the others to do the same. "I ordered for us," he said. Then, without any hint of levity, added, "And we're not having guacamole."

Smith glanced at Hedras, whose expression said nothing.

Aprile to Hedras: "Call the kitchen. Lunch in twenty minutes."

As his campaign honcho went to a phone in a corner and placed the call, Aprile said to Mac, "Whatever's said in this room doesn't leave it."

"Understood," Smith said, aware of the tension in his friend.

Hedras joined them. "Twenty minutes," he said.

"All right," Aprile said, sounding as though he was bracing for something unpleasant, "I won't take more time than necessary. You're heading for Mexico in what—nine, ten days?"

Smith nodded.

"I'd like you to go sooner than that."

"Oh? How much sooner?"

"A day or two earlier."

"I think I can swing it, although I'm not sure Annabel can."

It occurred to Smith as he said it that when dealing with such lofty echelons of government, it probably didn't, or shouldn't, matter what a spouse's schedule was. "But she can always join me later," he added.

Aprile ignored the modification. "I want you to go to Mexico, Mac, as my special envoy." He narrowed his eyes and looked at Smith, inviting a response.

"As part of my responsibilities as an election observer?" Smith asked.

"In addition to," Aprile said. "And strictly without credentials."

Mac's eyebrows went up. "You'll have to explain," he said.

Aprile replied, "I won't say I don't mean to be vague because that would be a lie. I *have* to be vague, Mac, for reasons I'll be able to tell you when your trip is over."

"Tell me what you can, Mr. Vice President," Smith said. "The blanks can be filled in later."

"Okay," said Aprile. "You're aware of the two murders at the Watergate."

"*Two* murders? The gentleman in the garage, yes. The young woman who fell from the east building? I wasn't aware it was murder."

Aprile looked to Hedras: "Why don't you fill Mac in, Chris."

Hedras had removed his gray tweed sport jacket and hung it

over the back of his chair. He shifted position, allowing him to face Smith and to cross his legs.

"The man killed in the Watergate garage, Morin Garza, was in Washington to provide information to a group known as The Mexico Initiative. Hear of them?"

Mac frowned. "Just recently. But I don't know anything about them."

"It's a lobbying group, Mac, although they don't claim to be. Never registered as such. Calls itself a think tank."

"What was Mr. Garza going to tell them?" Mac asked.

"What they wanted to hear," Hedras said. "Garza knew a lot about corruption in Mexico, especially union corruption."

Aprile interjected, "The Mexico Initiative is an organization very much at odds with the ruling PRI. They're small, but they have many supporters back in Mexico. The Washington office is headed by a man named Ramon Kelly. Ever hear of *him*?"

"No."

"A dedicated foe of the PRI. A champion of Mexico's disenfranchised."

"The young woman who fell—was murdered, you say—she worked for The Mexico Initiative, didn't she? At least that's what I heard."

Hedras said, "True. She was the organization's researcher."

"And you say it was murder. Have the police come to that conclusion?"

There was a knock at the door. Hedras opened it and allowed two waiters in short, crisp white jackets and black trousers to enter, carrying trays with covered dishes. The three men were silent as their lunch of consommé, jumbo shrimp on a lettuce bed, and rolls and butter were served, and water glasses filled.

"Anything else, sir?" a waiter asked.

"No, that's fine," Aprile said. "Thank you."

"The police?" Hedras said once they were alone again. "No,

they haven't come to that determination, although they're leaning in that direction."

Mac tasted his soup, savored it, then asked, "Was she killed for
the same reason Garza was? Because she knew something and
was about to tell someone else?"

"It appears that way, Mac," Joe Aprile said.

"All right," Smith said, "the next obvious question is who
would have been so injured by what these two people knew that
they'd resort to murder?"

Neither Aprile nor Hedras responded.

"Are you saying the PRI?" Mac said.

"Someone acting on their behalf," Aprile said.

"Hmmm," Mac said. "Any idea who that might be?"

"I thought you might find that out when you're in Mexico,"
Aprile said.

Mac sat back and dabbed at his mouth with his napkin. He
looked to Hedras, then to Aprile before saying, "Murder is a job
for law enforcement, not a law professor." As an afterthought:
"Or the CIA. They're good at coming up with information."

Aprile ran an index finger over his lips before saying, "Here's
where the vagueness comes in, Mac. The two murders here at
the Watergate are just symptoms, not the disease. There are ramifications far beyond finding out who killed these people, political ramifications that go to the heart of our relationship with
Mexico and its government."

Mac said to Hedras, "I sense you know quite a bit about this
Mexico Initiative, Chris."

"Some."

"Care to share some of that 'some' with me?"

Aprile replied, "Let's just say, Mac, that the work of The Mexico Initiative is not unknown to Chris, or me, or to others working with us. I know I'm imposing a heavy burden on you in
making this request. And you know all you have to do is say no."

He cracked his first smile since arriving. "Of course, I'm assuming you won't—say no."

"A safe assumption, Mr. Vice President. Who'll fill me in on what I'm to do, and who I'm to see in Mexico?"

"I will," Hedras said.

"All right."

"I prefer that we not meet again about this subject, Mac," Aprile said. "Certainly not here in the White House."

The comment struck Mac as odd, but he said nothing.

"I have to leave." Aprile stood. "Chris, why don't you and Mac spend a little time together this afternoon. Maybe take a walk, grab a drink."

Mac silently translated: Get lost and find a private place to talk.

"Okay with you, Mac?"

"Sure. Want to come back to the apartment?"

Hedras grinned, said, "Your place or mine? We're neighbors."

"Mine," said Smith.

The vice president left the room after shaking Mac's hand. Hedras and Smith exited the White House and walked slowly along F Street in the direction of the Watergate.

— — —

"That's a big dog," Hedras said after entering Smith's apartment in the south building.

"Big, and docile. Loves everybody and assumes everybody loves him. The worst he'll do is drool on your pants. Coffee? A drink?"

"I wouldn't mind some wine if you have it."

"Red or white?"

"White."

They settled in the living room, Hedras's wine in his hand,

Smith's nonalcoholic Buckler beer in a mug on a table next to him. "So," Mac said, "this organization, The Mexico Initiative, is allegedly at the root of—or is the cause of—the two deaths here at the Watergate. The vice president said it was someone acting on behalf of the PRI."

Hedras nodded.

"Is that your belief, too, Chris?"

"I don't know. But I'm not debating it with the boss. All I know for sure is that Kelly and his people at the Initiative are hell-bent on building a case against the PRI, which, of course—"

"Which, of course, *what?*"

"Which supports the vice president's posture on Mexico."

Mac sipped his beer. "I have a feeling you're not entirely in agreement with that posture?"

"Maybe not with his fervor, but I understand where he's coming from. There's a lot at stake. Treasury estimates that if our trading partnership with Mexico deteriorates, it could mean as many as a half million more illegal immigrants pouring over the border every year."

"I heard the president say that very thing," Smith said. "In a speech a week ago."

Hedras laughed. "It's not much of a secret that the president and Joe Aprile see Mexico through different telescopes."

"So I've heard," Smith said, smiling. "Chris, would I be off base in assuming that you and the vice president have a better idea of who carried out the killings than you're admitting to?"

"Just speculation, not worth discussing. About your trip, Mac. The vice president chose you for a number of reasons. One, you're someone he trusts implicitly. Two, you're on his commission studying U.S.–Mexican relations. Three, you'll already be in Mexico as an election observer. And four, you mentioned you'd be going on to San Miguel de Allende after the election."

"Why would *that* be of interest to him?" Mac asked.

"The person he wants you to meet with operates in that area."

" 'Operates'? As opposed to living there?"

"He's a rebel, Mac, a revolutionary, head of a group that broke off from Marcos's Zapatista National Liberation Army after the ninety-four insurgency in Chiapas."

"I remember that from what I read, and saw on TV. New Year's Day, wasn't it?"

"Yes. That crazy band of guerrillas sent the country's finances into a tailspin. Wall Street panicked, along with investors from every other country. American fat cats lost billions in a few weeks, thirty billion or more. A million layoffs of Mexican workers, hundreds of corporate bankruptcies. Stock in Mexican companies dropped by seventy billion."

"All due to the Chiapas revolt?"

"It triggered it, Mac."

"And President Scott came to the rescue."

"For which I give him a lot of credit. It was the biggest bailout of a country in history until the Korea save. It stabilized Mexico."

Smith took another sip and scrutinized the handsome young man sitting opposite him. Hedras was reciting the party line— but not necessarily that of Joe Aprile where Mexico was concerned. That aside, he was an impressive guy, Smith thought, demonstrably bright, filled with the requisite energy for such a job, and someone in and for whom Joe Aprile obviously had great trust and respect. *If I had a daughter, he wouldn't make a bad son-in-law.*

"Tell me more about this revolutionary I'm supposed to meet. Who is he?"

"His name is Carlos Unzaga, claims to be a direct descendant of Ignacio de Allende y Unzaga."

"And who was *he*?" Smith asked. "Mexican history is not my strong suit. Another revolutionary?"

"A general, a liberal idealist in the early eighteen hundreds. He hooked up with the famous Father Hidalgo to launch a revolt against the Spanish government. Paid for it with his life. He and the others had their heads lopped off. San Miguel de Allende is named after him."

"Interesting. You've obviously studied Mexican history."

"A little. I get a lot about San Miguel from Elfie Dorrance. She has a mansion there."

"So I've heard. This Carlos Unzaga. Why would he agree to meet with someone like me?"

"Because you'll be representing Joseph Aprile, vice president of the United States. Unzaga sent word through channels that he'll only meet with an Aprile envoy. Has to be unofficial, top secret. There's a hefty price on Unzaga's head."

"By the PRI?"

"By certain factions within it. They take a lot of unnecessary heat."

"The PRI?"

"Yes. There's lots to criticize there, but they've kept Mexico relatively stable for seventy years."

Smith decided not to contribute to a political debate over Mexico. He turned his attention again to the man he was to meet under clandestine circumstances.

"You said Unzaga sent word through 'channels' that he wanted to speak with someone representing Joe Aprile. What channels?"

"Can't say."

"The Mexico Initiative?"

Hedras answered with a blank stare.

Smith asked, "How do I make contact with him?"

"That's being worked out as we speak," Hedras said. "It will be in a public place. You and Mrs. Smith are staying at Casa de Sierra Nevada?"

"That's right. It's Annabel's hotel of choice whenever she's been to San Miguel."

"I'll fill you in as soon as plans are firm."

"You say all I'm to do is to hear Unzaga out?"

"Right. He claims he has information that will sink a lot of the PRI's leaders. Big drug payoffs to them, abject corruption, all the usual charges . . . but documented."

Smith scowled; he couldn't resist getting back into a political discussion.

" 'Usual charges'? You sound a little too dismissive, Chris. The problem with the stories of drug-fueled corruption in Mexico is all too real. I heard a Mexican newspaper editor the other day on NPR. He said drugs are such a serious problem in Mexico they're now considered a national security issue."

"I wasn't making light of it, Mac. It's a hell of a problem. I just think that the government needs help in fighting it, not criticism." His laugh was forced. "Don't tell my boss I said that."

"It's safe with me," Smith said. "Anything else to tell me?"

"Not at the moment. I brought a few clippings on Unzaga, thought you might want to learn a little about him. Colorful character, bigger than life, inspires loyalty from the *indigenas* who follow him—Indians, dirt farmers, the sort of people easily swayed by charismatic characters like Unzaga, Villa, Hidalgo. There's always somebody in Mexico to lead a revolt." He stood up. "Well, I'd better run. I've taken up a lot of your time, and I'm due back at the White House. I'm sure you know, Mac, how much the vice president and I appreciate what you've agreed to do."

"Sure. I'll look forward to hearing more. By the way, is there a specific date and place the vice president wants me to meet this Unzaga?"

"A day or two before the election. In Mexico City."

"But I thought—"

"Not Unzaga himself, his envoy. I have no idea who he is, but he'll make contact with you at your hotel there, set things up for later in San Miguel, where you and Unzaga will meet."

"All right."

Mac and Rufus walked Hedras to the door.

"Enjoying life in the Watergate?" Hedras asked.

"Very much, although I wish people would stop being killed here."

"I know what you mean. Might depress real estate values."

"That wasn't quite what I had in mind. Depresses me. Look forward to hearing from you."

Smith spent the rest of the afternoon running over a lesson plan for a law class he was to teach on Monday. Although his dean had given him carte blanche to leave his classes to a substitute professor when necessary to carry out his responsibilities for the vice president, he felt a compelling obligation to meet his teaching schedule whenever possible.

In anticipation of Annabel's return from the gallery, he laid out the ingredients for that evening's dinner—thoroughly washed romaine lettuce for a Caesar salad with a dressing he'd recently perfected, croutons ready to be crisped in the toaster oven, thin, free-range chicken cutlets he would sauté with wine and garlic, and a baguette—which he didn't have.

He went down to the mall and bought the bread at the pastry shop, successfully resisting, this time, a dessert. He returned to the south building and waited for the elevator. He stepped in and pushed the button for his floor. As the doors started to slide shut, a man suddenly appeared. Mac instinctively shoved his hand between the doors, causing them to open. The man stepped in, ignored Mac, ran a hand through his yellow, silken hair, and pushed a button with the other.

The elevator stopped at the floor beneath Mac's. The doors opened, and the man stepped into the hallway and disappeared.

"You're welcome," Mac muttered in the man's wake.

A simple thank you for holding the elevator would have been in order. High on Mackensie Smith's growing, shifting list of pet peeves was the current lack of civility.

CHAPTER 21

The Next Day
San Miguel de Allende, Mexico

The original portion of Elfie Dorrance's home in San Miguel had been built in the late 1700s, a classic example of churrigueresque architecture developed by the Spanish architect. Churriguera had wonderful visions, but committed few to paper. With scanty sketches to consult, the workmen had created a free-form work of art with pink stone, marble, and colorful tiles. The result was not harmonious, but certainly stunning. Additions over the years expanded the house all the way to the perimeter of Parque Benito Juárez, a sprawling, peaceful haven of juniper and soapberry trees, bougainvillea and dahlias, fountains, swarms of monarch butterflies and flocks of white egrets. The final addition under Elfie's direction created yet another wing with a rooftop terrace overlooking the park. Included in the renovation was an elaborate commercial water purification unit.

Elfie took her coffee and freshly baked cinnamon roll on a rear terrace. She'd arrived in Mexico City the previous night on a British Airways flight from London, and was driven the three and a half hours to San Miguel by a uniformed chauffeur always at her disposal when in Mexico. She'd slept soundly in the mountain village's customary nighttime coolness. Now the sun had risen, warming things, including the spirits—and memories.

— — —

This house had been purchased in 1974, the second year of Elfie's marriage to Charles Frampton, special White House counsel. Frampton had come to Washington from New York brandishing a distinguished family name. His father, Charles Frampton—tacking "Junior" onto a son's name was anathema to the family—earned his fortune manufacturing railroad equipment in upstate New York, and had made the preordained move from industrial success to political influence, never holding public office but wielding power behind a variety of thrones: confidant to governors, advisor to congressmen, banker to those whose conservative, Republican political directions agreed with his map of the world.

Elfie Dorrance and Charles Frampton met at a fund-raising party for the National Symphony. Washington rumormongers had much to say about this new couple. One popular topic had to do with opposites attracting. Elfie stood a foot taller than Frampton, which made more of a point of her natural, graceful, somewhat ample beauty. Frampton was slender and slightly bent, and wore his mouse-colored hair longer than would be expected of a White House counsel. Pale blue eyes, magnified behind quarter-inch-thick glasses, were perpetually wet, causing him to frequently wipe them with a handkerchief: "The Weeper" was his very unofficial nickname.

What Charles Frampton lacked in physical stature, however, he made up for in intellect. He was considered a brilliant lawyer, with an ability to shape arguments into such irrefutable positions that it was difficult, often impossible, to effectively attack them.

Frampton had two children from his previous marriage. They lived with their mother; that their father existed was more myth than tangible reality for them, so seldom did he visit, or otherwise acknowledge their existence.

Elfie and Charles married at a small, quiet ceremony at St. John's Episcopal Church on Lafayette Square, across from the White House, the "church of presidents," or some presidents, at least. Neither bride nor groom were represented by family. A cocktail reception for close friends followed at the Mayflower Hotel.

Elfie had been living in a relatively modest Georgetown row house since coming to Washington following the death of Dieter Krueger, enticed there by the wife of the British ambassador, who claimed that America's staid capital needed a dose of Elfie's spice and verve. Once married to Frampton, she set out to find a house befitting their status, falling in love immediately with the stately sixteen-room home near Dumbarton Oaks. Although she'd conferred with her new husband, she really didn't have to. It mattered little to him where he lived. His schedule at the White House left him no time to enjoy a home, and he gladly gave his bride a blank check.

The home in San Miguel was not as easily won.

She'd made many trips to Mexico at the invitation of well-placed Mexican friends, including Central Bank president Antonio Morelos, whose vacation homes included a secluded hilltop villa in San Miguel de Allende. One trip there was all

Elfie needed to contact a real estate agent and snap up the house near the park for the price of a modest tract house in the States.

"Fine. I have no intention of spending time in Mexico," Charles Frampton said when she informed him of her purchase. He was preparing to leave his post with the Ford administration to join a stalwart Washington law firm.

"It will be a good place to escape," she countered. "Now that you won't be at the president's beck and call, you'll have some time to relax. It's beautiful there, Charles, bursting with art and history. It's been designated a national monument, no traffic lights or neon signs or dreadful fast-food places. The weather is perfect, the people charming, and—"

They'd just settled in for their customary martini before dinner. He reacted to her litany of San Miguel virtues by dropping his glass to the marble floor, removing his glasses, and bringing his small face close to hers. He was red; his lips quivered. He growled, "I will not set foot in that filthy, disgusting country. That's the end of it, Elfie. Case closed."

Her husband had a sweet side to him, which he exhibited from time to time, usually when presenting her with a piece of jewelry—or when wanting her to come to bed after having soaked and scrubbed her feet so he could fondle and kiss them. But he'd also begun displaying a temper, generally fueled by the third or fourth martini. He'd been identified by political pundits as one of Nixon's favorite Oval Office drinking companions, which was true.

A few months after their blowup, Elfie announced she was going to Mexico for an extended stay to oversee renovations.

"How long will you stay?" he asked.

"As long as it takes to put it in order. I want it to be perfect, Charles, for you, because I know you'll come one day."

He displayed an infrequent smile. "Perhaps I will," he said. "When it's perfect."

Although Elfie made the house as nearly perfect as time and money could—she spent almost a million dollars redoing it—Charles Frampton never did see it. His drinking reached alcoholic proportions. He walked as though each step was searching for the ground, and was faced each morning with the choice of drinking vodka to steady his trembling hands and being drunk when he went to the office, or not drinking and shaking like a man with Parkinson's disease.

Elfie eventually stopped pointing to her husband's condition because it triggered angry outbursts. As with her second husband, Dieter, Elfie and Charles settled into a negotiated coexistence in their Washington home, with separate quarters and even more separate lives. She spent much of each year in London or Mexico. When in Washington, she threw herself into social and charitable causes, while her husband continued down his self-destructive slide.

Charles Frampton's funeral was held almost ten years to the day from when he and Elfie married. It drew a sizable crowd, and some genuine mourners. Those who'd worked with him in government and private practice were there to pay their respects. Elfie's multitude of friends also showed up and delivered customary expressions of sorrow, although they were well aware that any close emotional attachment to Charles Frampton had dissipated, then vanished—and that Charles had left his already wealthy widow with another small fortune to ease the pain of loss.

She flew to Mexico the day after the funeral and stayed a month, long enough to meet and fall in love with Jeremy Mahon, sixty-four, tall and lanky, distinguished, compellingly handsome, married, and on the *Forbes* list of the five hundred richest Americans. This last distinction was thanks to his worldwide construction firm, which had hundreds of millions of dollars in contracts with Mexico's ruling PRI to improve the country's infrastructure, and the income of Mexico's elite.

He divorced his wife in California, married Elfie the day after it became final, and the new Mr. and Mrs. Mahon swelled the ranks of jet-setters as they flew the globe together, a comely couple at the top of their game. Mahon's new wife introduced him to Washington's corridors of power, which not only provided him with psychic satisfaction; it was good for business. From Elfie's perspective, she was now "legitimate." She was a married woman again, no threat to her female friends, and had an elegant man on her arm.

But there was more than that. Finally, she'd met someone for whom her love was complete, physical and emotional, sent from heaven but hardly angelic: Mahon's sexual appetite and stamina hadn't heard of his sixtieth birthday. Elfie Dorrance's knight had arrived.

— — —

By eleven, Elfie was showered, exercised, massaged, dressed, and conferring with the chef and his staff brought in for that evening's dinner party for the U.S. ambassador to Mexico, his wife, and a dozen other guests.

"The ambassador is fond of lamb," she told the chef, "but his wife—a sour woman but harmless enough—is partial to salads and vegetables. I mean, she's not a strict vegetarian—I have a vegetarian friend who simply can't give up her bacon—but she is happier when her plate is filled with leafy green things."

"But she does eat some meat," the chef said.

"Oh, yes."

"The rack of lamb should be perfect," he said. "A small portion of meat surrounded by . . ." He laughed. "Surrounded by leafy green things."

"Splendid. Now, for Senor and Senora Zegreda . . . "

By noon, everything had been agreed upon for the evening. The chef was a young Californian who'd won accolades in two restaurants there, but who'd moved to San Miguel de Allende to establish its only gourmet catering service. With as many as four thousand Americans and Canadians living there, he was seldom without a commission. He went to work with his sous chef and pâtissier in Elfie's large, professionally equipped kitchen. The serving staff made its preparations under the watchful eyes of Elfie's live-in Mexican husband-and-wife team. The evening's liquor supply had been delivered, the gardeners had spruced up the front courtyard, and Elfie was free to go to lunch with the wife of the governor of Guanajuato, the state in which San Miguel was situated. They met in the stunning, lush garden restaurant of Casa de Sierra Nevada, proclaimed one of the world's finest small hotels.

"*Buen provecho!*" Elfie said, raising her glass of *agua de jamaica* in a toast to her luncheon companion.

"*Salud!*"

Corita Mendez and Elfie touched rims over the candle on the table, causing the purple hibiscus drink in their balloon glasses to twinkle.

"I wish you and Junipero could join us this evening," Elfie said.

"I wish that, too, but these plans were made months ago. We leave at four. Silao, Dolores Hidalgo. Campaigning is not fun for me."

"I suppose Junipero has to do it, Corita. The elections are days away. But—"

"He has done more of it this time. He says things are not as certain as they were. Who is coming tonight?"

"Fourteen people. The ambassador and his wife. Senor and Mrs. Zegreda. Antonio Morelos. His wife is ill. Viviana Diaz will be his table partner."

Corita Mendez laughed. "Lucky Antonio. Did he arrange for his wife to be sick?"

Elfie, too, laughed. "I suspect it wouldn't be the first time."

"And you?"

"Martin. Good old Martin, getting old but still a decent conversationalist. His wit is as brittle as ever."

Over a lunch of *antojitos*—appetizers known in Spanish as "little whims"—and a cup of onion soup for Elfie that she considered the best in the world—she'd had it flown to Washington for special occasions—they chatted about many things, mostly gossipy items about Mexican social and show-business notables. Then their conversation turned to more tangible politics, and the upcoming elections.

Corita's husband, Junipero, had been governor of Guanajuato for fifteen years, a PRI party kingpin whose reelection had never been in question.

Until now.

"What does Junipero say about the elections?" Elfie asked.

Corita's broad, smooth, copper face turned sober. "There could be changes this time," she said, "especially in Mexico City. Cardenas and the PRD look strong there. At least that is what Junipero says. He says governorships in Nuevo León and Querétaro could go to the opposition. Of course, I do not know any of this personally. Politics mystify me."

Me, too, Elfie mused, especially Mexican politics. "What about Junipero?"

"He says he is confident."

"I'm glad to hear that."

"I read that President Scott is concerned," Corita said.

"He certainly is. Cardenas is a leftist."

"The whole PRD, I think."

Elfie sighed and sat back, took in a huge tapestry and terracotta masks that decorated a facing salmon-colored stucco wall. Their two waiters stood poised to respond to their needs. Corita and Elfie were familiar faces at Casa de Sierra Nevada, and their respective positions in Mexican-American circles were known, and acted upon.

Elfie said absently, "A drastic change in government could be devastating to the economy."

"That's what Junipero says. He says the leftists will undo what has been established between your country and ours, the trade, jobs. There will be many reforms."

"Yes," Elfie said, thinking that Vice President Joseph Aprile would welcome those reforms, along with a weakening of the PRI's grip.

Coffee was strong and hot.

The two handsome women crossed the lobby, stopping to say good-bye to Gabriela, the hotel's multilingual concierge, who'd kept a watchful eye on them during lunch, waved to Mannix, the bartender—"The drink was heavenly," Elfie said—and went through the massive, heavy double wooden doors leading to the street, which was immediately beyond the door, separated from it only by a narrow cobblestone sidewalk.

"You will give my best to the ambassador and his wife," Corita said, taking Elfie's hand.

"Of course. Better your best than mine. He's an insufferable little man, don't you agree?"

Corita smiled. She knew her friend had set her sights on being ambassador to Mexico for years, ever since marrying Jeremy Mahon. Her disdain for the current American ambassador was worn on her sleeve—except, of course, when she was with him.

"Have a wonderful party," Corita said. "But of course, you always do."

"And campaign successfully. One thing we don't need is a change in leadership here."

— — —

Russell Cadwell, American ambassador to Mexico, and his wife, Priscilla, arrived in the ambassador's official car and were greeted warmly by Elfie in the expansive foyer. She led them to a room at the rear of the main wing where concertos by Boulez, Kurka, and Milhaud that featured the marimba came from speakers hidden in large plants. Other guests had already gathered.

"Good evening, Mr. Ambassador," businessman Manuel Zegreda said, coming to them and extending his hand. "Mrs. Cadwell." He bowed.

"Senor Zegreda," Cadwell said. "You look well."

"Why not? Living well is the best revenge, huh?"

The ambassador smiled; his wife's cheerless expression did not change.

Cadwell was a short, slight man; someone had once described him as being small and perfectly formed. The planes of his face were angular, his cheekbones pronounced, his chin clear and sharp, nose slightly hooked and thin. Once he'd begun to lose his hair, he'd taken to shaving his head, which made him seem even smaller.

He'd been appointed ambassador to Mexico by a Republican administration, more a matter of a pragmatic president demonstrating a nonpartisan approach to diplomacy than a reward for any unique qualifications.

Cadwell was a Democrat, albeit a conservative one. He was born in Oxford, England, the only son of a professor at the university. They moved to the United States when the young Cadwell was seven, his father accepting a teaching post at the University of Vermont. Russell became fluent in Spanish, and went on to teach Latin American history at the same school. It was there he met and married Priscilla, the unattractive daughter of a logging company founder. Using her family money, he mounted a run for governor in Vermont, lost, then drifted to Washington, where he held a variety of jobs in the State and Labor Departments.

His nomination as ambassador to Mexico caught everyone by surprise, including Cadwell. He'd been generous with Priscilla's money to the Democratic Party, not a nickel to the Republicans. But his past was so lacking in controversy, his visibility so limited, that those charged with confirming him, especially Democrats, were hard-pressed to deny the Republican president's choice.

And so Russell and Priscilla Cadwell moved to Mexico City, to his delight and her chagrin.

Scott, the in-sitting American Democratic president, had elected to retain Cadwell as ambassador, despite growing Republican displeasure with his performance. Critics of the administration's Mexico policy accused Cadwell of being nothing but a pawn of the president's trade-first policy, and of being too cozy with the PRI's leadership.

Elfie Dorrance's criticism of him was less specific, and more simplistic: He held the job she wanted. Therefore he was inept.

"You look lovely," she said to Priscilla Cadwell.

"Thank you."

"I love your dress. Did you buy it here?"

"New York. I'm afraid there isn't much to buy in Mexico for an ambassador's wife."

"Of course. Excuse me. I think another guest has arrived."

Martin Leff accompanied Elfie to the foyer to greet Viviana Diaz. Leff, a wealthy American ex-pat who'd moved to San Miguel twenty years ago because of its low cost of living, had never married. "He must be gay," it was said. Not so. Leff was asexual, and handsome, and bright, which enhanced his acceptability as an escort for women in need of a safe one.

"Ah, Viviana," Elfie said. "How wonderful to see you."

"I was glad I would be in San Miguel tonight," Viviana said, displaying a wide, ravishing smile familiar to anyone who followed Mexico's entertainment industry. She'd been a star in a succession of films, always playing the beautiful other woman using sexual wiles to steal leading men away from their true loves. Although she hadn't made a movie in more than five years, her presence, oddly, had grown, thanks to a succession of rumored affairs with leading politicians and businessmen, one ending in the tragic suicide of a wife.

"You know Martin."

"I don't believe so."

Martin Leff smiled. "No reason for the glamorous Viviana Diaz to know plain ol' Martin Leff," he said. "But I'm delighted to meet you." He spoke in an exaggerated baritone, and with precise pronunciation befitting his role as a nonthreatening gigolo.

They followed Viviana as she made her entrance into the cocktail room. All eyes went to her. To call her beautiful was to do her an injustice. She was more than that. Her large almond eyes were direct and challenging, her full, shining, and sensuous lips and large, white teeth creating the mouth of a temptress worthy of an Aztec myth. But it was her body that had brought her fame on the screen. Her breasts, precariously contained in the low-cut, black evening dress, were large but not vulgar, her waist strikingly small. Were her long legs visible that night, aside from glimpses afforded by a slit on one side of the gown, their symmetrical perfection would have been in evidence, adding to the spectacular effect.

Central Bank president Antonio Morelos, for whom Viviana would be a tablemate, quickly crossed the room, took her hand and kissed it, gave it up reluctantly, straightened, and said, beam-

ing, "I have looked forward to this evening with special pleasure
. . . ever since I learned we would be together."

Hardly the way to put it, Elfie thought, waving for a waiter.
She took Viviana's arm and led her away from Morelos to a knot
of guests talking with Cadwell.

"Ah, Senorita Diaz," Cadwell said, looking up at her. "How
good to see you again."

"Mr. Ambassador," she said. "Mrs. Cadwell."

Cadwell started to introduce her to others, all of which was
unnecessary. A waiter brought Viviana a flute of champagne, refilled others. Glasses were raised; the ambassador offered a flow-
ery toast.

Because everyone seemed to be having a splendid time over
cocktails, Elfie sent word to the chef to put dinner back a half
hour. Eventually, when she realized she couldn't postpone it any
longer, she announced it was time to go to the dining room.
There the conversation continued at its brisk pace, stories making their way around the elaborately set table in Spanish and
English, the universal language of laughter filling the room.

Dessert had just been served when the housekeeper whispered in Elfie's ear that she had a call. She started to say she
would call back, but the housekeeper told her where the call was
from, and from whom.

"Excuse me," Elfie said, standing, with the help of Martin
Leff, who leaped to his feet and moved her chair.

She went to her study, released the hold button, and said,
"Christopher. What a pleasure. I wasn't expecting you to call.
I'm having a dinner party—lovely time—and—"

"Sorry to disturb you, Elfie. I'm heading for Mexico tomorrow night."

"Oh? I thought you weren't coming until the elections."

"There's been a change."

"I hope you'll find time for me."

"Of course I will. I just got word that my father died."

"I'm so sorry. Had he been sick?"

"No, I don't think so. A sudden thing. Heart, I suppose. I'm flying to Boston in an hour for the funeral. I'll leave from there tomorrow night."

"Well, sorry for the bad news, but still, I look forward to seeing you. What's new in Washington?"

"The usual. I'll fill you in when I get there. Who's at the party?"

"The ambassador and his darling wife. Manuel Zegreda. Morales. Viviana Diaz."

"Really? Have you spoken with her?"

"Of course. She's a guest."

"No, I mean about—"

"I must get back to my guests, Chris. Sorry about your father. You were close?"

"No. I'll call from Mexico City."

"I'll send Maynard. Let me know your flight."

The party broke up at midnight. Elfie was effusive in her parting comments, assuring Russell Cadwell he was the best ambassador who'd ever served there, complimenting Antonio Morelos on what a charming companion he'd been to Viviana, joking with Manuel Zegreda and his wife that he would soon own all of Mexico, and lavishing praise on Viviana for how beautiful she looked, and her taste in clothes and jewelry.

"And how is your charming vice president?" Viviana asked Elfie as they stood in the foyer.

"Fine."

"I hope to see him again when he comes for the inaugural celebration."

Hopefully to honor the PRI candidate, Elfie silently said. "He'll be busy but—"

"Please give him my best."

"Of course."

Elfie stood alone in the foyer with Martin Leff.

"Some brandy?" he asked.

"No, I think not. I'm exhausted. Thank you, Martin, for being such a wonderful addition to the party, as usual. I'm going straight to bed."

"Well, then, I will take my leave," he said, sounding as though he were auditioning at a radio station. "Wonderful party, Elfie."

"You're a dear," she said, kissing him on the cheek and opening the door. "We'll be in touch."

She went to the room where the cocktail party had been held and told the bartender, who was packing up, to give her a cognac. She took it to her bedroom, stripped off her clothes, put on a pink nightgown, robe, and slippers, and went to the roof of the wing next to the park. It was deathly still there. A half-moon came and went behind clouds arriving from the west.

Elfie sat in a cushioned chair, propped her feet up on another, and drank from her glass. It was at times like this that she ached for Jeremy Mahon. It was nine years ago that he left for Russia on a business trip and did not return alive. He suffered a massive heart attack while there; his body was flown to San Miguel for burial.

There had been many proposals of marriage since then for Elfie, some of which she seriously considered. But Jeremy's death had left in her a lingering sadness that she knew would get in the way of another relationship. The thought of growing old alone was not pleasant. She'd reached a point in her life where it was—at least it seemed—preferable not to enter into a fifth marriage, unless, of course, another Jeremy were to surface. She doubted that would happen. And the trade-offs of marriage between well-placed people were less and less alluring. Instead, she'd contented herself with what had become a busy, fulfilling life outside herself, knowing the men and women who made things happen, becoming important to them, achieving a status in which what she thought and said mattered. And there was always a lover when needed.

She finished the cognac in a single swallow and went to the black wrought-iron railing. The cry of a nocturnal bird shattered the quiet. Then, a bat swooped low over her, causing her to cover her head with her hands and to scurry inside.

The bat kept attacking her in her dreams throughout the night.

She awoke groggy in the morning—and afraid.

Of bats?

Or of . . . ?

"True nobility is exempt from fear," Shakespeare said. That line came to Elfie as she huddled in bed, the covers pulled tight around her throat. Later, she got up, went to the window she'd closed against another bat attack, opened it, looked out over one of her gardens, the rising sun illuminating its glorious palette of colors, drew a breath, and said aloud, "The time for being afraid was years ago, darling. Be noble, be brave. The only thing we have to fear is fear itself."

She smiled with satisfaction. Most people assumed it was FDR who'd coined that famous saying in wartime. But Elfie knew it had been Thoreau in 1851: "Nothing is so much to be feared as fear."

It was the sort of knowledge that came in handy at dinner tables when someone pointed to Churchill, say, as the source of the sentiment, especially if that person was a bore needing to be put in his place. Besides having learned every nuance of hostessing, Elfie had collected hundreds of such tidbits, like hors d'ouevres, and was as skilled at dropping them into conversations as she was at creating ingenious menus and brilliant seating charts.

Chapter 22

The Next Day

Boston

" . . . man that is born of a woman is of few days, and full of trouble. He cometh forth like a flower and is cut down; he fleeth also as a shadow, and continueth not."

The funeral for Frank Hedras was held at Christ Church in Cambridge, across from Cambridge Common. It was a dim, rainy day around Boston; the church's interior, filled with light when the sun shone, was a somber gray this day, befitting the solemn occasion.

Chris Hedras sat with his now widowed mother in a front pew. To his other side was his older sister, Pauline, who worked part-time as a graphic artist, and her husband and two children. Chris knew that had his father died ten years ago, the church would have been filled. But this was ten years later, ten years in which his once prominent father had not only slipped into obscurity, but a disgraced one at that.

Following the service, they stood together on the sidewalk in front of the church, black umbrellas raised, awkward expressions of sorrow exchanged, mundane questions asked of those who owed their presence to a death.

"How is Washington?" Chris Hedras was asked by an uncle.

"Fine. Very busy."

"I hear you're the president's right-hand man."

"Well, not really. I'm on loan to the vice president for his campaign."

"I suppose he'll run," an aunt said, her tone mirroring her lack of interest in whether he did or not.

"I suppose so," Chris replied.

"Coming back to the house?" his sister asked.

"I don't know," Chris said. "I have to catch a plane."

"Your mother will be disappointed," said the uncle.

"Maybe for a few minutes."

"I have deli," said his sister.

"Uh-huh."

Chris looked to where his mother stood just inside the church's open doors, out of the drizzle. He hadn't seen her in more than a year, had forgotten how diminutive and frail she was. She'd borne the brunt of Frank Hedras's fall from grace, had been at his side when the front pages of the *Globe* and *Herald* and the six o'clock news reported his indictment on bribery and fraud charges, and had been at his bedside to nurse him through two heart attacks. Her quiet, staunch defense of her husband— his father—had, at once, impressed their only son, and caused a concomitant feeling of loathing.

Until his father's indictment, conviction, and one-year suspended sentence with five years' probation, the Hedras name in

Boston was one of which to be proud. It opened myriad doors for Chris Hedras, and he was quick to walk through them to reap the rewards once inside. Frank Hedras had been president of the city's most powerful labor union, a man to be reckoned with. You went to Frank Hedras the way you went to your clergyman, or neighborhood mob leader, when you needed help. Politicians counted on him to keep the labor peace, to keep the city working, the workers happy, the political machine greased and moving, the union members' tithings to the Democratic Party flowing without interruption. To be the son of such a man was an honor.

But then came the investigation, the sting, the secretly recorded meetings between his father and political leaders during which money changed hands, the arrest, and this man, who owed his son a future, was rendered impotent.

Chris Hedras had silently hated his father from that day forward.

Still, while most turned their backs on the senior Hedras, there were those who stood tall (and who still had something to gain by remaining in the Hedras fold), who helped the son with the bright future, the sterling academic record at Harvard, the good looks and ready smile, the developing political acumen, the understanding of why rubbing backs and greasing occasional useful palms and demonstrating loyalty to those who'd been loyal to you was the way it was done, the way things *got* done. There hadn't been many of his father's legion of friends who stayed the course once the disgraced labor leader sunk into an ever-deeper closed, bitter world, but those who did reached out to the son. It was the least they could do, was the way Chris viewed it.

"He wanted cremation," Pauline Hedras-Brady said.

"It was the scandal that killed him," a family friend said. "The heart attacks. How many? Three? Four?"

"It was the politicians that did it," the uncle said. "The Republicans. They set him up. He'd be alive today if . . . "

Chris said nothing, simply wondered at this need to rehash the past. It was so typically Boston; sports and politics, not necessarily in that order, dominating thought and conversation.

"You agree, Chris?" the uncle asked.

"What?"

"The Republicans. They were behind what happened to your father."

"Yes, I suppose so."

Chris hadn't seen Johnny Harrigan and his wife in the church. Now they came from it and stood on the steps, holding hands. The young man waved. Chris jerked his head in friendly response.

"Come with us," Pauline said. "We have the van. Plenty of room."

"We'll bring Mother," the aunt said. "She'll be so happy you're there."

— — —

The gloomy atmosphere at the church gave way, as it usually does, to more of a celebration of the deceased's life. Everyone soon had beer, wine, and sandwiches in hand at Pauline Hedras-Brady's unassuming house in Newton, a few miles outside Boston. A large urn dispensed coffee into Styrofoam cups. Cold cuts and cheese were rolled and arranged on two large plastic platters. Rock 'n' roll music from WHDH came softly from a boom box on the kitchen counter. Pauline had made a sheet cake for dessert.

"Man, it's great to see you again. Wish it was under more pleasant circumstances, but I guess that's the way it goes. That's life, I guess."

Harrigan, the young man Hedras had seen on the church

steps, was his best friend in high school. His wife, who'd immediately started helping Pauline in the kitchen, was named Mary.

"How've you been, Johnny?" Chris asked.

"Real good. Yeah, very good. I got married, you know. We
sent you an invitation."

"Right. I wanted to come but I was out of town or something."

"Yeah, man, I know. You must be racking up those frequent
flier miles, huh?"

"I do a lot of traveling. You, ah, still working for that company? What is it, ah—?"

"Hopkins. Sure. Been there ever since we got out of high
school. Doin' real good. I'm a supervisor now."

"That's great, Johnny. They must treat you good."

"They do. Nothing like you, though. The White House!" He
rapidly shook his open hand up and down to indicate he was impressed. "What's this guy like?"

"Who?"

"The president."

"He's, ah—he's good. Terrific."

Harrigan looked around as though about to spill a state secret. He lowered his voice: "To me, he really sold us out. You
know what I'm saying? This NAFTA thing. Man, that was a
dumb move. All those jobs goin' south. Good-paying jobs. What
'a those spicks get down there? A buck a day? No wonder we
can't compete. Know what I'm saying? Know what I'd like to
see?"

"What?"

"I'd like to see Joe Aprile get in the White House. He gave the
union a talk a couple 'a months ago. I was there. Shook his hand.
I think he feels about NAFTA the way we do. The union guys.
I think if he was president he'd shove NAFTA down the spicks'
throats. Right?"

"Well, maybe. It was great seeing you, Johnny. Nice of you to come."

"Hey, your father was good to me. Got me the job at Hopkins. Bailed me out when I had that—" He giggled. "When *we* had that hassle, huh?"

"Right. We'll catch up soon."

Chris started to walk away but Johnny grabbed his arm, used his conspiratorial tone again. "You still smoke a little?"

"Huh?"

"Mary and me still have a joint now and then." A whisper now. "Some coke, too. Nothing heavy duty. But you know, on the weekend. Only when the kid's asleep, though. To relax. I've got a great dealer at the plant. Only the best stuff. Says he gets it from some Mexican guy. Pure Colombian. You want some while you're in town? I got it out in the car."

"No, I—"

Harrigan pulled him close. "Man, remember that broad . . . what was her name? The one you banged in the car? Barbara— yeah, that's it. Man, she was hot stuff, huh? Rape! Bull . . . Man, your old man could fix anything. I'm sorry he died, Chris. I really am."

Chris managed to avoid Harrigan for the next half hour, until he and Mary left.

"I have to go, Pauline," Chris told his sister.

"I know. Momma's laying down in the bedroom."

"I don't want to wake her. I talked to her before. She looks old."

"She is. You really should try to get up to see her once in a while, Chris. How much longer will she be around?"

Chris felt a familiar anger well up at being chided by his sister.

She read his face. "I know how busy you must be in Washington. Thanks for coming."

The bedroom door opened and Hedras's mother emerged, slowly, sleep-induced confusion on her lined face.

"Chris was just leaving, Momma," Pauline said.

The old woman nodded.

"I have to get back," Chris said. "Business."

"I know," his mother said.

"Can't you stay another half hour?" Pauline asked. Her husband called for her from the kitchen. "Be right back," she said.

Hedras awkwardly shifted from one foot to the other.

"Go, Christopher," his mother said.

"Momma, I—"

"Catch your plane. I understand."

He was sure she *didn't* understand. No one did. This house, this city, these people were what he'd worked so hard to escape. His father's fall from grace—how stupid could the old man have been, taking petty graft?—had transformed Boston into a depressing, odorous sewer for Chris. He'd watched his father wither away, sitting in his worn chair, Daddy's chair, and being waited on hand and foot by his mother in their modest row house in South Boston, "Southie." Before the sting, there had been a steady stream of visitors to the house, his father's cronies sucking up to him for favors, politicians seeking his union's blessing, union officials huddling with him late at night in the finished basement. The few who bothered to keep coming were pathetic in Chris's eyes, symbols of smallness of mind and even smaller ambitions.

He winced as he looked into his mother's tired eyes, shifted his gaze to the floor. He was, at once, ashamed at the revulsion he felt, yet justified in feeling it.

Pauline rejoined them. He kissed her cheek. "Come down to Washington. Bring the kids. There's lots to see there. I can arrange something."

Pauline said to her mother, "We could all go. Wouldn't that be fun, to see Washington? With an insider, no less." She laughed.

Mrs. Hedras managed a small smile. "Very nice."

"Maybe we will," Pauline said brightly, "if Jack can get some time off. Maybe some weekend. You're flying back to Washington?"

"Mexico. I'll be there until the elections."

"Elections? In Mexico?"

"Yes. They have them."

She returned the kiss. "Take care."

"You, too, Pauline. It was great seeing you."

He turned to say good-bye to his mother, but she'd retreated into the bedroom, slowly closing the door behind her.

— — —

He used his frequent flier miles to upgrade to first class. After a layover in Chicago, he boarded another plane for Mexico City. Before boarding, he placed a call on his cell phone to San Miguel de Allende.

"Hello, Chris," Elfie Dorrance said. "Where are you?"

"Chicago. Boarding a plane for Mexico City."

"Give me the flight number. I'll send Maynard."

"No. I have to stay in Mexico City a day or two. I'll call when I'm free."

"All right. How was the funeral?"

"How is any funeral? Grim."

He slept most of the way to Mexico City, eschewing the meal service. It was a fitful sleep, and he awoke in a sweat an hour before landing. He asked the flight attendant for a beer. As he sipped it, he thought of the day, of his father and mother, his sister's house, what the priest had said during the funeral, his conversation with Johnny Harrigan.

He knew that had he stayed overnight in Boston, he would have taken his high school buddy up on his offer. He didn't use coke nearly as frequently since coming to Washington as he had in Boston, but there were times when its kick, its ability to alter thought, its magical quality to bury bad karma in a haze of euphoria were needed, and welcomed.

This was one of them. Lately, there seemed to be more and more.

CHAPTER 23

That Same Day
Washington

Ramon Kelly, president of The Mexico Initiative, muttered to himself as he left police headquarters. The detectives who interviewed him seemed oblivious to the obvious, that Laura Flores had been murdered by Mexicans acting on behalf of the government of Mexico. At one point he'd slammed his fist on the table and called them incompetent.

"Calm down, Mr. Kelly," Detective Wendell Jenkins said. "Just tell us what you know as fact, and we'll take it from there."

"You don't understand, do you?" Kelly said. "You're treating this as some crime of passion, the act of some demented individual who just happened to pick Laura as a victim. I'm telling you that . . ."

The interview—Kelly did not view it as an interrogation, so inept was the questioning—lasted an hour. Kelly hadn't thought it necessary to dress differently for the police than for any other day of the week. His well-worn jeans, cowboy boots, button-down shirt, and sweater, selected from a dozen in his dresser drawer, represented a uniform of sorts. But no matter what he wore—and he had a few suits, even a tuxedo for those occasions demanding formality—it was his face that caused people to look at him a little longer than they might at others. His heritage of a gringo father and a Mexican mother of Aztec lineage had resulted in curly red hair, a broad brow, copper skin, and a Milky Way of brown freckles covering his upper face, particularly around his cheeks, nose, and blue eyes. Guessing Ramon Kelly's origins was never easy.

Kelly apologized on his way out, explaining that Laura Flores was a special friend.

"Don't sweat it," Detective Peterson said, walking him through the squad room to the main entrance. "I understand."

"Thank you," Kelly said.

"But you know what?"

"What?"

"We're not incompetent, just overworked and underpaid."

Kelly managed a thin smile.

"Give a call if you think of anything else. Have a good day, Mr. Kelly."

He returned to the Initiative and closeted himself in his office, asking that no calls be put through. He spent an hour making notes in a small notepad. At noon, he announced he would be out for the afternoon: "I can't be reached. Call my machine at home at the end of the day and tell me who called. I'll get back to some of them from Mexico. See you in a few days."

He walked two blocks to the garage where he'd parked his gray 1992 Honda Accord, paid, put in a tape of Astrid Hadad, Mexico's answer to Madonna, and slowly drove south on Seventeenth Street until veering off onto the access road to the

George Mason Memorial Bridge. He reached the historical port town of Alexandria, hometown of George Washington and Robert E. Lee, found a parking space on Union Street, got out of the car, and entered the Union Street Public House. Ferguson was already there, at the bar. Kelly took a stool next to him.

"Traffic?" Jim Ferguson asked.

"Am I late?"

"No. Just wanted a traffic report."

Kelly smiled. "What are you drinking?"

"Virginia Native. They brew it especially for here."

"Oh?" To the bartender: "A Virginia Native."

"Hungry?" Ferguson asked.

"No. A little. I spent an hour this morning with the police."

"An inspiring experience."

"Yeah."

"So, shall we talk and order, or order and talk?"

Kelly looked around. The bar, the room itself, was filling up. "Let's find a table."

"Upstairs."

They carried their beers to the second floor and settled in a private, cozy nook. Ferguson ordered crab cakes, Kelly a club sandwich.

"Fill me in," Ferguson said when the waitress left the table.

While Kelly recounted his morning with the police using his notepad, as well as sharing other information regarding the deaths of Laura Flores and Morin Garza, Ferguson sat quietly and erect. His twenty years as a naval intelligence officer were written all over him: salt-and-pepper hair cut short and close to his temples, eyes clear and seldom blinking, skin youthful and unblemished for a forty-five-year-old man, but not surprising considering the discipline of his life—daily vigorous exercise, never a cigarette, an occasional beer usually left half consumed.

His approach to dress was also different from Ramon Kelly's.

For twenty years he'd proudly worn the military uniform dictated by the season. Now retired from the navy, he was seldom seen without his civilian uniform—immaculate blue blazer, white shirt, tie, gray slacks, and shoes polished to a mirror shine.

The arrival of their lunch temporarily interrupted Kelly's monologue, which lasted through coffee. Ferguson said little, waiting for natural pauses to ask an occasional question.

"I think that covers it," Kelly finally said.

Ferguson's mouth tightened into a thin line as he digested what Kelly had told him, and his crab cakes.

"Well?" Kelly asked. "What's the next step?"

"Not my call," Ferguson replied. "I'll pass on everything you've told me. They'll decide what to do with it."

"I'm afraid they'll do nothing."

"That's always a possibility where politics is involved."

"I spoke with Laura's father last night."

"Tough duty. What did you tell him?"

"Just that I was sorry for what happened to his daughter, that we were friends."

"Did you get into any of what you've told me?"

"No. I didn't think it was appropriate, considering his ties with the PRI. It wasn't easy not saying anything. His daughter was killed by his own friends."

"That's a little harsh, isn't it? Everybody in the PRI isn't a killer."

"Everybody in the PRI, Jim, at least everybody with something to lose if it goes down, will do whatever is necessary to keep their status quo."

Ferguson's lucent green eyes said nothing to betray what he was thinking.

Kelly said, "I'm flying to Mexico tonight to see Laura's father."

"Sure you should?"

"Why shouldn't I?"

A twitch of his eyebrows was Ferguson's response.

"Something has to be done," Kelly said.

"That's out of our hands."

"I'm not used to having things taken out of my hands. That's what the Mexican leaders and fat cats want from us, just keep quiet, let the drugs and drug money roll, rape the country and its people until—"

Ferguson held up his hand. "A word of advice?"

"What?"

"Back off, Ramon. Just keep doing what you've been doing, gathering information, finding out things that will help him formulate a workable policy."

"And keep my mouth shut."

"That, too. I'll pass along what you've told me, and I'll keep you informed—to the extent I can—on what steps are being taken."

"And what about Laura? And Garza? Just fallen soldiers in the war? Unmarked graves? Expendable?"

Ferguson waved for the check. The two men said nothing as Ferguson paid cash, counted out a tip, nodded, and stood. They went downstairs, where the bar was even busier than an hour ago.

"What time's your flight?" Ferguson asked.

"Ten."

"Have a good trip, Ramon."

"Thanks."

As they passed the bar on their way to the door, Ferguson paused to watch a game of bar dice being played between a customer and the bartender. The customer rolled the dice. He lost. Others at the bar laughed.

The customer shook his head, ran his hand through his long, flaxen hair, turned, and said to Ferguson and Kelly, "Not my lucky day."

— — —

While Kelly drove home to pack for his trip, Jim Ferguson went to Foggy Bottom, entered a narrow storefront on Wisconsin Avenue, next to a French restaurant, and a block away from Annabel Reed-Smith's art gallery. A temporary sign in the window read COMING SOON: CLOTHES FOR THE DISCRIMINATING WOMAN. A hastily erected wall separated the small front area from a larger room to the rear.

"Hi," Ferguson said to the young woman seated at a desk with a phone, computer, fax, and copy machines.

"Hi."

"Mind getting us some coffee?"

"Sure."

She left. Ferguson took her place at the desk and dialed a number. It didn't go through. He tried again. Still no luck. The third try succeeded.

"Hotel Majestic," a woman with a heavy Spanish accent said.

Ferguson spoke in perfect Spanish: "Mr. Hedras's room, please. Christopher Hedras."

Hedras came on the line.

"Jim."

"Hi. What's up?"

"I had lunch with Ramon today."

"Yeah?"

"The police interviewed him this morning about Ms. Flores's death."

"And?"

"Nothing special. He gave me a rundown on what he's come up with the past few days." Ferguson consulted notes he'd made in the car before leaving Alexandria and filled Hedras in on what had transpired at the restaurant.

"That's it?" Hedras said.

"Yes. That's it."

"Thanks for the call, Jim."

"I promised I would. Ramon's flying to Mexico City tonight to meet with Ms. Flores's father."

"He is? Where's he staying?"

"He didn't say."

"I'll try to catch up with him. Take care."

The young woman returned with two coffees as Ferguson hung up.

"You don't mind getting coffee for us, do you?" Ferguson asked.

"No, of course not. Besides, I know you really don't want coffee, just time alone with the phone."

Ferguson's grin was boyish, a kid caught in the act. "See you in the morning," he said. "I'll bring the coffee."

CHAPTER 24

That Same Afternoon
The South Building–the Watergate

Mac and Annabel sat on their terrace overlooking the Potomac. She'd come home early that day, leaving the gallery in the hands of a young assistant, an art history major at GW. Mac had taught that morning, and the experience hadn't done anything for his customary pleasant disposition.

"They're bright," he told her after she'd delivered a platter of cheeses and two nonalcoholic beers to the terrace. "They wouldn't have been admitted if they weren't bright. But they don't seem to get it."

"Get what?"

"What law is really all about. They seem to want the law to conform to their thinking, support their views of life and society. But law can't be what they *want* it to be. It's what it is."

She cocked her head, smiled, and patted his arm. "Remember what Swift said."

"Jonathan Swift?"

"I learned it in law school. He said, 'Laws are like cobwebs, which may catch small flies, but let wasps and hornets break through.' "

"I didn't learn that in *my* law school."

"Laws aren't as black and white as you'd like them to be."

"And they aren't as subject to flimsy interpretation as my students would like them to be."

"Cheese?"

"Please. The Camembert. On one of those wheat crackers."

"So, Professor Smith, tell me more about this James Bond mission you're about to go on for Joe."

"Hardly that," he said. "Joe wants me to—I always feel funny calling him Joe—"

"Call him Joseph."

"Not what I meant. He wants me to go to Mexico a few days earlier than planned. I'm to meet with some unnamed fellow in Mexico City, who will tell me how to contact this Unzaga in San Miguel."

"And this Unzaga is a revolutionary."

"According to Chris Hedras."

"And he's to tell you things that are calculated to drive a stake in the PRI's political heart."

"A little too dramatic, but basically correct."

"And what about your heart?"

"What about it? I passed my last EKG with high grades."

"Certain people in the PRI might like to drive a stake into Unzaga's heart—and those he confides in."

"I'm sure he's not the most popular fellow in Mexico, but let's not overstate it."

"Let's talk fact, then. You do know, I assume, what happened to Villa and Zapata. You do know your history."

"Killed."

"Assassinated. Assassination's long been a major sport there. Strange. The Mexican people—average Mexican people—are so gentle and loving, yet it's always been such a violent country."

"True. And how about us? But I'm not leading a rebel army against the government. All I'm doing is meeting with someone in a public place, hearing what he has to say, and reporting it back to—"

"Back to who?"

"Chris Hedras, I suppose."

"For Joe Aprile's ears."

"Yes, which I find intriguing."

"So do I. Why does Joseph Aprile, vice president of the United States, want this sort of information? He has other intelligence sources. It sounds as though he's deliberately undercutting the president."

"That's not a surprise anymore, is it? Anybody you talk to who's tapped in to Joe's campaign expects at least a modest rift over Mexican policy to go public any day."

"Still, I'd like to know what use he intends to make of what you learn."

"I suspect we'll know that in due time. I suggested using someone else, a CIA type or an all-purpose, experienced diplomat. But evidently Unzaga has made it clear he won't talk to anyone involved with our government, at least officially. He's specified that he'll only meet with a person personally chosen by Joe. Sure you can't break loose a few days earlier, come with me from the start?"

"I'd love to, but I'm on that panel at Catholic. I helped put the program together. I can't miss it."

"I understand. Just wish you could."

"I'll catch up with you in Mexico City, then on to San Miguel. I'm really excited about the trip, Mac. I love San Miguel. It's so unique. You'll love it."

"I'm sure I will."

"Why can't this Unzaga just write down what he knows and mail it to you?"

Mac laughed. "Did Zapata or Villa send letters?"

"They should have. Maybe they'd have lived if they did. I have one of our days in San Miguel all planned out for us."

"Oh?"

"The Casa de Sierra Nevada owns a five-hundred-acre ranch a few miles outside of town. They'll pack us a picnic lunch, put some margaritas in a thermos, and we'll spend the day there, maybe do a little riding."

"I'll pack my spurs."

"Good."

She got up, came to where he sat, and hugged him from behind. "You go have your clandestine meeting with Mr.—"

"*Senor.*"

"With Senor Unzaga. Do your patriotic duty for our friend, our next president, as they say, and save the rest of the time for us."

"Okay."

"Promise?"

"Absolutely."

She straightened up, went to the railing, and took a deep breath. "Mexico. I can't wait." She turned: "As Scarlett said to Ashley in *Gone With the Wind,* 'We'll go to Mexico and everything will be marvelous.'"

— — —

The exchange on the terrace between Mac and Annabel was typical, Annabel knew, of the way they sometimes approached serious subjects.

Their marriage was based upon a solid principle—that two strong individuals are more likely to succeed as a couple than a relationship in which one partner's uniqueness is subjugated to the other's. They'd discussed that need early in their relationship, and were in happy agreement that such would be the linchpin of their marriage. But there were times—this was one of them—when, in an effort not to tread heavily on either one's decisions, disagreement was couched in banter, a tap dance of sorts that made points without mounting a frontal assault.

Mac's decision to act as special envoy had not pleased Annabel. She understood why he'd agreed; her husband was not a man to shy away from challenge. Annabel also knew that Mac's friend, Joe, would not have asked him to undertake the mission if it were not of considerable importance. Mac was undoubtedly aware of that, too.

Still, she wished he'd said no. She couldn't come straight out and attack the wisdom of placing himself in a dangerous situation. It wasn't her role, not in a marriage based upon individualism. But if she could switch roles at that moment, she would have told him to go back to Aprile and tell him to find someone else. Mac could fulfill his role as election observer, and then enjoy a few days in San Miguel without having to meet some caballero with bandoliers slung across his chest, a sombrero the size of a manhole cover, dedicated to overthrowing his government and everyone in his way.

She couldn't do that—in so many words—and so she'd contented herself with asking questions. She'd kept everything positive, focusing on the holiday aspects of their trip rather than his simultaneous mission. If he were to decide not to go through with it, it would be a decision *he* came to upon reflection and analysis.

Annabel went to bed early that night, leaving Mac browsing the latest issue of the *Washington Monthly*.

"Feeling okay?" he'd asked.

"Tired."

He tilted his head up to receive her good-night kiss. "Pleasant dreams, Annie. I'll be along shortly."

Her dreams that night were not pleasant. They were filled with dread, represented by a huge, hairy, swirling black mass in which Mac was caught and that kept moving away from her no matter how fast she ran—reaching, calling his name, coughing from the dust it kicked up, invoking God in loud screams, her body failing from exhaustion, seeing his tormented face one last time as the mass lifted him into the air and away from her forever.

Annabel Reed-Smith was not by nature fearful. But if one thing could inject terror, it was the occasional, fleeting but edged thought of not having Mackensie Smith in her life.

She awoke early, more fatigued than when she'd gone to bed. She looked over at him sleeping, kissed his forehead, got out of bed, and turned on the drip coffee maker. She sat at the kitchen table and tried to recapture the nightmare's essence, but it was too elusive.

A few minutes later he joined her—"Smelled the coffee, Annie"—and reminded her of the nice day she had in store; nightmares no longer on the agenda. They were together in their new home. The sun was coming up; the weather forecast was fine. And in a few hours she'd be having a second coffee with her friend and former college roommate, Carole Aprile, and another friend, Rosie Brown, who was in town with her husband for a convention.

"Feeling better?" Mac asked, filling their mugs.

"Much. Nothing like a good night's sleep."

"Good. I'm heading for the shower." He paused in the doorway. "Did Scarlett O'Hara really say that in *Gone With the Wind*?"

"Absolutely."

He laughed. "Being married to you is like going to college, Annie. Scarlett was right. Everything *will* be marvelous in Mexico."

CHAPTER 25

That Same Morning

"You had a call while you were showering," Annabel said when Mac reappeared scrubbed and polished.

"Who?"

"I wrote it down." She handed him a slip of paper.

"I don't know any Jim Ferguson."

"He said he's working with Joe."

"A new addition to the campaign staff, I guess. I'll call him when I'm dressed. What time is your girls' morning out?"

"Ugh! Why is it that when men get together, it's a meeting? When women get together, it's a so-called girls' night out? Or in this case, a morning."

"Just a slip of the sexist tongue, Annie. When are you, Carole, and Rosalie *meeting*?"

"Ten. At Carole's house. I admire her for trying to find time for a normal life outside being second lady."

"I always admired Gene McCarthy for suggesting on national television that a president take a day off every week to read poetry, or listen to music."

"Didn't exactly go over with the voters."

"Ah, what do they know?"

Mac dressed for the day while Annabel was taking her turn in the shower. Then he returned Jim Ferguson's call.

"Mr. Ferguson, Mackensie Smith."

"Yes, Mr. Smith. I'm doing some work for the vice president. He told me that you'll be traveling to Mexico in a few days and wanted me to catch up with you before you leave."

"I see."

"The vice president felt I could offer a few things to make your trip go more smoothly. Sort of a last-minute briefing."

"Sounds good to me."

"Would you have an hour today? Later this morning?"

"I have a tentative lunch date. How about eleven?"

"That'll be fine."

"Where?"

"State Department Building? Only a few minutes' walk from the Watergate."

"Yes, it is. I'll ask for you?"

"Yes. Appreciate the time, sir."

A military type, Smith decided.

When Annabel came from the bedroom, Mac was about to walk Rufus. He told her of the meeting he'd scheduled with Ferguson.

"So, who is he?" she asked.

"He never did say, but we're meeting at State."

"Maybe he wants to offer you an ambassadorship."

"I'll take it, provided it's to a place with a moderate climate. You'd better get going. Carole is as punctual as Joe."

"I know." They kissed. "Enjoy your meeting. What's for dinner?"

"Out. I've been a slave to the kitchen lately."

Another kiss and she was gone.

Before walking the dog, Mac placed a call to Joe Aprile's campaign headquarters in the 600 building. One of the VP's senior advisors came on the line.

"Sid, Mac Smith. Just a quick question. I'm meeting this morning with a gentleman named Jim Ferguson. He says he's working on the campaign. I haven't met him before."

"Good man, Mac. Navy, retired, worked in intelligence. He's advising us on intelligence matters."

"Oh. Just wanted to know who I'm meeting with. Thanks for the info."

Mac decided to take the Dane on an extended walk that morning. He circumvented the 600 Office Building, pausing to take in the Kennedy Center and Saudi embassy across the street, stopped to chat with a friend who'd just taken out coffee from Cup-A-Cup, then headed down Virginia Avenue to where it intersected with Rock Creek and Potomac Parkway. It took him a few minutes to navigate the heavy traffic to safely reach the perimeter of the park. Rufus found a sign—THOMPSON BOAT CENTER—to be of olfactory interest, added his own signature to it, and they proceeded in the direction of the boat center. They'd almost reached it when Mac heard his name called. He turned to see Jiggs Machlin, chief of staff to Wisconsin Democratic Congressman Philip Broadbent, jogging his way.

"They let you out for a run?" Mac asked. "I thought Congress was in session."

"We get an hour for lunch, an hour for exercise, and an hour for sleep," Machlin said. "I'm into my run hour. How've you been, Mac?"

"Just fine. You?"

"I'd be a hell of a lot better if Curtain would get off his crusade to nail the president over the eternal matter of campaign finances."

"I saw your boss discussing it on CNN not long ago. Is Curtain going ahead with hearings?"

"Yup. He's got the votes. Phil's tried everything short of threatening to cancel his parking space. You know Curtain. I swear the man tortured little furry animals when he was a kid."

"He'd better not try it with *this* furry animal," Smith said, patting Rufus's head. "When's it about to pop?"

"No idea. Curtain says that unlike previous fund-raising investigations, he's got the smoking gun this time."

"Any idea what it is?"

"No. Typical Curtain tactic. Get the public convinced there's something real to nail the president with, keep it going as long as you can, then let it fade away. How's things with Joe Aprile?"

"Okay, I suppose."

"You know, Mac, if Curtain and the committee does have something tangible on the president, Joe will take the hit just as hard."

"I know."

"Funny, but I went along with Clinton and Scott on our Mexico policy. Now I'm not so sure."

"Always two ways to look at anything, Jiggs. Well, I won't hold you up. You're running out of run time."

"Yeah. Give a call one of these days. We'll grab some lunch."

"Love it. Soon as I get back."

"Where you going?"

"Mexico."

"That's right. The elections. You're on the observer team." He patted Rufus. "Does he take you out for walks often, Mac?"

"When he's in the mood, Jiggs, and when I let him know I have to go."

Mission accomplished, Mac and Rufus headed back to the Watergate. As they waited to cross the intersection, Smith saw the man who'd been rude when Mac had held the elevator door for him. He wore a black leather jacket and jeans, and was leaning against a tree. He'd been looking at Mac and Rufus. When he saw that Smith noticed him, he slowly pushed away from the tree and walked in the direction of the boat center.

Mac returned to the apartment, paid a few bills, and set off for his eleven o'clock appointment.

— — —

Annabel, Carole Aprile, and Rosalie Brown met in the vice president's official residence, the Admiral's House, on the grounds of the Naval Observatory on upper Massachusetts Avenue. A curious place, she thought for the umpteenth time. It had been built in 1893 as a home for the observatory's superintendent. In 1928, the superintendent was asked to leave and the house became home for various chiefs of naval operations. In 1974, Congress decided the vice president of the United States deserved an official residence and designated the Admiral's House, a comfortable home of Victorian architecture, with a turret, a few dormers, and a turn-of-the-century porch that wrapped around three sides.

Rosalie, a congenitally good-natured woman, was first to leave the reunion, having to join her husband, George, at a social event connected with the convention he was attending.

"She's amazing," Carole said when she and Annabel were alone in the kitchen and fresh cups of coffee had been poured. "As bouncy and exuberant as she was in school."

"It's those southern genes," Annabel offered. "I'm glad to see George doing so well."

"Even if he is a rock-ribbed Republican. They're fun. We've got to find more time to spend together. Maybe when—"

Annabel laughed. "If you're about to say that you'll have more time when Joe is out of office, forget it. He'll be our next president—for eight years. *Then* you'll have time."

"I know. I wish. I don't wish."

Annabel sat back and observed. While Carole had been upbeat during the previous hour, Annabel sensed it had taken some effort. Now, Carole's brow furrowed, and her bright green eyes dimmed.

"Want to tell me?" Annabel said.

"Tell you what?"

"What's on your mind. I'm not a mind reader but I'm pretty good on faces, starting with the pre-Columbian."

Carole smiled, nodded, placed her elbows on the table, and cupped her chin in her hands. "I feel pre-Columbian. Do you ever worry about your marriage, Annabel?"

"In what way? I had a nightmare last night that Mac was abducted—or something—and was gone forever."

"Scary."

"Very. But I suspect you don't mean nightmares."

"No. Do you ever worry about other women?"

"And Mac? No."

"Never?"

"Never say never, huh? Sure. Mac is a handsome man, among other things. He turns heads on occasion, and I sometimes wonder—just for a second or so—whether he's noticed and might be interested in an admirer. But I never question whether he's faithful."

"Lusting in his heart, maybe, like Jimmy Carter?"

"A fantasy now and then? Of course."

Annabel waited for Carole to speak. When she didn't, she asked, "Are you concerned about Joe?"

Carole pursed her lips, closed her eyes for a moment, and said, "Yes."

"Why? Has something happened?"

"Do you mean have I walked in on Joe and another woman? No. I have no tangible evidence that Joe is being unfaithful, just this nagging, painful feeling that he might be."

"I'm listening, Carole. And you don't have to go any further. But I'm here, always will be for you and Joe."

Carole placed her hand on Annabel's. "I know. Thanks. Sometimes I feel so isolated in this house, the Secret Service always looming, Joe traveling all the time, the kids away at school. I don't think I was cut out for this life."

"I'd say you were perfectly cut out for it, Carole. You'll be one of the country's best first ladies."

"Annabel, ever since Joe made that series of trips to Mexico—remember, six or eight months ago?—he's changed. He's become distant, preoccupied."

"Wait a minute, Carole. If I were vice president of the United States and was poised to run for the presidency, I think I'd be preoccupied, too."

"This is different."

"How so?"

"It's a personal detachment, Annabel. Between us, man and wife. Woman's intuition? Chalk it up to that. I just know something's changed with him that goes beyond the office and his ambitions."

"Have you spoken with him about it?"

"I've tried. Joe is the most level-headed, even-keeled person I know."

"Not bad credentials for a president."

"But when I have tried to broach the subject, he shuts down.

It's not like him. We've always had an open marriage—not the sixties' version—the lines of communication have always been open, no matter what the subject."

Annabel took her empty cup to the sink, turned, and leaned against the counter. "Is there a specific woman?"

"You'll laugh."

"Which might be a good thing."

"She's an actress."

"Oh?"

"Viviana Diaz."

"I don't think—oh, the *Mexican* actress. I've never seen any of her pictures. All I know about her is from the tabloids. There was some scandal where a wife—killed herself?—over her husband's affair with her?"

"That's right. She's a very beautiful woman."

"Yes, if the pictures haven't been retouched." Annabel sat at the table again. "Okay, let me get this straight. You think Joe might be involved?"

"Yes."

"Why? Remember, I'm a lawyer. Every question is followed by another question. Why do you think that?"

Carole took a deep breath. "Joe came back from one of his trips to Mexico talking about her. That was fine. He met many Mexican celebrities, political leaders, big honchos. But then he went *back;* the president had him almost commuting there for a while. The drug thing and all that. He returned from that second trip a different person. That's when the change started, Annabel. And there are the pictures."

Pictures?

For the first time since Carole had raised the subject, Annabel wondered whether there might be something to her friend's fears.

"What sort of pictures?"

Carole read the dismay on Annabel's face. "Not those kind of pictures, Annabel."

"What kind, then?"

"Of Joe and Viviana Diaz together. Parties, receptions. He brought a ton of them back with him from one of the trips, emptied them from his briefcase one evening. He didn't show them to me. They were in a pile of things on his desk. I saw one sticking out and looked. She seemed to be wherever he went in Mexico. There was even a shot of just the two of them on a balcony."

"But there are always pictures when the vice president travels."

"I know that. And all but that one picture include many people, political bigwigs, businessmen, embassy types, security men. But damn it, Annabel, there's a look on his face—on her face, too—that says to me they are happy to be together, that they're involved in some way beyond photo ops."

"Could I see them?"

"I don't have them. They were gone from Joe's desk the next morning. I suppose they're at his office. I haven't asked."

"Look," Annabel said, "I don't want to question your ability to read your husband's face in photos, Carole, but you might be reading things into it that are—well, wrong."

"Paranoid, you mean?"

"I wouldn't use the word, but yes, seeing things that aren't there. I suppose it's natural after being married a long time to wonder whether things are the same, whether too many opportunities are presenting themselves to the other spouse."

"You may be right, Annabel. I'd certainly prefer to think that way. My head tells me that's the case. My heart says something else."

"Trust your head," Annabel said, not sure it represented her true feelings, but it seemed the right thing to say. In truth, there was no reason to summarily dismiss Carole's fears. But in a world of philanderers, there were certain men who simply did not fit that mold. Joe Aprile was one of them. So was Mac. For Annabel, they lived by a set of standards a cut above those men who easily fell prey to what seemed, at times, a legion of predatory women out there enticing them.

"Still . . ."

"I feel like I'm one of those women spilling over on an afternoon TV talk show."

"What do you want me to do, Carole?"

"Do? Nothing. You've already done, sitting here listening to me. And I'm embarrassed to have gone on like this. How about you, Annabel? That nightmare sounded dreadful."

"It was. I suppose it has to do with Mac's trip to Mexico."

"You're going together."

"No, we're not. Not at first. He's going . . . "

Should she mention Mac's trip on Joe Aprile's behalf? Carole obviously didn't know.

"Mac's going a few days before I do."

"Why the change in plans?"

"Your husband."

"Joe?"

"Yes. He's asked Mac to do something for him while he's there, before the election."

"Oh."

"I'll be catching up with him. We'll be in San Miguel."

"Lucky you. Staying with Elfie Dorrance?"

"No. The Casa de Sierra Nevada. But I'm sure we'll see her."

"Thanks, Annabel."

"No thanks needed. I just wish we could do this more often. We really should."

They stood and embraced.

"And put this business about Joe and Viviana Diaz out of your head. She's not his type. *You're* his type."

—   —   —

Mac Smith entered the lobby of the nondescript Department of State building and took an elevator up to the elegant Edward Vason Jones Memorial Hall, which served as State's official foyer. Its stunning decor presented a dramatic contrast with the cold, austere "modern" entrance downstairs.

The foyer was but one of many rooms renovated in the mid-1980s, the eight-million-dollar budget covered exclusively by private sources, including a half-million-dollar gift from Elfie Dorrance.

Mac glanced into the adjoining entrance hall, resplendent in Oriental rugs, English cut-glass chandeliers, and rich, ornate paneling. He and Annabel had attended several events at State; the rejuvenated rooms ranked among their favorite Washington venues.

A man walked with erect bearing and military precision as he came through a door in the entrance hall. His hand shot out. "Jim Ferguson."

"Mac Smith."

"Thanks for making yourself available. This way, please."

Ferguson took them to a small conference room on the seventh floor where another man waited. He stood at their arrival and introduced himself to Mac: "Richard de LaHoya, Mr. Smith."

LaHoya was a solidly built Hispanic; Mac judged him a middleweight, were he to enter a ring.

"Dick is with State's Latin American division, the Mexico desk."

"I'm sure you know Herman Winkler," Mac said.

"Sure," LaHoya said.

"We're friends."

"Herman's a good guy," LaHoya said, demonstrating for the first time the hint of a Spanish accent.

"Yes, he is."

"Seat?" Ferguson said, indicating a chair at the table.

When they were seated, Ferguson said, "Dick de LaHoya and I have been briefed on your trip to Mexico, and the reason for it."

"As an election observer?"

"And as special envoy for the vice president."

Mac said nothing. He wanted them to establish how much they knew, not get it from him.

Ferguson must have sensed that was the case. "As I understand it, you'll be meeting with Carlos Unzaga as part of your trip."

Smith said, "That's right."

"And you'll be contacted in Mexico City by one of Unzaga's people to set up the actual meet with Unzaga."

"That's what I've been told."

"How do you feel about it?"

Mac pulled his head back slightly and smiled. "I'm not sure what you mean by that."

Ferguson said, "We just want to be sure that there's no chance of you changing your mind."

"Why would I?"

"You aren't being paid for this. You aren't an official member of government being assigned this task. You could, at any juncture, decide not to go through with it."

"Maybe you should give me the reasons I might make that decision," Smith said.

"All right," said Ferguson. "There could be an element of risk involved. Of course, we'll do everything to minimize that risk."

"I've considered that, and agree it's a minimal risk. Let me assure you, Mr. Ferguson, that if I hadn't been personally asked by the vice president to do this, I wouldn't. Joseph Aprile is a good friend. And I'm a good soldier—for good causes and good friends, especially when he's the vice president. Now, how about being a little more specific about the risks."

Ferguson looked to LaHoya. "Richard?"

LaHoya thought for a moment before saying, "Unzaga is a wanted man, Mr. Smith. He's not the only guerrilla leader in Mexico determined to overthrow the government, but he's an effective one, not at all flamboyant like the others. He has a quiet, single-minded dedication to his goal."

"I was aware there was a price on his head," Smith said. "Chris Hedras filled me in on that."

"I know," Ferguson said. "But I thought you might benefit from a little more detail about the man you'll meet. That's why Richard is here. He's just come back from Mexico."

"I'm listening," said Smith.

LaHoya opened a file folder; TOP SECRET was stamped in red. He began to read: "Carlos Unzaga, age thirty-one, born in Celaya, south of San Miguel de Allende, father a farmer. Mother died when he was seven. Two sisters, one older, one younger. Educated in the States, Purdue University, degree in agricultural engineering, top student, three-point-eight grade average. Disciplinary problems, threatened two professors who didn't give him a straight four . . . "

He read for ten minutes. When he was finished, he closed the folder and sat back, his expression asking for Smith's reaction.

"You say Unzaga is unusual because he didn't come from the sort of abject poverty that usually spawns revolutionaries," Smith said.

"Not to be misunderstood, Mr. Smith. His family was poor. But in Mexico, there is poor, and there is poor. In the south, poverty is at alarming levels. In the north, and in the mountains, it tends to be a little better."

"He split off from Marcos's National Liberation Army," Smith said. "He operates a totally separate army?"

"Yes," Ferguson responded. "The usual ragtag bunch, poorly equipped, almost no training. But they're dedicated. When you don't have anything, you don't have anything to lose."

"And you also say that Unzaga's army, and others, are financed through well-connected liberals in Mexico City."

"Correct," LaHoya said.

"Militarily, he's considered far less a threat than others in Mexico," Ferguson said. "It's his intellect and sophistication that scares them. He's as much at home in wealthy society as he is in the jungle and mountains. People tend to listen to and believe him. He's charming and persuasive, according to our intelligence."

"This is all very interesting," Smith said, "and I'd like to learn more. But let's get back to risk. I was in Hollywood six months ago. I had lunch at a trendy place, filled with the standard nubile starlets and smooth-talking producers. At the next table were two gentlemen and a beautiful young woman. They were trying to convince her to appear in some film they were planning to shoot. One of the men said, 'There's risk here.' She replied with great sincerity, 'I'm heavy into risk these days.' I thought it was a funny comment, typically Hollywood." He thought of Annabel. "I'm not heavy into risk these days, gentlemen. I'll be meeting Mr. Unzaga alone?"

"That's the plan. In a public place."

Smith smiled. "I can leave my Banana Republic outfit home? No clandestine meetings in a steaming jungle?"

Ferguson laughed, stood, and went to the end of the conference table. He perched on it and said, "But we're going to add a few twists to the plan to make it risk free."

"Such as?"

"Backup people close by when you meet him. A procedure in place to allow you to abort every step of the way. Frankly, I don't see anything to worry about. You'll be meeting in a public place mutually acceptable to both sides. You'll be alone—except for your backup team."

"I assume he'll have backup people nearby, too."

"Almost certainly. The point is, once Unzaga's Mexico City representative contacts you and tells you the time and place of the meet, you'll run it by us. If we see any problem, we'll scrap the project."

"I take it I'll have people to confer with in Mexico City."

"Absolutely," Ferguson said.

LaHoya handed Mac a piece of paper.

"Simple chain of command," said Ferguson. "You'll be at the Majestic hotel. So will our people. It's right on the Zócalo, the center of town."

"I know it," Mac said. "I've stayed there."

"Good. You remember the bar on the seventh floor?"

"Yes. There's a restaurant just outside it, on the terrace."

"Restaurant Terraza. Good food."

"As I recall."

"That's where you'll make contact with everyone, Unzaga's people and ours."

"The restaurant?"

"The bar or restaurant."

"All right. And all I'm to do when I meet with Mr. Unzaga is hear what he has to say, remember it, and report back."

"Right."

"Report back to who?"

"One of our people in San Miguel de Allende. You'll be given his name when you're there. Unzaga might give you documents. At least we hope he will."

"Proof of some of what he claims?"

"Right again."

Ferguson took a chair next to Mac and put his hand on Mac's shoulder. "We're making this sound like some high-flying covert operation, Mr. Smith. Hardly that. Unzaga said he'd only talk through a nongovernment type personally selected by the vice president. The veep chose you. Should involve nothing more than a half hour's conversation, if that, and a story to dine out on later. Much later." He looked at LaHoya: "Anything else Mr. Smith might find useful, Richard?"

"I don't think so."

"Any questions?" Ferguson asked Smith.

"Just one."

"Shoot."

"What do you intend to do with this information?"

Ferguson glanced at LaHoya before replying, "Analyze it."

"And?"

"Not our call."

"Whose call is it?"

No answer from either man.

"The vice president?"

"Mr. Smith, there are some things that simply can not be discussed at this point, even if we had the answer to your question. I will say, however—and I'm sure I'm not telling you anything you don't already know—I will say that the future of relations between this country and Mexico is going to depend upon many things, not the least of which is the sort of information someone like Unzaga possesses. What he knows certainly isn't the whole story, just a small piece. But foreign policy works best when it's based upon many small pieces woven into a bigger, more complete picture. That's all I can say."

Smith stood. "I appreciate your time," he said. "If you're worried that I might change my mind, don't be, unless, of course, something comes up that would cause you to cancel things. I assume the vice president knows we've met."

"Of course."

"Good. No need to see me out. I've been here before."

They shook hands, and Smith left the building.

"Dine out on the story, indeed," he muttered to himself. One thing Mackensie Smith didn't need was dinner table stories provided by others. He had plenty of his own.

On the other hand, he had to admit to himself as he walked back to the Watergate that there was a certain appeal to spending a portion of his trip meeting with a Mexican rebel leader. There were plenty of people who would enjoy hearing about such an adventure. Or, at least, one. Annabel.

He had to smile.

Maybe having a new story for their dinner table wasn't so terrible after all.

Chapter 26

That Same Day

Mexico City

Ramon Kelly stepped from his modest hotel in the Bosque de Chapultepec neighborhood of the city. He'd arrived late and slept late. It was almost noon.

He wedged his way through the milling crowd on the street. Every inch of sidewalk not occupied by a *mercado*—vendors who sold everything from monkey flowers and roses to stuffed tortillas, enchiladas, and meat wrapped in banana leaves—was taken up by Mexicans and tourists. The city's pervasive toxic pollution cast a mawkish yellow-green haze over everything and everyone.

Nothing had changed.

It had been close to a year since Kelly had revisited his place of birth. There hadn't been any reason to return. His parents had left Mexico two years earlier to live in Chile, where his father had taken a job with another oil company. Ramon didn't need

to be in Mexico to reinforce his images of the country and its
largest city, home to a quarter of Mexico's population. He lived
with those images day and night, as though they were on a continuous loop of film: the pollution of the cities and the dusty
roads outside them, the hopeless expressions on the indigenous
farmers as they scratched in tracts of dirt they didn't own to stave
off hunger; the constant festivals in which music and vividly colored costumes numbed the pain for a few hours; smoke pouring
out of chimneys of the north's *maquiladóras,* the foreign-owned
assembly plants just south of the U.S.-Mexican border, polluting
and killing. Sometimes Ramon Kelly had to will away those images, so torturous were they.

What had the American Medical Association called the border between the United States and Mexico? "A virtual
cesspool."

In contrast to those whom Kelly considered "his people" were
the nation's wealthy elite, the politicians and businessmen, drug
lords and money launderers who raped the country with greater
violence than Cortés and his armies. At least the Spaniards had
left behind a culture. These contemporary "conquerers" took
everything, leaving only scorched earth and hollow souls.

Many considered Kelly a zealot with a maniacal commitment
to impoverished Mexico. "You're too strident," he'd been told.
"Back off or you'll accomplish nothing." The last time they'd
been together, his own father said, "I'm proud of you, Ramon,
for caring. But those who scream loudest are heard the least."

Ramon knew there was wisdom in that advice, and he sometimes attempted a more conciliatory tone in his approach. But
those exercises invariably failed. There were always the visions,
the images that had been burned into his brain from his earliest
days. And now there was Morin Garza and Laura Flores, returned home in separate boxes for burial, because they'd cared.

For Garza, his decision to cooperate had been more pragmatic than idealistic. Still, he risked his life and the life of his family to right wrongs.

Laura Flores had shared Ramon's passion, perhaps not with his fervor, but shared nonetheless.

And like Garza, she was dead.

Because they believed in something.

There was no reasoning with those in Mexico who held the power. Bargain? Futile. Appeal to their sensitivities, to their religious convictions? A coarse joke.

He squeezed into a battered green-and-white Volkswagen Beetle and gave the taxi driver an address in the clearer, healthier hills to the north. It took twenty minutes to break free of the city and begin the ascent on a road running through long rows of huge cardon cactus until the junipers and pink, red, and fuchsia bougainvilleas replaced them.

The driver turned onto a wide, winding road that passed large, handsome houses set back behind pink, white, and yellow masonry walls. He stopped outside the one with the number Kelly had given him.

"You want me to wait?" the driver asked. "No charge to wait."

"*Gracias,* no," Kelly said, paying, and unfolding his way out of the small vehicle.

The taxi pulled away, fumes pouring from its tailpipe. Kelly approached a heavy wooden gate. There was a buzzer to the right. He pushed. A voice came through a small intercom high up on a post.

"Who is it?" a woman asked in Spanish.

"Ramon Kelly."

"*Un momento.*"

The gate had a small opening covered with metal mesh through which Kelly could see the front entrance. A man came

through it and slowly crossed a circular red-brick drive. He un-
latched the gate and opened it enough to see the visitor.

"Ramon Kelly. I have an appointment with Senor Flores."

The man was short and heavy. He wore a multipocketed tan
vest over a black T-shirt. The edge of a shoulder holster pro-
truded through the vest's opening.

For a moment, Ramon wondered whether the man was
about to usher him inside or slam the gate in his face. Then, he
stepped back and said, *"Adelante!"*

"Gracias."

Kelly had been in the homes of the Mexican wealthy before;
still, this extravagant decor was a surprise. The floor of the entrance hall was gleaming red-and-white hand-cut marble. A
large hammered-copper sculpture dominated one wall; Kelly
recognized it as having come from Michoacán, a fine example of
a votive offering to the saints crafted by Tarascan Indians.
Crossed swords defined the wall opposite, causing Kelly to recall
words to the Mexican national anthem: "Mexicans, ready your
swords and saddle to the call of war . . . "

"Wait here," the man said, disappearing down a short hallway
and through a door at its end. Ramon waited nervously, moving
from foot to foot. He suffered a fleeting doubt about his clothing: jeans, a blue chambray work shirt, cowboy boots, and light
tan windbreaker. Perhaps he should have—

"Senor Kelly."

Ramon turned to see Oswaldo Flores approaching, his hand
outstretched. He was tall. He wore a navy blue blazer, gray
slacks, brown tasseled loafers, and a teal silk shirt open at the
neck to display a heavy gold chain and cross. "Welcome to my
home."

"I am sorry to be here under such unfortunate circumstances.
I wanted to attend Laura's funeral but—"

"No need to explain. Washington is very far from Mexico

City. Sometimes too far, sometimes not far enough. Come. Where we can be comfortable."

The living room of Flores's home was spacious and warmly appointed. The walls were filled with eclectic and expensive art—an original Diego Rivera, Frida Kahlo self-portraits, a huge religious painting by Miguel Cabéra, and three stunning examples of Fernando Gracia Pónce's abstract works.

"Please, sit," Flores said, indicating a small floral couch. A leather-inlaid coffee table separated the couch from two high-backed red leather chairs. Flores took one of them, lighted a cigarette, and released a stream of smoke into the air. Kelly had stopped smoking two years ago and now wished he hadn't.

"The funeral was, as you would expect, a sad day for all of us," Flores said. His voice was deep and well modulated, his words chosen carefully. There was discernible sadness in his voice, but his brown eyes did not mirror it. They fixed on Ramon with the unblinking persistence of a surveillance camera.

"A terrible experience," Kelly said. "Senora Flores? How has she taken it?"

"Not well. She and our two other daughters have gone to our country home to rest. I was to accompany them but business keeps me here."

"Of course."

The silence was awkward.

"Would you like a drink?" Flores asked. "Lunch will be served in a few minutes."

"No need for that," Kelly said.

"Then I will have to eat alone. The drink?"

"A Coke?"

Flores's fleshy lips parted in a smile. "You have become a true American," he said, going to the door, where a housekeeper stood. He returned to his chair. "Of course, Coca-Cola is but one of so many American ideas that are now part of our culture.

It is very popular here, too, *sí*? But we do not drink the Diet Coke. Did you know that? I have a friend who works for Coca-Cola. They did studies. We drink more soft drinks per capita than any other nation, but not diet sodas. Do you know why, Senor Kelly? Because Mexicans consider diet drinks to not be manly. Not machismo enough."

"Interesting," Kelly said.

"Of little importance, unless you are selling Coca-Cola. I am glad you are here, Senor Kelly. There is so much of Laura's recent life that I do not know, do not understand. Naturally, when she chose to go to the States to school and then to remain there, her mother and I were deeply disappointed. We have the tradition that—" He waved his hand. "But you know of Mexican tradition. You are Mexican."

"You're speaking of an unmarried young woman not leaving the family home until marriage."

"Yes, of course. Tradition is important. Don't you agree?"

"Some traditions."

Kelly's Coke was delivered, along with a glass of *anejo* tequila, aged and rare.

"To Laura," Flores said, holding up his glass.

Kelly didn't return the toast.

"Perhaps you can help me understand, Senor Kelly. As you know, Laura and I did not have a great deal of communication in past months. But I always had the impression she was happy in her life. When the call came—unfortunately, her mother took it—it was as though *we* had died. I am sure you can understand that. It haunts me that she should become so unhappy that life became unbearable. So young, with so much to offer. What could have caused her to become so sad, so despondent that she would take her own life?"

"She didn't," Kelly said flatly, sipping his Coke.

Flores's eyebrows went up. He leaned back, crossed his legs, and said, "Please explain."

Kelly chewed his cheek and thought for a moment before saying, "Senor Flores, I am not here to cause you any more grief than you've already endured. But Laura's death has grieved me, too, very deeply. We were good friends. We worked closely together, shared many things."

"Lovers?"

"Much more than that. We were comrades. We believed in what we were working for."

" 'Comrades.' That sounds political. Communistic."

"Call it what you will. No, we were not communists. But we *were* dedicated to seeing things change here in Mexico."

"Things are always changing," Flores said.

"But not for the better."

"You have established yourself as the judge of what change is good or bad for our country?"

"I have established myself—and so did Laura—as one of the judges of inequality in this country. You needn't remind me that I am Mexican. I am proud to be. But I am ashamed that ten percent of the people here own eighty percent of the wealth. I am ashamed that my country's leaders become rich with money from the drug runners and corrupt businessmen. I am ashamed that my country's police live by *la mordida,* lining their pockets from the very people they are supposed to be against. Yes, Senor Flores, I am ashamed of many things in my country. As was Laura."

"I see," said Flores.

The housekeeper entered carrying lunch on a tray, but Flores waved her away.

"You come here to my home at a moment of great personal tragedy to talk political nonsense. You visit me presumably to pay your respects, yet you sit and insult me and the memory of my dead daughter."

"I meant to do neither, Senor Flores, and I apologize if that is what you take from what I have said. You believe Laura took her own life. But that is not true. Do you know of Senor Garza? Morin Garza?"

"Who is he?"

"A man who came to believe also in our vision for a better Mexico. Like Laura, he was killed because of his beliefs."

"I am a patient man, Senor Kelly, but I am beginning to run out of patience. You tell me my daughter was killed. Murdered! Who did this?"

Kelly slid forward on the couch and extended his hands. His voice took on urgency. "Senor Flores, Laura was killed by the very people with whom you have forged such a close alliance. Your business associates. The politicians who are responsible for your television station, this house, the cars, the country home."

"You're *demente*!" Flores said.

"No, sir, I am not mad. Laura was a fine researcher. She had uncovered information potentially very damaging to the PRI. Garza had come to Washington to testify about the filthy corruption of our leaders. Both lost their lives as a result."

Flores stood, still holding his glass. He shook with anger, the amber liquid in it undulating and threatening to spill over the sides. "You will have to leave," he said, his voice no longer calm.

"Sir, please hear me out. What I say is true. And because it is, I would expect you as Laura's father to share my anger at those responsible for her death. I would expect you to come forward to tell of a system that fosters the murder of innocent people whose only sin was to *care*. I urge you to stand tall in your daughter's name and to—"

Flores answered by flinging the contents of his glass in Kelly's face. The edge of an ice cube broke the skin on one cheek. Kelly put his hand to the wound, pulled it away, and saw blood on his fingertips.

Flores shouted a man's name. Moments later, the armed guard who'd escorted Kelly into the house appeared.

"Get him out of here," Flores said.

The man took steps in Kelly's direction. Kelly held up his hands, said in Spanish, "Stay away. No need to hurt me. I am leaving." He walked brusquely past the security guard, flung open the front door, and stepped outside, where another burly man blocked his way. Kelly stepped around him and headed for the gate, broke into a run, clumsily undid the latch, and stumbled into the street. He looked back; the two armed men stood next to each other, eyes trained on him.

He started down the hill; he was on the verge of tears. He walked for ten minutes, his throat tight, eyes burning, heart pounding. An unmarked four-door blue Ford came up from behind. The driver stopped, said through the open window, "You want a taxi?"

"*Sí*," Kelly replied.

"Get in."

"How much to the city?"

"Not much."

"How much?"

They agreed upon a price.

As they headed for the center of the city, Kelly clenched his hands into fists and closed his eyes. The driver worked for one of many private car services in Mexico City that pick up street passengers. He glanced repeatedly in the rearview mirror and saw the strange-looking young man with red hair and freckles covering his copper skin curled into a corner of the rear compartment. A crazy man, he thought. On drugs.

He turned. "Hey, you pay me now, okay?"

"What?"

"Pay me now."

"Yeah. Okay."

As Kelly fished for money in his pocket, the driver again looked in the mirror. The battered tan Volkswagen that had fallen in behind from where he'd picked up his passenger was still with them, maintaining a constant distance.

"*Gracias*," the driver said as Kelly handed money over the seat.

They approached the Bosque de Chapultepec district on Campos Elíseos. Traffic was thick and slow. The clear air of the highlands was only a memory now in the heavy, smothering pollution.

A truck had broken down, bringing traffic to a halt. Kelly sat up straight and peered out the window, tried to judge how close they were to his hotel.

"I'll get out here," he said, opening the door.

As he did, the tan Volkswagen, which had been directly behind, pulled alongside. A man in the passenger seat holding an Ingram submachine gun leaned out the window and pointed it at Kelly. Kelly saw the weapon, giving him a split second to throw himself back across the rear seat before the Ford was riddled with bullets, glass flying, metal ripping, the sound and smell of gunfire engulfing the rear compartment.

The firing stopped. Kelly reached and opened the opposite rear door. He scrambled through it, fell onto the road on his hands and knees, and desperately crawled to the other side, oblivious to the chaos behind him, horns blaring, the Volkswagen's out-of-tune engine screaming as the driver drove up on a sidewalk, knocking down pedestrians and vending stalls until finding a hole in the traffic and escaping down a side street.

Kelly looked back. His pants were torn, his knees and the heels of his hands bloodied. Women continued to scream, men ran as fast as they could to leave the scene. No one seemed to notice Kelly sitting on the curb, dazed and in pain.

He slowly got to his feet and walked in the general direction of his hotel.

— — —

The driver of the tan Volkswagen pulled into a gas station and went to a pay phone. The shooter remained in the car smoking a cigarette.

The driver said into the phone, "It's Mynor."

"Where are you?"

"Chapultepec."

"It's done?"

"*Sí.*"

"He's dead?"

"*Sí.* I think he is dead."

"You *think?*" the angry voice said.

"He must be. Dozens of bullets. We were next to him."

"He had better be dead, Mynor."

"He is dead. Yes, I am certain of it."

— — —

Later that night, Alfredo Montano, the man who'd taken the call from the Volkswagen driver in his office in a hangar at Mexico City's Benito Juárez Aeropuerto Internacional, entered one of dozens of cantinas lining the airport's main access road. There he met with two people, a man and a woman.

The woman worked in the central passenger control center and had informed Montano of the flight Ramon Kelly had taken to Mexico City the night before.

The man had followed Kelly from the airport to the hotel, and called to Montano to tell him where Kelly was staying.

Montano handed each of them an envelope containing

money. He then bought a round of drinks: They poured salt on the backs of their hands, bit into lime wedges, licked the salt off, and downed shots of cheap tequila. That was followed by *sangrita* chasers—"little blood"—a cocktail of chilies, tomato, and orange juice.

"*Felicidades!*" Montano said, raising his glass.

"*Salud!*"

"*Salud!*"

Chapter 27

Later That Afternoon
Mexico City

Had the terminal at Mexico City's airport not been so vast and crowded, Ramon Kelly and Chris Hedras might have bumped into each other.

Kelly had checked out of his hotel the minute he returned and taken a cab directly to the airport, where he booked a seat on the next flight to New York.

Hedras, after a day of meetings, had a car service deliver him to the airport for a flight to León, an hour and a half from San Miguel de Allende, where he was met by Maynard, Elfie Dorrance's chauffeur.

"Chris, darling," Elfie said when she greeted him at the front door. She was wearing a flowing, floor-length purple-and-white caftan and had spent the past three hours lolling in a hot tub, and enjoying a facial and massage. "Good trip?"

203

"All right. You should get them to build an airport here in San Miguel. I hate the ride from León."

"It can be pretty."

"Seeing those armed thugs lined up when you come through the villages is no thing of beauty, Elfie. I could use a drink."

She watched him head for the party room and the bar, an amused expression on her face. He could be such a petulant child, she thought. But that was part of his youthful appeal. Foul moods in her older male friends were inevitably played out as disagreeable grouchiness.

She followed him into the room, where he poured tequila over ice and took a quick swallow.

"I didn't think you'd be able to break away," she said.

"I didn't either," he said, finishing the drink, pouring another, and slouching in a cushioned white wicker chair. He'd loosened his tie and undone the top button of his shirt. His hair was tousled; his dark shading of beard and tired eyes generated a look of fashionable dissipation.

"How did your meetings go in Mexico City?" she asked.

"Okay."

"Who did you meet with?"

It was an admonishing laugh. "Anything else you'd like to know? Who I slept with, maybe?"

She'd been playing along with his surliness. Her taste for it was now gone.

"I suggest you get off your high horse, Chris, and answer my questions."

Her stern tone wasn't lost on him. He sat up a little straighter, rubbed the sleep from his eyes, and said, "A few of the twelve. We met at Pasado's house. A palace. It's in the Polanco district. He's got—"

"I've been at Pasado's home a number of times, Chris. I don't need a house tour. Who was there?"

"I told you. Some of the Mexico Twelve."

"Pour me a drink. Light. Rum and a splash of soda. I'll ask again. Who specifically was there?"

Elfie knew each member of the so-called Mexico Twelve, a dozen of Mexico's wealthiest men who'd secretly gathered one night prior to the 1994 elections and had remained a close, closed club ever since.

Before the '94 elections, there had been growing concern about the ruling PRI's primary source of money, the government itself. It was time for the private sector to offer more financial support to the party. Each of the twelve men feasting on smoked salmon and steak that Tuesday evening in February 1993 were asked to pay financial tribute to their source of wealth, the PRI and its president. By the time they'd climbed into their limousines to leave, they'd each pledged an average of twenty-five million U.S. dollars—a total of seven hundred and fifty million.

Hedras named four men who'd been at his meeting. "They're pouring money into the newspapers like never before," he added, "to make sure the PRI's news is on the front page. Those reporters are getting rich, too. They rack up the money."

"Senor Zegreda wasn't there?"

"Yes, he was. I forgot. We can't forget him, can we?"

"I would say not. Did you get to see the ambassador while you were in the city?"

Hedras laughed. "The distinguished Russell Cadwell, ambassador to Mexico? I spent an hour with him at the embassy. Nervous as a cat. He knows his cushy life is over if Joe wins."

"*When* Joe wins. What did you talk about?"

"The elections. Joe's trip here for the inauguration. His arthritis, his wife's sciatica. He said he had a nice time at your party."

"Everyone did. You would have enjoyed it, too, Chris. Viviana was her usual radiant self."

"She sure brings out a man's carnal best."

"Oh? Has she brought out *your* carnal best?"

"On occasion."

"You're staying through the elections?"

"Uh-huh. I convinced Joe I could be of more use to him here as an advance man than holed up in DC. He's cooling his campaign activities for a few weeks, affairs of state getting in the way, I suppose. I could use a shower."

"By all means. Gina took your bags to your room. You know where it is."

He stood and stretched travel stiffness out of his body. "What's for dinner?"

"I thought we'd go out. Sierra Nevada."

"Great. Do you know what I was thinking about on the flight?"

"What?"

"Their onion soup."

"I thought you might have been thinking about me."

"Oh, I was, Elfie. Almost every minute."

She came to him, placed the back of her hand against his rough cheek, smiled, and said, "I'm glad you're here, Chris."

Later, showered and shaved and wearing a red cashmere robe that had been hanging in the closet, Chris Hedras unpacked his luggage. He'd almost finished when the door opened.

Hedras grinned. "You never knock, do you?" he said.

"I don't have to knock. Doors open for me all by themselves."

Her arrival hadn't surprised him. He'd expected it. He was waiting.

— — —

The first time they'd made love was a year ago, in Washington, the evening of a party she'd hosted for a former White

House press secretary whose book about his experiences had just been published. Elfie had flirted with Hedras all evening; at least he took it as such. He wasn't looking for sex that night because he'd had plenty of it in the afternoon at his apartment, his partner an old flame from Boston who was visiting Washington. It had been like old times, snorting a line of cocaine and thrashing about in his bed, on the living room floor, later in the shower.

Had it not been the infamous Elfie Dorrance, he would have passed, maybe gotten a phone number for future reference but nothing beyond that. But it *was* Elfie Dorrance, and the contemplation of making love to a woman her age exerted a strange and compelling pull on him. He'd heard all the rumors—well, maybe not *all* of them—that she was a woman whose sexual appetite and prowess had made not only four husbands happy, but a variety of other men as well.

It happened as though it had been scripted, and the two of them were acting out parts in a pantomime. He'd intended to leave and had already retrieved his coat from the hallway. But the way she looked at him said he was to stay. And he did. When the last guests had left, she took his hand without a word, led him up a wide, carpeted staircase, down a hall, and into her bedroom, illuminated by two small table lamps next to the king-size bed.

"I think this is where we're supposed to be," she said into his ear, running her hands down his shirtfront. There was something surrealistic about the scene for Hedras, and powerful. Everything seemed to be magnified: the smell of her, the sensuality of her voice, the ritual of achieving nakedness and her incredible smoothness. He was almost a nonparticipant as she guided him through the motions that led to her pleasure.

Was he expected to stay the night? he wondered when they were finished, and she'd retreated to the bathroom. She answered the question when she returned: "Having you spend the night would be a delight," she said, "but I'm afraid it won't do."

She kissed his cheek at the front door and wished him a pleasant evening.

— — —

Now, in San Miguel, she closed the door, slipped out of her purple velvet slippers and came to him barefoot. His boyish grin had returned; her smile was less innocent. She raised her lips to him, which he met eagerly with his own. Her hands undid the sash of his robe. She slipped it off his shoulders, leaving him naked and aroused. Elfie stepped back to allow room to strip off her caftan. Now she, too, was naked. "You're very beautiful," he said as they walked hand in hand to the bed.

"Thank you," she said. "So are you. Two beautiful people doing what beautiful people should be doing. And not another thought about onion soup, Chris. That would disappoint me—and you wouldn't want to do that, would you?"

CHAPTER 28

That Same Night
Washington

For Mac and Annabel, deciding where to go for dinner usually involved a choice between sticking to tried-and-true favorite spots where they were regulars, or sampling any one of the new restaurants opening every week in the nation's capital. Washington's reputation as a city of great monuments and bad restaurants was no longer deserved, thanks primarily to the influx of ethnic populations and interesting food. The gastronomic bar had been raised considerably.

This night, they opted to try something different, Cafe Atlantico, near the MCI Center. Friends who'd recently visited it came back raving about what they called its "*nuevo* Latino" menu.

"*Nuevo* Latino?" Mac said on their way to the restaurant on

Eighth Street, at the edge of the city's small but vibrant China-
town. "I distrust any restaurant with 'new' food."

"Peter and Waldine say the bar serves *mojitos.* And they rec-
ommend the house special for dinner, quail stuffed with wild
mushrooms."

"*Mojitos,* huh? The original Havana recipe? Maybe Papa
Hemingway will be there."

"Or Elvis."

They declined seats in the third-floor cigar smokers' dining
room, settled in the smoke-free section to enjoy their tangy lime
mojitos with an appetizer of spicy patties of ground chicken on
polenta canapés, in a cooling fresh mango sauce.

"To Papa," Annabel said, raising her glass.

"I think I saw him at the bar as we came through. *Salud!*"

"So, what's the latest on the trip?" she asked.

"Originally, we were scheduled to leave in five days. But since
our friend the VP wants me to go early, I thought I'd book
something four days from now. That okay with you?"

"Would it matter if it wasn't?"

"Do I detect a hint of pique?" Mac asked.

"No, you do not. I just meant that when your vice president
sends you on a special mission, it takes precedence."

"Just as long as you understand, Annie."

"Oh, I do. Besides, I have wonderful news."

"You do?"

"Yes. I got a call today from that dealer in San Miguel I've
bought things from before. Hector?"

"Sure. That baked-clay head—where was it from, Chiapas?—
was stunning."

"One of my favorite pieces. I think I may have it sold. Anyway, Hector called to say he's come upon two magnificent
Mayan vases, one carved in human form. He's giving me first
look."

"That's wonderful, Annie. And you know you can trust him, unlike a few other so-called dealers in your business."

"The point is, Mac, I think I'll leave a few days early, too."

"But you have that seminar at Catholic University."

"I called Susan to check on flights. She can get me on a late one the night of the seminar from Dulles to Dallas. I'll have just enough time to make a connection to León through Mexico City."

"Sounds good. But why the rush?"

"I don't want to miss out on seeing what Hector is offering. Besides, that would give us an extra day or two together."

"But I'll be in Mexico City through the elections."

"I know. I'll go straight to San Miguel, examine the vases, make a decision, and head right back to Mexico City. Being there with you during the elections will be exciting."

"Sounds good to me. Shall we order?"

They arrived back at the Watergate a little before eleven.

"Nightcap?" Mac asked.

"In the hotel?"

"Yes. We can celebrity watch."

The Potomac Lounge was packed. Every table was taken, and a large group gathered around the grand piano, where a pianist hidden by the crowd belted out a rollicking blues tune. Annabel peeked over some shoulders, turned to Mac, and said, "It's Stevie Wonder."

"He must be appearing in town," Mac said.

"At the Kennedy Center. I read about it."

Mac spotted a couple getting up from a small table closer to the bar and guided Annabel to it.

"That's Stevie Wonder," the waitress said when she came for their drink order.

"I know," said Annabel. "Just an impromptu performance?"

"Yes," the waitress said, unable to contain the excitement in

211

her voice. "He did the same thing last year when he was in town. Played till four in the morning."

Mac checked his watch.

Annabel laughed and took his hand. "We won't stay that long. Just this one drink."

An hour later Mac paid the check and they prepared to leave. Stevie Wonder was still performing; the crowd hadn't thinned.

"Ready?" Mac asked.

He'd no sooner stood and was pulling out Annabel's chair when he saw a familiar face approaching.

"Mac," Jim Ferguson said.

"Hello," Smith said. "Enjoying the music?"

"Just got here. Frankly, I was looking for you."

"Oh? This is my wife, Annabel. Annabel, Jim Ferguson."

"Hello."

"I took a chance that you might be in the hotel," Ferguson said. "I called a few times and left messages."

"We were out to dinner."

"Any chance of a little private time together?"

Smith looked at Annabel. "Now?" he said to Ferguson.

"Tonight. Doesn't have to be this moment."

"I suppose so. Why don't I take Annabel back to the apartment and—"

"You two go talk," she said. "I'll stay right here and soak up the music."

"Sure you don't mind, Mrs. Smith?" Ferguson asked.

"Not at all. Just don't forget I'm here."

"Impossible," Mac said. He kissed her cheek and followed Ferguson from the lounge, the sound of many out-of-tune voices singing "You Are the Sunshine of My Life" filling the lounge and lobby.

Smith and Ferguson went out to the circular drive in front of the main entrance. It was a clear night, a cool hint in the air of the coming season.

"Where to?" Mac asked.

"Let's just walk."

They went to stairs leading down to the Watergate's mall, empty and dark at that time of night. Ferguson stopped at a metal table, looked around three hundred and sixty degrees, then up to low roofs overhanging the mall.

They sat.

— — —

Mac had been gone only a few minutes when a young man approached Annabel at her table. "Would you mind if I shared this table with you? It's the only empty seat in the place."

Annabel hesitated, then smiled and said, "Please do."

He took the vacant chair and waved for the waitress. "Buy you a drink?"

"Thank you, no," Annabel said. "I'm afraid my husband will be returning shortly, but you're welcome to stay until he does."

"Cognac, please," the man told the waitress. "And a glass of water." To Annabel: "Sure I can't buy you something? It's the least I can do."

She shook her head. "One nightcap is enough."

They said nothing else to each other until Stevie Wonder took a break. Annabel turned to the man: "Do you live in the Watergate?"

"Yes. The south building."

"Then we're neighbors," she said, extending her hand. "Annabel Reed-Smith."

"Pleased to meet you. I'm new to the building."

"So are we. Do you work close by?"

"Pretty close. You?"

"I have an art gallery in Georgetown. Pre-Columbian art."

"I like art."

"So do I. That's obvious, I suppose, owning a gallery."

"What does your husband do?"

"He's an attorney. Well, he was. He teaches now. Law at GW."

" 'First, kill all the lawyers.' "

"Pardon?"

"Shakespeare, wasn't it?"

"Yes. *Henry IV.* Literally, 'The first thing we do, let's kill all the lawyers.' By the way, I'm an attorney, too."

"I thought you owned a gallery."

"I was a lawyer before that."

"No offense."

"None taken. Stevie Wonder is going to play again. I'd like to listen."

— — —

"What you've told me is shocking, Jim." Smith and Ferguson had gotten on a first-name basis.

"And obviously part of a pattern. Will you meet with Ramon?"

"Of course."

"He left Mexico City late this afternoon, flew to New York. He'll be on the next shuttle. He's coming straight to my apartment. He should be there in two, two and a half hours."

"Where is the apartment?"

"The west building."

"You live in the Watergate, too?"

"Just temporarily. A short-term sublet."

"I didn't think short-term sublets existed in the Watergate."

"It can be arranged." He gave Smith the apartment number.

"I won't go back with you," Ferguson said, standing. "Please give my best to your wife and apologize for dragging you out in the middle of a concert—and the middle of the night."

"She'll understand. It's not the first time."

———   ———   ———

The young man at Annabel's table stood when Mac arrived. "I confiscated your chair," he said. "Your wife was gracious enough to let me sit down."

"Yes, she is a gracious lady."

"Thank you," the man said to Annabel. To Mac: "It's all yours."

Mac sat next to his wife.

"What's his name?" Mac asked.

"I don't know. He didn't say. He lives in the south building. Hasn't been there long."

"I ran into him a few days ago."

"Oh?"

"I held the elevator for him. He didn't thank me."

"He was polite enough to me. He suggested killing all the lawyers."

"He suggested *what*?"

"Quoting Shakespeare. Poorly."

"Why would he say that to you?"

"I told him you were a lawyer."

"Oh, that justifies it. Ill-mannered twerp."

"He's a neighbor. Be neighborly."

"We have to leave."

"All right."

"I'll be going out later."

"Later? Tonight?"

"Yes. I'll explain when we get home."

They paused close to the piano while leaving the lounge.

"Isn't he wonderful?" Annabel said.

"Who, the guy with the polyester hair?"

"No. Stevie Wonder."

"Yes, he certainly is. Come on, lady, I've got some things to tell you."

CHAPTER 29

Later That Same Night
The West Building–the Watergate

The apartment in the Watergate's west building to which Smith had been summoned had all the trappings of the quintessential safe house. The furniture was of rental variety and quality, cheap and functional—two green-vinyl club chairs, a couple of wobbly floor lamps, Scandinavian-inspired kitchen table and chairs, cotton throw rugs, a small TV, and faded color photographs of Washington tourist attractions bunched together on a wall of the living room.

It was one of the smaller apartments in the Watergate's residential buildings. Gigi Winston of Winston and Winston, the Watergate's preeminent real estate agency, had shown Mac and Annabel fifteen apartments when they were looking to buy, including even the smaller ones to give them a sense of the range of what was available. A 950-square-foot one-bedroom without a view was going for $135,000. A luxurious two-bedroom on the river was priced at $695,000. Plenty to choose from.

Ferguson was alone when Mac arrived. "Thanks for coming," he said.

"My dog got a rare treat tonight," Mac said. "A walk after midnight. Where is Kelly?"

"On his way. He went home first. He'll be here in a few minutes. Drink?"

"No, thanks. You don't live here."

"No. It's a—convenience. For out-of-town guests."

"Uh-huh. Have anything cold? Club soda? Ginger ale?"

"Pepsi."

"Sold."

Ferguson had no sooner handed Smith a glass when the lobby attendant buzzed: "Mr. Kelly to see you."

"Send him right up."

As always happened when someone initially met Ramon Kelly, his curious facial features were noticed first, then the rest of him. He wore what he'd worn on the flight, wrinkled chino pants, a nubby red-and-green V-neck sweater that had seen too many wash cycles, and high tan work boots. His face drooped with fatigue; he hadn't bothered to comb his red hair since the attack earlier that day.

Kelly and Smith shook hands after Ferguson's introduction. Kelly looked at Ferguson, then said to Smith, "I don't mean to be rude, but I don't know you." To Ferguson: "Would you please explain?"

"Sure," Ferguson said. "Let me get you a drink. Pepsi?"

"A beer?"

"Yes."

Smith and Kelly took the club chairs. Ferguson pulled up one of the dining table chairs to form a tight circle. "Let me explain Mac Smith's presence, Ramon. He's a distinguished member of the faculty at George Washington University. He's also a close personal friend of the vice president. He's on the observer team for the Mexican elections, sits on a commission studying American–Mexican relations, and . . . and he's undertaking an assignment for the vice president as his special envoy."

"To Mexico?" Kelly asked.

"Yes," Smith said.

Kelly sat back and drew a deep breath. He'd replayed the attack in his mind over and over since leaving Mexico. Now it was time for him to recount what had happened. It was time to be debriefed.

"The point is," said Ferguson, "Mac Smith is very much wired into what's going on. Because he's going to Mexico, I wanted him to hear firsthand what happened to you today. Start from the beginning, from the moment you climbed on a plane here in Washington. Every detail. I'll run a tape. We've got all night."

Mac thought of Annabel asleep in their bed and hoped it would be quicker than that.

Kelly's play-by-play of his trip took a half hour. Smith was impressed with his recall and use of language. This was a bright young man who'd almost lost his life today in Mexico City. Had the assassination attempt succeeded, Mac knew, it would have meant that two members of the group known as The Mexico Initiative had been killed. And, of course, there had been Morin Garza, who'd also lost his life, allegedly because of what he was about to tell The Mexico Initiative. Even the most dedicated believer in coincidence couldn't justify this series of events.

Ferguson turned to Smith. "Pretty chilling, huh?"

"Yes."

"Of course, it's nothing new in Mexico these days."

"That's the most chilling thing of all," Smith said. "Mr. Kelly, you say Laura Flores's father became angry with you, tossed a drink in your face, and ordered you from his house. He's also, as you indicate, a man who owes his wealth and position to the PRI. His daughter might have been murdered by the very people closest to him, or at least her death ordered by those people. Do you think he was the one who set the gunmen on you?"

"It's possible."

"I'd say probable," Ferguson said.

"But you also say he was gracious in welcoming you and asked about his daughter's recent life. That doesn't sound to me like someone planning an assassination of his guest."

Kelly managed a small smile, held up his empty bottle to Ferguson in a gesture asking for another, and responded to Smith's comment.

"I like to think the best of people, Mr. Smith, but—"

"Please call me Mac."

"Sure. I'd like to think Flores was seriously grieving and couldn't possibly think of having me killed. But you can't make that assumption about anybody in Mexico these days, at least not the ones tied to the PRI. They've got so much to lose if the party goes down in this election. But more important are the ramifications if this country changes its stance on Mexico, gets tough, demands real reform, not the sort of lip service it's been getting. Remember, Flores knew I was coming to Mexico, knew exactly where I'd be this afternoon."

Smith thought for a moment. "Was he the only person who knew your schedule today, Ramon?"

It was Kelly's turn to ponder for a second. "No, of course not. The people in my office knew I was going to Mexico, but I didn't tell them I was seeing Flores." He laughed. "There's only two others in the office besides myself."

"Who else knew?" Smith asked.

"I did," Ferguson replied.

"We had lunch yesterday," said Kelly. "I told him I was going. But I don't think I mentioned what I'd be doing there."

"You said you'd be seeing Flores," Ferguson said.

"Right, I did."

"Who else?" Smith asked.

"The airline, I guess," Kelly said. "But they don't give out that kind of information."

"Chris Hedras knew," Ferguson said. "I called him in Mexico City after we had lunch."

"Anyone else?" Smith asked.

Ferguson and Kelly looked at each other.

"I don't think so," Kelly said. "It was a last-minute trip, spur of the moment. I packed a little bag and took off after calling Flores to ask if I could see him."

Smith asked Ferguson, "Who else did you tell besides Chris?"

Ferguson shrugged. "No one that I can recall. No, I'm sure I didn't mention it to anyone else. No reason to."

"Why Chris Hedras?" Smith asked.

"Because he's part of the team."

Smith stood and walked to the window, which was covered with heavy drapes. He parted the folds and peered at the neon sign of the Howard Johnson's Premier Hotel across Virginia Avenue.

Kelly said, "I have to figure that it was Flores who told people where I'd be. Maybe he didn't do it with the intention of setting me up to be killed, but it's only natural for him to tell close associates I'd be visiting his house. That's all it would have taken. Let's face it, I'm not the most popular person in Mexico these days."

Smith turned. "Do you have any information, Ramon, that would link up the attack on you with Ms. Flores's death?"

"Sure. We both work for—she *worked* for—the Initiative. It's no secret we're an information-gathering organization with the goal of changing U.S. policy toward Mexico. She'd come up with some powerful new proof of corruption involving PRI leadership and the private sector. Some of it even had to do with her own father."

"Did her father know this?" Smith asked, reclaiming his chair.

"I don't think so. What I haven't been able to figure out was why Laura was at that party the night she was killed. The Initiative and the Mexican-American Trade Alliance aren't exactly on the same page."

"It was the guy she was dating," Ferguson said.

"What guy?" Kelly tensed in his chair.

"The fellow she was seeing from the Mexican-American Trade Alliance," Ferguson said. "Chapas. Jose Chapas."

"Laura was dating *him*?" Kelly said, incredulous.

"That's the information I get from police sources. Nothing official, of course, but the source is good."

"Damn!" Kelly said, hitting the arm of his chair with his fist. "She never told me."

Ferguson and Smith said nothing.

"She was at the party with him?" Kelly asked.

"The way I hear it," said Ferguson, "she didn't go to the party with him. But he'd invited her."

"What about questioning him?" Kelly said.

"The police did, of course. He left the party before she did."

Smith said, "I asked you, Ramon, who knew of *your* movements in Mexico City today. But what about Laura Flores? Who knew where she'd be that night, and the damaging information she'd uncovered? By the way, what was that information—*specifically*?"

Kelly looked to Ferguson.

"Go ahead, Ramon. Mac is on the team."

Kelly said, "It had to do with two assassinations. One was Luis Donaldo Colosio. He was a political protégé of President Salinas. Shot in the head. The official investigation determined it was a lone gunman, and a deranged one at that. No conspiracy, no involvement by anyone else. Laura had been collecting information from sources in Mexico that the killing had been arranged by some of the PRI's 'dinosaurs,' the old guard who didn't like Colosio's call for more open government."

"The second?" Smith asked.

"Jose Francisco Ruiz Massieu. He was general secretary of the ruling party and was about to become the new majority leader in Congress. He was also an in-law of then President Salinas. They called him 'Pepe.' Very well liked. Another reformer. Everybody had a theory about why he was killed. Some claim he was a bisexual and was hit by a lover. The drug men hated him because his brother, a prosecutor, was coming down hard on one of the cartels. Like with Colosio, Laura had been putting together a case against those same PRI dinosaurs for Massieu's assassination."

"Was it in writing?"

"What?"

"What she'd uncovered? Had she put it down on paper?"

"No. By design. She briefed me verbally every day. There were some notes. They're in the office safe."

Smith decided to press on. He felt as though he were back in court cross-examining a witness.

"What about this Mexican-American Trade Alliance?" he asked. "The group Jose Chapas works for? You indicated your group and it are at odds."

"Sure, we are. They're for the status quo when it comes to American-Mexican relations. Keep the fat cats getting fatter. They lobby hard in Congress, spread money around."

They spent another half hour discussing the situation. Mac Smith continued to question hard.

Ferguson brought the meeting to an end. "I'm glad you had a

chance to hear what Ramon had to say, Mac. I thought that since you'll be representing the vice president in Mexico, you ought to be brought up to speed on everything."

"Can I ask you a question, Jim?" Smith said.

"Anything."

"Were you acting unilaterally in having me here tonight?"

"Meaning?"

"Is the vice president aware of what happened to Ramon today, and about this little get-together?"

Ferguson ignored the question by putting his arm about Kelly's shoulders and walking him to the door. "I'd lay low for a while, Ramon," he said. "You may want to leave the city until after the elections. Take a vacation. There's money for it."

"Maybe," Kelly said. He turned: "Nice meeting you, Mac Smith."

"Same here."

When Kelly was gone, Ferguson said to Mac, "To answer your question, the team keeps the vice president abreast of everything, Mac. Yes, he knows about the attempt on Ramon's life, and that I wanted you present when I debriefed him."

" 'Debriefed him.' 'The team.' What connection does Joe Aprile have with all of this? I mean, what *official* connection does he have—with this 'team'?"

"Let's just say, Mac, that what this team comes up with will have a profound impact upon not only the vice president's run for the presidency next year, but the future of U.S.-Mexican relations. I can't be more specific than that."

"And I won't press you. Thanks for the Pepsi. I think I'll get home."

"Of course. You must be tired. I am, too. That was wonderful, wasn't it, having a star like Stevie Wonder just sit down and start playing the piano for fun. Must be a nice guy."

"Must be. I'll be leaving for Mexico in a few days. I'll be at home until then, getting ready for the trip. Give me a call if there's anything else you want to cover."

"I will. Thanks again for allowing me to pull you away from that wonderful wife of yours. A truly beautiful woman."

"Inside, too. Good night, Jim."

CHAPTER 30

Two Days Later

Washington

The seminar at Catholic University was convened to examine the health of Washington's artistic community, focusing especially on what could be done to encourage the city's young painters and musicians. Annabel was one of six panelists; Mac, who sat in the front row, experienced the sense of pride he always did when his wife was in the limelight.

As was too often the case, however, such a panel of experts invariably included someone whose didactic posture unbalanced the discussion, prolonging it beyond productivity. The growing annoyance of other panelists was palpable as this individual droned on, challenging everything said by his colleagues at the speaker's table, and causing members of the audience to check watches and shimmy in their seats.

Annabel took advantage of the long-winded speaker's need

for a drink of water to break in with, "This has been an interesting, and I feel useful, discussion. But as I mentioned earlier, I'm due to catch a plane and will have to leave. Thank you so much for including me."

Mac took her hand as she stepped down from the stage. They left the auditorium and went to the car.

"Well, how did it go?" she asked when they were on their way to National Airport.

"Fine, until your colleague decided he was doing a one-man show."

Annabel laughed. "He does go on. Might have been tolerable if any one of his ideas made sense." She glanced at the car's digital clock. "We'll just make it."

"Provided we can find the gate in the new terminal."

Because they were running late, there wasn't time for Mac to accompany Annabel inside. He pulled up in front of the terminal, jumped out, came around, opened the door for her, and grabbed her bag from the backseat.

"I miss you already," he said.

"Me, too, but it's only for twenty-four hours. I'll meet up with you tomorrow night at the Majestic."

"I'll be there. Smooth flight, Annie."

"Don't forget to drop Rufus at the Animal Inn."

"First thing in the morning."

"Oh, and remind Sandy and Bernadette he needs his allergy medicine."

"Okay. You'd better get inside. I'm sure they've already called your flight."

They hugged and kissed, and he watched her disappear into the terminal, turning to blow him a final kiss. He drove to the Watergate, walked Rufus, poured himself a shot snifter of Blanton single-barrel bourbon, and settled in to watch the eleven o'clock news. It led off with a replay of a press conference held by Indiana Republican Congressman Dan Curtain late that afternoon. Curtain read a terse statement announcing that his Government Reform and Oversight Committee would open hearings in a month into the administration's campaign fund-raising activities during the last two elections:

"The hearings will show the American people conclusively that this administration's fund-raising activities clearly violated federal statutes in a number of areas, including the funneling of foreign donations through a system of front organizations and companies, in particular those representing Mexican business and political interests. In addition, witnesses, and the evidence they bring forth, will prove that these hundreds of thousands of dollars of illegal donations included money generated by Mexico's infamous drug cartels and laundered through these front organizations and business entities."

— — —

Joe Aprile and his wife, Carole, sat together in pajamas and robes on a couch in a small room of their residence, the only light in the darkened room glowing from the television.

"Is there the sort of evidence he's talking about?" Carole asked quietly.

"Not that I'm aware of. It's a typical Curtain technique. Talk enough about evidence that isn't there and everybody eventually forgets to ask to see it."

"But there must be something," Carole said, using the remote to turn down the volume.

"Oh, I don't doubt that there is," her husband said ruefully. "Fund-raising has gotten so out of hand, especially since its 'reform,' that it's impossible to know the source of every donation. You just have to trust your people and hope they've followed the law."

"'Front organizations,'" Carole said. "'Money laundering.' Sounds like something out of *The Godfather.*"

"What's Spanish for 'godfather'?" he asked.

"*El padre Dios?* I don't know. Why?"

"I warned the president going back to the first election."

"Warned him about what?"

"Mexico. The PRI's agenda to get us to look the other way while they do business as usual. The businessmen championing NAFTA and lending support to the campaign."

"Legally?"

"On the surface. But it's too easy to hide the true sources of money, Carole. The Mexicans, among others, are masters at it. They've had to be to launder billions in drug money. I told him we needed to put in place a checks-and-balances system to keep tabs on funds coming into the campaign from foreign sources, particularly Mexico. I told the Democratic National Committee people the same thing, and they assured me they had. But going after big money to finance a presidential campaign is a heady challenge for too many people. It's like a game, coming up with a bigger contribution than the next guy. Can you top this? Hedras and I talked about it many times when he was on the president's staff. That's why I wanted him for my campaign. Chris sees it the way I do."

"Surely if there's any validity to what Congressman Curtain is saying, it won't be applied to you next year."

He said nothing.

"Will it?"

Joe turned, took her hand in his, and looked into her eyes. "Carole, I'm afraid there is some credibility to what Curtain is charging."

It was her turn to be silent.

"I can't be specific—I mean, I could be but I won't. I've been receiving new reports over the past year on Mexico and its avenues and alleys of corruption. Some of these reports point to illegal contributions into our campaign of money, big money, by certain Mexican interests."

"Can't you just give it back?"

"Some has already gone back, but it's damn near impossible to trace it all, nail down its *real* sources."

"What sort of reports have you been getting? From whom?"

"Various people. I set up a channel of information through a group here in Washington that has good sources in Mexico."

"A task force? A government group?"

"No. I had to keep it unofficial, outside the White House and away from the administration."

"Does the president know?"

"No. Frankly, I don't know how much longer I can continue to publicly support his all-positive positions on Mexico."

"That's been coming for a long time."

"I suppose it has."

"What is this group that's feeding you information?"

"A think tank. Chris set it up for me. I—"

"The one that young woman worked for, the one who fell from the roof at the Watergate?"

"Yes. The Mexico Initiative."

"Is there any connection with . . . I've heard it wasn't suicide, that she might have been thrown from the roof."

"I know. And there was an attempt on the Initiative's director's life in Mexico City a few days ago."

Carole stiffened; her gasp filled the room.

"Carole."

"Yes?"

"I'm thinking of announcing that I won't be a candidate for president next year."

"How can you not? A vice president in a popular administration is expected to carry the mantle. It would throw the party into turmoil."

"What about the turmoil it would cause for us?"

"I've never shied away from challenges, Joe."

"I know you haven't. Maybe it's me who wants to shy away from conflict, get out of the sniper's scope, get up in the morning worrying only about what the weather is going to be."

Her smile didn't reach her eyes.

"What we both need, I think, is a vacation," she said. "You always say the biggest problem we have is not having time to think, and that mistakes happen that way."

"Vacation? I don't see two days of leisure strung together for a year or more."

"We could carve a couple of days out for ourselves. A weekend."

"Maybe after Mexico."

"Mexico! It's ripping you apart, isn't it?"

"I suppose it is."

"Annabel left for there tonight. Mac is going tomorrow. Annabel told me you're sending Mac to do something for you."

"She said that? It's true. I asked him to act as a special envoy for me."

"Something involving this Mexico Initiative?"

"Yes."

"Joe, is what you're asking him to do dangerous?"

"No. He's just meeting with someone, that's all. An hour out of his trip."

He wished she'd said something in response.

"I'm ready for bed," she said, standing and yawning.

"I think I'll sit up awhile."

"I spent some time today going over my calendar for the next month. I have your trip to the inauguration on it. I assume I'll be going with you."

"I'd rather you didn't," he said, not looking at her.

"Oh? It's expected, isn't it, that your wife accompany you on an official visit?"

"Sure, but that can easily be covered. The president can send me anywhere he wants. He doesn't have that power over you."

"Joe, I—"

"Please, Carole. Not now."

"Good night, Joe."

"Good night."

— — —

Mac Smith finished packing at midnight, aside from last-minute things to add in the morning. He went over a standard packing list he always consulted when traveling. This one had a number of items added in ink, most having to do with his role as an election observer.

Dressed for bed, he went out onto the terrace, where a humid breeze came off the Potomac, the river's ripples catching the light from a half-moon. Like the city's stately buildings and monuments, the Potomac was synonymous with Washington, flowing incessantly like the political process that defined the city, that *was* the city. Rufus was at his side, leaning against his hip.

"You be good for Sandy and Bernadette," Mac said, rubbing the Dane's large head.

Rufus looked up and panted, which Mac and Annabel considered a smile.

"And let them give you your medicine without a hassle. Got that?"

His hand was licked in response.

In bed, Smith's thoughts were positive.

He'd been blessed with a fine first wife and son, then cursed when a drunk driver killed them in a head-on collision on the Beltway. He'd been one of Washington's top criminal attorneys until he could no longer cope with the inimical system of criminal jurisprudence—and with the death of the two persons he loved most in the world. Now, he had Annabel, lovely, loving, and decent Annabel, who'd brought spark back into his life and gave him something to fervently nurture and protect.

Sometimes, it was when things were best that fears were worst, fears of things coming unraveled, calamity striking when not expected, losing the special reasons for things being so good.

Fortunately, sleep interrupted this increasingly morbid series of reflections. He slept soundly and awoke refreshed.

Chapter 31

The Next Day

San Miguel de Allende, Mexico

It had been an arduous trip to San Miguel.

The Mexican taxi driver who took Annabel on the hour-and-a-half ride from the León airport was no older than eighteen, she judged, and drove with the wild abandon of youth. His car was battered; it ran more on oil than gasoline and he stopped twice at gas stations to add quarts. Annabel asked in Spanish a few times that he slow down when taking hairpin curves full bore, but each request resulted only in a moment of sanity until his foot rammed the accelerator to the floor again.

More disconcerting was passing through small towns consisting of nothing but the road, and a string of ramshackle houses and restaurants. Even at that late hour, their passage was narrowed by milling crowds of men, women, and children. Some of the men openly carried weapons and glared at the taxi as the driver slowed to avoid hitting someone. After they'd passed through the first such town, Annabel leaned forward and mentioned the armed men, tales of abduction in Mexico very much on her mind.

The driver laughed, reached across the seat, and held up a baseball bat. Somehow, his display of a Louisville Slugger did not ease her concerns.

The Casa de Sierra Nevada was aware she'd be arriving late and had staff waiting for her.

"¿*Como está usted*, Senora Smith?"

"Fine. Tired, and still shaking from the taxi ride."

"You should have had our limousine pick you up."

"I know, but in my haste leaving Washington I forgot to re-quest it. I will need it late tomorrow afternoon into Mexico City. I'm just happy I'm here—and definitely ready for bed."

"You'll be in a suite at our building in the park, Senora Smith. I hope that is suitable."

"Perfectly suitable," Annabel said. "I saw those suites the last time I was here. It's a lovely setting."

"*Sí*, very quiet. Come, the car is waiting."

The Sierra Nevada's Hotel-in-the-Park, adjacent to Parque Benito Juárez, was only a minute's drive from the main building at 35 Hospicio, in the center of town. On other visits, Annabel had stayed in one of five suites in that main building, which also housed the restaurant, bar, and reception desk. Ten separate buildings in all comprised the Casa de Sierra Nevada, a total of thirty-seven rooms and suites.

The staff laid out Annabel's luggage, and gave her instructions on the suite's amenities. When they left, Annabel drew a long sigh of contentment and took in her surroundings.

Mac and Annabel had enjoyed opulent hotel suites before, and this rivaled the best of them. It was huge, the sitting room and sleeping areas larger than their living room in the Watergate. An open picture window at one end afforded a splendorous view of the formal gardens and park beyond. The twenty-foot-high ceilings were whitewashed brick with rough-hewn timber beams, the floors terra-cotta, the walls a delicate yellow. Large watercolors of parrots—parrot paintings were throughout the hotel—held prominent positions on the expanse of walls.

The king-size bed was covered in the same fuchsia fabric as the long sofa and stuffed chairs. Above the headboard was a massive black carving of the Mexican "Tree of Life," with multiple tiny butterflies and flower cup candleholders woven into the pattern. A free-standing fireplace with a conical hood reaching up to the ceiling spanned the sitting and sleeping areas.

The bathroom was the size of a New York City studio apartment. Twin gold sinks were sunken in black marble vanities. A window offered an inviting view of a terrace. Logs in the fireplace had been ignited, casting a copper warmth over the room.

Annabel kicked off her shoes and plopped down on the couch. A heavy wooden table held a vase with two dozen crimson roses and a cut-glass bowl of fresh fruit. Two envelopes rested beside them.

Annabel opened the first.

Senora Smith: Welcome once again to the Casa de Sierra Nevada. I trust your accommodations are to your liking. We chose the park suite as a quiet place for you and Senor Smith. I look forward to meeting him when he joins you. In the meantime, please call upon me at any time for your needs. I look forward to personally welcoming you tomorrow.

Gabriela.

She opened the second envelope.

Annabel, dearest—How dare you sneak into San Miguel without giving me adequate warning to host a proper party for you.

You know you are always welcome as a guest in my home, although the hotel probably offers you and your darling husband a more private setting for what I'm sure is a perpetual honeymoon. Call me your first spare moment.

Love, Elfie.

Annabel tossed the note on the table, sat back, and laughed. She'd met a number of Washington's omnipresent social hostesses, each a formidable presence in her own right, but none approaching Elfie Dorrance for sheer magnitude. What most impressed Annabel about Elfie was her ability to push people to the edge of animosity but then, operating from an innate sense of limits, know how to keep them from falling off that edge and loving every minute of their trip to the precipice.

Annabel had never been to Elfie's San Miguel home. Her previous trips to the lovely village had been strictly on business; Elfie never even knew Annabel would be there. She seemed to remember Elfie mentioning it was on a park. *This* park? Annabel wondered.

She went to the window. By leaning out and looking to her right, she could see lights on in a few homes even at that late hour. Was Elfie entertaining in one of them?

After a shower, and wrapped in one of the hotel's thick terrycloth robes, Annabel emptied her suitcase, placing selected items in a smaller, empty bag she'd brought along for the trip to Mexico City. She and her husband had made a study of effective packing for a trip, thinking everything out and listing items on their respective computer-generated lists, including an ample supply of plastic bags of varying sizes, the first thing packed by every savvy traveler. That chore completed, she sat on the broad windowsill and listened to the cries of nocturnal birds, the only violators of the night's stillness.

"God, things are good," she said aloud in a breathy voice. The minute she did, she silently reminded herself not to be cocky, not to assume that life was a continuing embarrassment of riches and fat times and glowing sunrises and sunsets. It was more like the stock market, she thought as she got into bed, sometimes climbing steadily until something, or someone, did something that caused it to fall; a bull or a bear life, optimistic one day, fearing the worst the next.

Annabel was not a religious person in the sense that she devoted much time or thought to it. But she did, on occasion, say a soundless prayer. This night, she thanked someone she didn't know—wasn't even sure existed although she preferred to think he or she did—for Mac and their life together, for Rufus, for the good preparation her parents had given her, for so many wonderful friends and . . . and for Mexico and its elections.

"Let it go smoothly," she said aloud, her voice heavy with sleep. "Let it be good for Mexico."

CHAPTER 32

The Next Morning
The South Building–the Watergate

Mac Smith locked his suitcases and made a final inspection of the apartment, checking that timers on selected lights and a small radio were properly set, and adding a few items to a note he'd written to their housekeeper, who'd stayed with them after their move. He'd deposited Rufus at the Animal Inn that morning, guilty at condemning the large beast to confined quarters but taking solace from the love lavished on the Dane, and other four-legged wards, by the kennel's owners.

He called the lobby desk. "This is Mac Smith. I need a cab to National."

"Right away."

Instead of waiting for a call that the cab had arrived, Smith decided to wait in the lobby. He placed his bags by the front door and glanced about. The rude young guy from the elevator, who'd sat at Annabel's table in the Potomac Lounge, was in a chair reading a magazine. Mac went over to him. The young man looked up.

"Mac Smith. We met at the impromptu Stevie Wonder concert."

"Right," the young man said, running a hand, as usual, through his satin hair.

"We've never been properly introduced." Smith extended his hand.

The young man took it, not getting up.

"Well, welcome to the building, although we're new here, too."

"So your wife said."

"Have a pleasant day."

Smith walked away, again dismayed at the young man's lack of social grace. He hadn't stood, nor had he given his name. "Slug," Smith muttered under his breath.

"Cab is here, Mr. Smith."

"Right. Thanks. See you in a week or so."

As the taxi drove off, Mac looked back at the glass-walled lobby, where his new, disrespectful neighbor stood near the door, his face empty, eyes trained on the cab.

— — —

"Welcome to the Majestic, Senor Smith," the desk clerk said.

"*Gracias,*" Smith said, accepting a pen with which to fill out his registration card. "Have others from the election observer team arrived?" he asked.

"No, not yet. The elections are two days from now. They are due in tomorrow."

"I thought I'd jump the gun a little," Mac said, smiling and sliding the card across the desk. "Relax for a day before getting to work."

"A good idea, but it is hard to relax with the elections, huh?"

The clerk spoke the truth.

—   —   —

The trip in from the airport was tortuous, the streets chock-ablock with vehicles and pedestrians. The taxi passed beneath thousands of large, colorful posters proclaiming the virtues of the PRI's candidate for mayor of Mexico City, Alfredo del Mazo. Noticeably fewer and smaller banners for the PRD candidate, Cuauhtemoc Cardenas, and PAN's Carlos Castillo, fluttered in a warm breeze from wires strung across the streets and wide avenues. Music from mariachi bands came from unseen places, melding with the pungent aroma of food stalls and the pervasive acidic smell of pollution.

Mac felt the excitement in the air as the taxi inched along. This nation of more than seventy-five million people was poised on the brink of its first taste of free and democratic elections since 1911. All the political parties had supported far-ranging judicial reform in the election process, and had agreed upon transparent and understandable rules covering campaign financing and media access.

Still, the reigning PRI remained the dominant force, a hegemonic political juggernaut that had ruled Mexico for seven decades, controlling every aspect of the nation's daily life. Whether its public proclamations of support for an open election would translate into action remained to be seen. But if the forecasts were accurate, the PRI's grip on power was in jeopardy, especially in Mexico City, where the winner of the mayoral race would emerge as the leading presidential candidate in the 2000 elections.

— — —

Although he hadn't requested a room with a view of the Zócalo, the city's vast main square, second largest in the world, trailing only Moscow's Red Square, his suite looked out over this hub of Mexico City's life since the Aztecs founded their capital there in 1325. He opened the windows and allowed the square's sounds to reach him, took in the buildings surrounding it, anchored by Palacio Nacional, which housed the president's official headquarters and contained some of Diego Rivera's finest murals; myriad museums; other government buildings; and the Portal de los Evangelistas, where public scribes assisted the illiterate in writing their legal documents and love letters.

His suite contained a TV with a remote, a mini-bar, a radio, a king-size bed, a desk, and two comfortable armchairs. Not the most luxurious hotel room he'd ever been in but perfectly serviceable.

He placed a call to the Casa de Sierra Nevada in San Miguel de Allende.

"Senora Smith's room, please."

After a pause: "Senora Smith is not here. May I take a message?"

"This is her husband. Do you know if she's left for Mexico City?"

"Un momento, por favor."

Gabriela, the concierge, came on the line. "Senor Smith, this is Gabriela."

"Oh, yes, Annabel often speaks of you."

"That is nice to hear. She left an hour ago for Mexico City. By our limousine."

Mac checked his watch. She'd be arriving in about three hours. He was glad she was in the hands of the hotel's limousine driver, not a suicidal Mexican cab driver.

"Gracias," he said.

"My pleasure. I look forward to seeing the two of you when you return to San Miguel."

"Right after the elections. I'm looking forward to it, too."

It was seven o'clock. He decided to wait until Annabel arrived before having dinner. But he was hungry. He pulled the room service menu from the desk and had started to look through its snack section when the phone rang.

"Hello."

"Senor Smith?"

"Yes."

"This is Raul Telo. I am associate director of the IFE, the Federal Election Institute. I was told you had come a day early and thought we might have an opportunity to meet informally, before the others arrive."

"That would be fine. I'm expecting my wife in a few hours but was about to grab a snack."

"Perfect. Allow me to buy you a drink and some *entreméses.*"

"I'm afraid you've lost me."

"Appetizers. The snacks you mention."

"Oh. All right."

"I will call you from the bar in, say, a half hour?"

"I'll be waiting."

Telo stood at the entrance to the Majestic's Bar El Campanario on the seventh floor when Smith arrived. He was small in stature, a wiry man in his forties with a black pencil mustache, thinning black hair combed straight back, and wearing a green suit, yellow shirt, and brown tie. There was a second man with him, considerably taller and larger, with a round, flushed face, white walrus mustache, and dressed in a tan suit and open-necked red silk shirt. Telo introduced him as Alberto Palomino.

"My pleasure," Palomino said, shaking Smith's hand. "Welcome to Mexico City."

Telo suggested they take their drinks on the terrace, over-looking the Zócalo. Once seated at the only vacant table, next to the railing, Telo ordered three bottles of beer and a platter of assorted hors d'oeuvres. "We had better enjoy some beer now," he said, smiling. "Tomorrow, no alcohol is served."

"The day *before* the elections?" Mac said.

"*Sí,*" said Palomino. "And election day. We are serious about doing it right."

"That's good to hear," Mac said. He glanced out over the railing to the Zócalo, where thousands of people had gathered; bands played, dance troupes in Indian costumes performed, and a general spirit of celebration prevailed.

"The people are hopeful," Telo said, raising his beer glass in a toast. "To the beginning of a new democratic era in Mexico."

Mac and Palomino clicked the rims of their glasses with Telo's.

Palomino said, his glass still in the air, "And to our good friends, the Americans. To you, Senor Smith, for being here to help us."

A six-piece mariachi band—three high-pitched *vihuelas,* a large bass guitar called a *guitarron,* a trumpet, and a violin—dressed in tight, studded black pants, embroidered white shirts, gaudy yellow jackets, and huge black felt sombreros came to the terrace and began playing, loudly. The three men at the table had to raise their voices to be heard.

When the band took a short intermission, Telo announced he had to leave. "I would like to stay longer," he said, "but I must attend a meeting with the staff. It was a pleasure meeting you, Mac Smith. I will see you at the briefing tomorrow morning."

"I'll be there."

When Smith and Palomino were alone, Mac said, "I take it you're involved with the election commission, too." Palomino smiled, shrugged, said, "In a sense." He motioned for a waiter to bring them another round, sat back contentedly, looked at Smith, and said, "I suppose having to have foreigners watching over us at election time strikes you as somewhat pathetic, Mr. Smith."

"Not at all. Soon, I trust, it will no longer be necessary. You said you were involved with the election commission 'in a sense.' In *what* sense?"

"You might say I am a supporter. I suppose I have been rude. I apologize for that. I am a professor and writer."

"What do you teach?"

"Political science."

"And your writings?"

"The same subject. I am not a published author, although I am working on a book."

"The elections play a part in your book?"

"Oh, yes. The day after tomorrow will signal a great change in our country."

"In leadership?"

"I believe so. The PRI will lose its grip on Congress, and the PRD and PAN will begin to assume a greater role in our political destiny, *si Dios quiére.*"

"God willing?"

"*Sí.*"

"I take it such a change would please you."

"Of course."

The sudden presence of another person at the table caused both men to look up. It was a young man with a large box suspended from a leather strap about his neck. Two small wire cages were side by side, close to his body. Each contained a live canary. The rest of the box was taken up by two sections sunken into it to allow their contents to be level with the surface. Each contained what appeared to be hundreds of tiny pieces of folded paper, yellow on one side, pink on the other.

"What have we here?" Mac asked, laughing.

The young man answered, "Your future, senor. You choose one of the birds and it will perform for you, then pick your fortune from the papers."

"An ornithological fortune-teller," Smith said, laughing. "No, thank you."

"Perhaps you should," Palomino said.

"Really? You vouch for the birds' accuracy in predicting futures?"

"I vouch for how useful it might be to you. I must leave, Senor Smith. The bill has been paid."

Before Smith could respond, Palomino stood, slapped Mac on the shoulder, leaned close to his ear, and whispered, "Don't disappoint the birds. They have much to tell you." He threaded his way through the tables and was gone.

"Senor?" the young street performer said. "Your fortune?"

"How much?" Smith asked.

"Whatever you wish to give Pauchito and Estelita."

"The birds' names?"

"Sí."

"All right." Mac fished pesos from his wallet.

"Your fortune in English, of course."

"Of course."

He opened the door to one of the cages and the canary hopped out onto the folded papers. "This is Estelita," the young man said. "She will choose your fortune. But first she wishes to entertain you."

Mac watched with a bemused expression as the tiny yellow bird went through its trained paces. It picked up a small hat with its beak and flipped it up onto its head, then shook it off. It rang a bell, stopped when instructed, then rang it again on command.

"Wonderful," Mac said. "I didn't know you could train a bird to do things like that."

"Only Pauchito and Estelita," the man said. "The only two birds in the world."

"I see."

Mac realized they were being observed by bemused customers at other tables.

"Now, for your fortune, senor." To Estelita: "Pick the right one. Be careful."

The bird turned in circles on top of the yellow papers, dipped its beak into them, and came up holding one.

"Your hand, senor."

Mac extended his hand palm up. Estelita dropped the yellow paper in it.

"*Gracias,*" Mac said.

"*De nada, senor. Buenas noches.*"

He walked away.

Had Palomino not urged him to engage the street performer, Smith would have simply tossed the unread yellow paper on the table when he left. But Palomino's insistence had been more than simple encouragement. He had wanted Smith to do it.

"What does it say?" a man at an adjacent table asked, laughing.

Mac said, "I haven't looked yet."

The paper unfolded like an accordion. Mac put on his half-glasses to read the minuscule print.

"Long life and riches?" the wife of the man at the next table asked.

Mac grinned, replaced his glasses in his pocket, and said, "Exactly. Would you expect anything else?" The paper accompanied his glasses into his pocket.

Smith went to his room and picked up a book he'd started on the plane, P. D. James's new crime novel, *A Certain Justice*. As much as he was enjoying it, the long day caught up with him and he eventually dozed in the chair, to be awakened by the ringing phone. "Senor Smith, this is the desk. Senora Smith is here."

"Good. Send her right up."

Annabel burst through the door with high energy, followed by a bellhop carrying her bags.

"It is good to see you," she said, embracing him.

"Good trip?"

"From San Miguel? Fine. A limousine with a professional driver sure beats a local taxi. He was sane."

Mac laughed. "Glad to hear it—and see you here in one piece."

After the bellhop was tipped and had departed, they hugged and kissed again, less self-consciously this time. When they disengaged, Annabel took in the suite. "So, this is home for the next few days."

"Not bad, huh?"

"Wait'll you see our suite in San Miguel." She looked out the window to the Zócalo. "Nice location."

"Yes, it is. I held off on dinner, although I did have a couple of beers and a snack."

"Alone?"

"No." He explained who he'd been with.

"Sounds pleasant."

"You hungry?"

"Yes, but nothing heavy. Room service?"

"Sure. Here's the menu. Whatever you order is fine."

They nibbled, drank wine, and switched between CNN, pulled in by the hotel's satellite dish, and Televisa. The Mexican channel played a succession of *telenovelas,* popular soap operas, interrupted every few minutes by a barrage of commercials extolling the virtues of various PRI candidates. Some ran as long as six minutes. The opposition's TV exposure was virtually nonexistent.

"How can they call this a fair election when the television is controlled by one party?" Mac muttered. "Supposedly, all parties agreed to open media access."

"Can't happen overnight," said Annabel. "Just as long as polling places are open to all, and the ballots are counted fairly."

"I suppose you're right, but I'll include it in my report all the same."

"I talked to Elfie before I left. She's throwing a party for us when we arrive."

Mac grinned. "Any excuse for a party."

"Chris Hedras is there."

"Really? Got to sneak out of Washington for a few days?"

"Evidently. Have you heard anything yet about your furtive tryst with the revolutionary?"

" 'Furtive tryst.' That's redundant. Besides, we're not lovers meeting for a clandestine smooch."

"I hope not."

" 'Tryst' is when lovers sneak off."

" 'Tryst' is any secret get-together."

"Yes."

"Glad we agree."

"I mean, yes, I've heard something."

"What?"

He took the yellow accordion-folded paper from the dresser and handed it to Annabel.

"What's this?"

"Read it."

"I can't without a magnifying glass."

"Here."

Mac gave her a thin, wallet-size sheet of magnifying plastic he always included on his travel list. Annabel positioned herself beneath the room's strongest lamp, closed one eye, and deciphered the Lilliputian writing.

"What does it mean?" she asked, handing it to him.

"It was supposed to be my fortune."

"Your *fortune*?"

"Yes." Mac briefly explained the canaries and their act. "Obviously, it isn't my fortune. Or maybe it is in some perverse sense. At any rate, it's instructing me to meet someone tomorrow afternoon at two o'clock at El Angel, on the Paseo de la Reforma, in Zona Rosa. The Pink Zone. El Angel is a famous statue, a monument to independence from Spain."

"And the canary picked this out for you?"

"No. I wasn't watching that closely. I assume the young man made sure Estelita came up with it."

"And who is Estelita, if you don't mind my asking?"

"The canary. Her brother is Pauchito."

"Of course he is. Her brother. Mac, don't you think whoever is setting this up could be a little more direct?"

"Sure. But remember, Mexico is a nation of masks. Everybody isn't quite what they seem to be. Besides, when you're running a guerrilla operation dedicated to toppling your government, directness can get you killed."

He was sorry he'd said it.

"Mexico is the moon's navel," she said.

"Huh?"

"That's what Mexico means. 'The moon's navel.' "

"That's good to know."

"What are you going to do?"

"Stroll over to El Angel tomorrow at two. The briefing for election observers is at ten, scheduled to finish up at noon. We'll be given our polling place assignments. We meet again in the evening for a reception, to which you are invited. In the mean-

time, you and I will go look at El Angel. I've seen it. It's beautiful, very tall and gold. A little sight-seeing wouldn't hurt."

"Do you think they'll approach you if I'm with you?"

"We'll just have to see. Maybe you can browse a few shops
while I give them a chance. It's a nice part of the city. Paseo de
la Reforma is very fashionable."

"Have you reported this to the backup people you were
promised would be here?"

"I don't know who they are. No one's contacted me. If they
do, I'll tell them about it. By the way, how did your meeting with
Hector, the dealer, go in San Miguel? That's why you went there
in the first place."

"I bought something."

"Did you?"

"I'll have to draw against the gallery's line of credit."

"That much, huh?"

"Yes."

"Well, Annabel, it's been a long day. I suggest we get to bed."

"Hector propositioned me."

"He did? That weasel. What did you say?"

"I told him I was sexually sated by my husband, and that I was
in for a long night of lovemaking when I got to Mexico City."

"You didn't?"

"No. But if affairs of state can be so subtle they're delivered
by a canary named Estelita, I can get subtle, too."

"Not *so* subtle, Annie."

"But I've made my point."

He pulled her close and ran his hands over her back—to start.
"Yes, you certainly have made your point, Mrs. Smith."

CHAPTER 33

The Next Day

Mexico City

The briefing for the international election observers was held at the Palacio de Bellas Artes, a huge, ornate theater complex on Angela Peralta. Mac knew there would be representatives from many countries, but was surprised at the number—four-hundred men and women welcomed by the director of the International Republican Institute, and receiving a stirring pep talk about the importance of their roles in the next day's election. Participants were given a folder with their names on them when arriving, containing last-minute instructions and the locations of the polling places to which they were assigned.

The briefing broke precisely at noon. Mac and Annabel met for lunch at Prendés, where they enjoyed paella valenciana, then headed for Paseo de la Reforma, arriving at the base of the 188-foot-tall golden-winged El Angel at precisely two. The throng of

252

chilangos, Mexico City dwellers, was swelled by tourists snapping photographs of the city's enduring symbol of freedom.

"What now?" Annabel asked.

"I'll just wait around, give it a half hour. I hope whoever's supposed to contact me knows what I look like. I sure don't know what he looks like."

"Meet you back here in a half hour?"

"Right."

Mac watched Annabel's long-legged gait take her across the avenue to a succession of expensive shops but she quickly disappeared from his sight as the crowds swallowed her. He decided to slowly circle the statue, giving whoever it was he was waiting for a chance to spot him.

He checked his watch frequently. Twenty minutes passed, then twenty-five. He started to return to where he and Annabel had parted when a wizened, stooped man carrying a large rack of helium-filled balloons and gaudy pinwheels approached and asked if Mac wished to buy one.

"No, *gracias,*" Mac said, waving him away.

"For your lovely wife," the man said in English. "To take with you to San Miguel."

Mac looked into the man's eyes. They were Indian eyes, hard and determined. The message emanating from them was unmistakable.

"All right," Mac said, fishing for pesos in his pocket. He handed the vendor the money and was given in return a green balloon on a stick.

"*Gracias,* senor," the vendor said, shuffling away.

"*De nada.*"

He felt a little foolish, standing there holding a balloon, and wished he had a child with him to justify it. Annabel arrived a few minutes later and raised her eyebrows at the sight of his purchase.

"For you," Mac said, bowing slightly from the waist and presenting it to her.

"Is this——?"

"Hang on to it. Don't let it float away."

They returned to the hotel. The minute they were in the suite, Mac examined the balloon. A vague shadow inside indicated a foreign object. "Hold your ears," he said, puncturing the rubber skin with a ballpoint pen. He tore the wound open and removed a single slip of paper.

"What does it say?" asked Annabel.

"Here."

Be at La Terraza, at the Jardín in San Miguel, two days after the election at nine in the morning.

"Canaries and balloons," Annabel said, handing the paper back to Mac. "A high-tech undercover operation."

"You'll have to tell me where La Terraza is."

"Tell you? I'll take you there. It's lovely, Mac, right on the main square. All the newspapers are delivered there each morning. The ex-pats pretty much start their day at the Jardín—coffee, newspaper, local gossip—pop into the bank and post office. We'd be going there even if you weren't instructed to. Still no word from your alleged backup team?"

"No. We'd better get ready for the reception. It's at the Four Seasons. Oh, by the way, I'll be poll-watching tomorrow near Chapultepec Park, by the zoo. Part of a team of six, two Americans, two Brits, a German, and a Chilean."

"Exciting."

"Yes, it is. I hope everything goes smoothly."

"I prayed for that night before last, in San Miguel."

"Did you? Then it's assured. No God would dare refuse you, Annabel. First in the shower?"

"No, you go first. What a nice thing to say."

"About you and God? Just reciting theological fact. Only be a minute."

— — —

"Ambassador Cadwell," Mac said after being introduced to the U.S. ambassador to Mexico. "Mrs. Cadwell."

"A pleasure to meet both of you," Cadwell said. "My good friend Elfie Dorrance often speaks of Mr. and Mrs. Smith with great fondness."

"We'll be seeing her in a few days," Annabel said. "We're going on to San Miguel after the elections."

"So are we," Priscilla Cadwell said. "We escape this city whenever we can." Her pug nose moved, as though smelling something fetid.

Although the official reception was held, in part, to allow election observers from different countries to mingle socially—and with their Mexican hosts and hostesses—birds of a national feather tended to flock together, including the large American contingent. Mac and Annabel chatted with dozens of people over the next hour. When they eventually found themselves alone for the first time that evening, Mac asked, "Ready to leave?"

"I think so."

"Good. A few good-byes and—"

"Mackensie Smith?"

Mac and Annabel faced a forty-something-year-old man with a broad face, wide, open smile, and close-cropped salt-and-pepper hair.

"Yes," Mac said, extending his hand.

"Ron Pacie. I'm with the embassy."

"This is my wife, Annabel."

"Yes, I know. A pleasure, Mrs. Smith."

"Quite a party," Annabel said.

"Our Mexican friends know how to entertain. Possible to steal your husband for a few minutes, Mrs. Smith?"

"Borrow him? Yes. Steal him? I'm afraid not."

Pacie laughed gently. "Strictly a short-term loan, Mrs. Smith. Only be a minute."

The two men walked a dozen feet to the empty end of one of multiple bars set up in the large function room.

"Jim Ferguson told me to look you up," Pacie said.

"Did he?"

Smith immediately realized this was the team's contact.

"How's everything going?"

"Fine."

"Any approaches yet?"

"About?"

"San Miguel."

"As a matter of fact, yes. I've been contacted by a canary named Estelita and a balloon salesman, name unknown."

Pacie didn't smile.

"I was told to be at the El Angel statue this afternoon. I went and was sold a balloon—a green one. In it was a message telling me to be at a certain place in San Miguel de Allende two days after the election."

"What place?"

"The town square. A restaurant with a terrace overlooking the square. Nine o'clock in the morning. That's about it."

"Okay. If you have anything else to report, any problems, you can call me at the Majestic, room four-ten."

"I thought you were with the embassy."

"I am."

"Live in the hotel?"

"For a few days. I don't want to keep you from your wife any longer. Oh, Jim asked me to pass along some news. Not very pleasant news, I'm afraid."

"Yes?"

"Ramon Kelly has been killed."

Smith's stomach muscles knotted, then relaxed. "In Washington?"

"Yes."

"Thanks for the information."

"And thanks for the chat. We'll be in touch."

Mac rejoined Annabel.

"I take it your backup has surfaced."

"Yeah."

"What's the matter, Mac? You're pale."

"Ramon Kelly has been killed. Looks like they're more efficient at killing in Washington than they were in Mexico City."

"He's the—"

"Yeah, the one I met with at Ferguson's apartment in the Watergate. Ferguson suggested to Kelly that he take a long vacation, become low-profile. He should have listened. Come on, Annie, let's get out of here. I'm not in a partying mood."

Chapter 34

Two Days Later

Mexico City

MEXICO HOLDS FREE, DEMOCRATIC AND FAIR ELECTIONS

CAPITAL GOES TO CARDENAS

MEXICO'S GOVERNING PARTY LOSES CONTROL OF
CONGRESS ENDING 7-DECADE MONOPOLY

PAN ESTABLISHES ITSELF AS RULING PARTY OF THE
NORTH

MEXICO CITY PRI PRESIDENT
ANNOUNCES HE WILL STEP DOWN

The day after Mexico had gone to the polls, Mac and Annabel
watched TV election coverage and read newspaper accounts in
their suite at the Majestic.

But all the headlines weren't uplifting.

MEXICAN GUNMEN SLAY 45

IN SOUTHERN INDIAN VILLAGE

KILLERS BELIEVED LINKED TO RULING PARTY

ZAPATISTA SUPPORTERS

PLAN DEMONSTRATION IN MEXICO CITY

TENS OF THOUSANDS EXPECTED

"Still, a day to celebrate," Annabel said, packing while watching TV.

"Agreed," said Mac. "Overall, everything went smoothly. There are reports of attacks on a few polling places in Chiapas, but here in the city there wasn't a hint of trouble."

"You're finished up with your official poll-watching duties?"

"Yup. Except I have to contribute to the official report when we get back. My input will be positive, aside from the obvious domination of the media by the PRI."

"You'd better pack," she said. "The limo will be here before we know it."

The phone rang. Annabel answered. It was a call from San Miguel.

"I spoke with Gabriela," Elfie Dorrance said. "The hotel's limo is on its way. You should be back here in San Miguel by four."

"Provided we're not kidnapped en route," Annabel said.

"If you are, I'll pay the ransom. The party—*your* party—is shaping up nicely for tomorrow night. Can't wait to see you. How is your handsome man holding up?"

Annabel glanced to where Mac had started placing things in his suitcase. "Holding up very well, I would say."

"Good. I want him in fine fettle tomorrow night. Lots of inside stories about the election."

"I'll pass that along. Call you when we get in."

They had a late breakfast on the terrace overlooking the Zócalo. Below, the city was still in the midst of a massive public celebration of the election and the changes it promised for the country. The boisterous pro-Zapatista crowd had begun to gather in the square.

"Finally, the PRI has lost its grip," Annabel said after their huevos rancheros—fried eggs on steamed corn tortillas covered with a tomato sauce—had been served. "It must be a breath of fresh air for the people."

"The elections have loosened their grip—a little," Mac said. "But Mexico has a long way to go and the PRI still has a vise on most heads." Mac fell silent, his expression somber.

"Ramon Kelly?" Annabel said.

"Yes. It taints everything for me."

"Is there someone you can call to find out more?"

"I suppose, although I'm not sure I'd get much information at this juncture. You said Chris Hedras is in San Miguel. I assume he'll know something."

"Why him?"

"He seems to be in the thick of everything. He's the one who set up my meeting in San Miguel with this guerrilla leader, and he's obviously been working closely with The Mexico Initiative."

"Where Ramon Kelly worked."

"Right. Kelly was the head of it, and the young woman who fell to her death from the east building was its research director. Add to that the fact that the murdered Mexican union leader—Garza was his name—had come to Washington to tell Kelly and his group what he had on PRI corruption. If there is such a thing as coincidence, it doesn't apply here."

"How involved is Joe Aprile with Kelly's group?"

"I don't know specifically, but it was obvious to me when we met at the White House that he was certainly in the loop. You know, it's easy to chalk up the killings to PRI officials trying to hang on to power by getting rid of anyone with evidence that could strip it from them. Too easy. These same people could become even more desperate now that the electorate has spoken."

"Have you heard from Pacie again since the reception?"

"No."

"Maybe you should call him."

"To tell him what?"

"To tell him we're going to San Miguel de Allende on our first and only honeymoon, and that a meeting with some rebel leader isn't on our agenda."

"I've considered that."

"You have?"

"Sure."

"And?"

"I'll play it by ear, take it a step at a time. If things don't look right to me, I'll say exactly that."

Annabel scrutinized her husband, the morning sun splashing across his craggy face. This was a man, she knew, who would not take unreasonable chances with his life or with hers. She'd never known anyone with a mind like Mackensie Smith's, open to all ideas but questioning them with precision, like a surgeon removing cancerous cells; wise yet not allowing wisdom to dominate every decision at the expense of intuition and insight; proud and humble at once, suffering fools but only to the extent it didn't take away their dignity; angry at injustice, accepting of the human condition.

"Mac."

"What?"

"Do you know I love you very much?"

"Hadn't a clue."

He spotted their waiter: *"La cuenta, por favor."* He signed their name and room number to the check and they returned to the suite. They were about to call for help with their luggage when the phone rang.

"Mac Smith."

"Mac, Chris Hedras."

"Hello, Chris. We were just talking about you."

"Favorably, I hope."

"No reason to be unfavorable. Is there?"

"Depends on the day. Mac, I know you've made contact with Ron Pacie."

"Yes."

"You're coming to San Miguel today."

"Leaving any minute. We'll be seeing you at Elfie's party tomorrow night."

"I'd like to see you before then."

"That shouldn't be a problem, although Annabel and I are looking forward to some unencumbered time together. Nonofficial time."

"And I wouldn't think of taking up too much of that nonofficial time. Would you call me when you arrive?"

"Sure. Where are you staying?"

"At Elfie's. Second-best hotel in San Miguel. You're staying at the best."

"I don't think she'd appreciate being number two, Chris."

"And she'll never know it from me. I'll be waiting for your call."

Other members of the U.S. delegation to the election observer team staying in the Majestic were in the lobby when Mac and Annabel came downstairs. The feeling was one of victory. Hands were shaken, backs slapped, and expressions of "having done it" exchanged.

"It's a great day," one of the observers said to Mac. "I'm proud to have been a part of it."

"I share that feeling," Mac said.

"Going to the airport?"

"No," Annabel said. "We're staying in Mexico for a few days. San Miguel de Allende."

"Where's that?"

"Colonial Mexico. In the hills, the middle of the country."

"Keeping the celebration going?" someone said, laughing.

"Something like that."

Another round of good-byes preceded their climbing into the limousine and heading for San Miguel de Allende, more than 450 years old, a national monument, home of the acclaimed Instituto Allende art school and, depending upon the time of year, home to that other monument to money, cosmetics, and physical fitness, Elfie Dorrance.

— — —

"Well, what did Chris want?" Annabel asked her husband as they strolled hand-in-hand through Parque Benito Juárez. The sun was setting over the Santa Rosa Mountains, the park's tall, graceful trees rendered as silhouettes against a golden sky.

"To tell me he'll be my contact here in San Miguel."

"Your backup?"

"In a sense. I'm to let him know the plans for meeting Mr. Unzaga."

"Good. At least Chris is someone you know. Better than strangers popping up all the time. You saw Elfie when you went over to meet Chris?"

"Yes. She was disappointed you didn't come with me."

"I wanted to save seeing her house for tomorrow night's party. I assume it's baronial."

"Not really. Lovely, though. You'd think she was planning an inaugural ball. People all over the place getting ready for the party."

"*Our* party."

"I'm sure she's told everyone coming it's *their* party. An old hostess's trick. I only spoke with her a few minutes. Chris and I took a walk on the grounds. Not sure where her property leaves off and the park begins."

"Happy?"

"Very. The suite is magnificent, and I'm anxious to see the town tomorrow."

"You'll love it. The art institute is interesting, and the library—I think it's the largest or second-largest bilingual library in Latin America; the ex-pats congregate there—is a joy. We'll have breakfast at a wonderful little outdoor cafe called La Buena Vida, in a little alley across from the American consulate. Superb fresh-baked cinnamon rolls and yummy café con leche. Then we'll go to the Jardín and wait for your next set of instructions from persons unknown."

"You should hire out as a tour guide, Annie."

"The only person I want to guide is you."

"We're having dinner at the hotel?"

"Yes."

"The onion soup is as good as you say?"

"Even better. Come on, let's get back and have a drink to celebrate our honeymoon. They have more than seventy brands of tequila and . . ."

— — —

As Mac and Annabel enjoyed the outdoor bar connected to the Sierra Nevada's parkside suites, a battered, tan two-door Chevy sedan navigated the final steep and winding road into San Miguel and pulled up on to the sidewalk in front of a cantina across from the art institute. Two men sat in the back. The driver got out, yawned, stretched against stiffness developed during the ride, and casually took in his surroundings. He was about to open the rear door for his passengers when he saw two armed *federales* crossing the street fifty yards from him. He paused until the officers had passed from his view, took another look around, then opened the door and nodded.

The first man out of the car was big and bulky. He adjusted his shoulders inside his suit jacket and rearranged the handgun tucked into his waistband. He, too, surveyed the street. Satisfied, he motioned for the remaining man to exit.

Carlos Unzaga slid across the seat and stepped out into San Miguel's cool twilight. A heavy black mustache covered his upper lip and drooped down the sides of his mouth. His black hair was thick and unruly, causing his head to appear to be too large for his short, slender frame. He wore a beige unconstructed sport jacket, blue slacks, and a lightweight white V-neck sweater.

The driver stayed by the car as the other two men crossed the street and entered the institute's spacious, airy courtyard. They walked quickly, the larger man's ponderous steps in marked contrast to Unzaga's lithe movements. After covering two sides of the courtyard, they went through an open arch and down a set of concrete steps to a vacant artist's studio. Unzaga closed the door behind them and flipped a wall switch. The big man positioned a chair by the door and sat heavily in it while Unzaga went slowly from one unframed painting to another tacked up on the walls, moving his head from side to side for a better viewing angle.

A few minutes later, the door opened and two people entered the room, a man of advanced age and a young woman. Unzaga came to them and they embraced, pressing cheeks against each other's.

Unzaga and the two new arrivals huddled in a corner and spoke in hushed tones for twenty minutes while the big man maintained his watchful position at the door. Then, after another series of physical farewells, Unzaga and his bodyguard retraced their steps to the car and got in. The driver started the engine, turned, and asked, "Where?"

"Guanajuato," Unzaga said.

Forty minutes later they entered the capital of the state of Guanajuato, made rich from its silver deposits, and home to one of Mexico's leading universities of music and theater. The car struggled as it climbed and descended a labyrinth of twisting cobblestone *callejónes,* alleys, that defined the colonial city, until reaching the Irapuato Highway, which took them to their destination, the southwest suburb of San Gabriel de la Barrera. There they came to a stop behind a nondescript white house.

Inside, two women had just finished setting a table for dinner. Unzaga greeted them, went to a small bedroom, and removed the mustache and wig, revealing a youthful, smooth, sensuous face graced with large, soft, dark eyes. Aside from the remnants of a scar running from the side of his right eye to his ear, it was a face to inspire poets and challenge artists.

Unzaga was joined at dinner by four other people. The mood was jovial. The women served steaming bowls of tortilla, Aztec soup, and platters of *tortillas por manos,* handmade *almuerzo* and *lonche* tortillas. Toasts were offered to the PRI's loosened grip on Mexico. Although Unzaga joined them, he did it without any overt display of celebration.

"Hey, Carlos, why so glum?" Unzaga was asked. "A new day dawns for us, huh?"

"Just the beginning," the rebel leader said. "The PRI still controls the country. Those *campesinos* slaughtered in Chiapas didn't benefit from the election. Not much has changed here. Perhaps one day, when other nations refuse to do business with the leadership and their businessmen stooges, there will be true reform. What has changed here in Guanajuato? The PRI still controls this state. The fat fool, Mendez, wins again. No, nothing has changed and it will never change as long as those across our borders refuse to deal fairly with us. Until then—"

"Until then we must be grateful for what we are given, Carlos," offered the oldest person at the table, a gaunt man in need of a shave and wearing a black patch over his left eye. "The people have spoken. The PRI is not as strong as it was a day ago."

Carlos sat back and fixed the older man with a hard stare. "The PRI will do what all weakened animals do. They will become more vicious, more willing to spread the blood of our people. I have bad news to tell you."

Silence fell over the table.

"Ramon Kelly has been assassinated."

"*El zanahoria?*" someone said, using Kelly's nickname, "the Carrot."

"*Sí.* In Washington."

Curses intermingled with invocations of God were muttered.

"This is not the time to step back," Unzaga said. "It is the time to intensify our efforts to influence those stripping our country through NAFTA to think again, to reconsider their stance."

Later, Unzaga sat on a bench beneath a gnarled tree with the older man. It was past midnight. The cups of strong, sweet *café olla* they'd carried with them from the house had grown cold.

"I meant no offense, Carlos," the man said. "I suppose I have been here long enough to be lulled into a sense of gratitude for the smallest of things."

"I understand. And I did not mean to be disparaging of your wisdom. But I am right in this."

"Yes, you are, my son, and I stand with you."

"Tomorrow's meeting with the gringo is set?"

"*Sí.* All precautions have been taken."

"You will deliver the envelope as planned."

"Of course. It is better to have me do it than to have you carry it with you to the meeting."

"I agree. This *americano,* Smith. He is a close friend of their vice president, Aprile."

"That is true."

"The information I will give him must be passed on to the vice president."

"There is no question that it will be, Carlos. Whether he will act upon it remains to be seen. But we are told Senor Aprile is a man of honor and compassion. If that is true, he will have no choice when he becomes president but to take a hard stand against the leadership here as it exists."

The men finished their coffee. An almost full moon had been obscured most of the night by low clouds. As Unzaga looked up into the sky, it broke free for a moment, illuminating the untended orange grove in which they sat. Darkness reappeared as suddenly as it had been broken. Unzaga placed his hand on the older man's arm and said, *"Ya se mira el horizonte."*

"*Sí,* Carlos, you have always been able to see the horizon, the day when we will be free of a brutal and corrupt regime. May God grant me enough years to be here when that day arrives."

CHAPTER 35

The Next Morning
San Miguel de Allende

It had rained for an hour in the early morning, enough to flood the cobblestone streets and send water cascading down them. Now, at eight-thirty, the deluge was a memory and the sun shone as if new.

The Jardín was busy as Mac and Annabel took a table on the terrace of the restaurant overlooking the town square. They'd eaten breakfast at La Buena Vida; the cinnamon rolls lived up to Annabel's advance billing as had the soup the night before at Casa de Sierra Nevada. Mac was struck with the number of non-Mexicans on the streets and in the square. San Miguel's large expatriate population was vibrant and visible, mostly older men and women looking to stretch their retirement dollars while enjoying the pleasing climate and colonial ambiance.

A truck arrived at the Jardín. Men who'd been waiting for it eagerly unloaded bundles of newspapers, lining them up on a low wall and taking money from the crowd that had gathered.

"Think I'll see what today's papers say about the election," Mac said, standing.

"Go ahead. I'm not moving."

The terrace was now filled with customers, mostly non-Mexicans, who'd settled in with their papers and coffee. It occurred to Annabel that if Mac's next instructions came from a Mexican, as she assumed they would, that person would stand out among the expatriate Americans and Canadians gathered that morning.

She looked across the street and saw Mac, newspapers under his arm, watching one of a half-dozen men carrying palettes of balloons, pinwheels, and mechanized stuffed animals for sale.

Not another message in a balloon, she thought.

Mac started back to the restaurant. As he waited for a break in the chaotic traffic, Annabel noticed a tall, heavy man with a white walrus mustache come up behind and follow him across the street. Mac reached the table; the man was only a few steps behind.

"Mac," Annabel said, indicating with a nod there was someone with him.

Mac turned. "Senor Palomino."

"*Buenos días.*"

Mac said to Annabel, "Mr. Palomino was one of the people I enjoyed a beer with before you arrived at the Majestic."

"Oh." She extended her hand.

"I thought it was you in the square," Palomino said in a loud voice, "but wasn't sure. A nice coincidence seeing you here in San Miguel."

"Won't you join us?" Annabel said.

"Gracias."

"Mr. Palomino is a professor and author in Mexico City, Annabel. Political science."

"You must have found the election fascinating," she said.

"Extremely." He took a Cuban cigar from his jacket pocket and lighted it with skill, careful to keep the flame from actually touching the tip. "I pity American cigar smokers," he said. "Your Cuban embargo deprives them of such pleasure. Here in Mexico, we do not have such a problem. We travel freely to Cuba. Do you have friends here in San Miguel, Senor and Senora Smith?"

"As a matter of fact, we do," Mac said. "From Washington."

"Elfie Dorrance?"

Mac and Annabel laughed. "I take it you know her," Annabel said.

"We've met. Will you be at her party tonight?"

"Yes. Will you?"

"No. But her parties are always the talk of San Miguel. It seems half the town is involved in one way or another."

Palomino drew contentedly on his cigar and observed the passing scene on the street and in the Jardín. It was during that contemplative moment that Mac and Annabel glanced at each other, realizing simultaneously it was Palomino who would deliver Mac's instructions on where and when to meet Carlos Unzaga.

"Would you excuse me," Annabel said. To Mac: "I'd better use the cash machine in the bank before we forget."

"Good idea," Mac said.

When she was gone, Palomino said in a quiet, matter-of-fact voice, "A lovely woman. And extremely instinctive."

"All that and more," Mac said.

"I assume you really don't need cash at this moment."

"Correct. And I assume you have something to tell me."

"That's right. Surprised at the messenger?"

"Nothing surprises me in Mexico, Senor Palomino, although I must admit I expected someone of the ilk who follows guerrilla leaders."

Palomino chuckled, drew on his cigar. "An unkempt peasant farmer with a machete."

"Something like that."

"Carlos Unzaga has many followers, Mr. Smith, who do not fit that mold. His major base of support is in Mexico City. It is his source of money. You'd be surprised at how many financially comfortable Mexicans care more about the plight of the impoverished masses than the wealthy elite."

"I take it you're in that category."

"Decidedly so. I'm sure your wife will be returning soon, and I have somewhere else I must be. There is a festival tonight in San Miguel. It is relatively new here, borrowed from the strolling *estudiantes* of Guanajuato. Familiar with it?"

"No."

"Students in Guanajuato have been strolling through the streets and singing for, maybe, forty years. A lovely event. The students wear sixteenth-century costumes, carry candles, and lead everyone through the streets while making music. The tourists like to wear costumes, too, and join in. It starts at El Chorro, at eleven."

"I have a party to go to."

"It wouldn't be a problem, would it, to leave a little before eleven? Make your excuses, say your farewells, and depart. No one would question why a man would want to be alone with such a beautiful woman as your wife."

"I'll be wearing a tuxedo. Ms. Dorrance's party is black tie."

"Perfect. You'll be in costume. It's a very popular event with

272

our American and Canadian friends living here. They turn out in elaborate costumes, including tuxedos. Very festive."

"Where is El Chorro?"

"Convenient for you. Have you seen the public tubs where local women wash their clothes?"

"It's right outside where we're staying, near the park."

"Exactly."

"And how will I know Mr. Unzaga?"

"Simple. Look for me. We'll join the procession together, enjoy the music, walk until reaching a small cantina on Aldama. It will be open to serve those enjoying the festivities. Very small, owned by someone who believes as we do."

"What's it called?"

"No matter. You and our mutual acquaintance will go inside, where there is a private room in which you can talk."

"I was to meet him at a public place."

"What could be more public? A parade, music, singing, a cantina. I trust you realize that there are people in our government who would like very much to see Carlos Unzaga dead."

"I've heard."

"He is risking much in meeting with you. It took months of planning and discussion before it was agreed to seek out someone in whom we could trust, someone not officially involved with your government, and someone who has influence with your Vice President Aprile."

"My wife is aware of what I'm doing," Mac said. "She wondered why Unzaga didn't simply package up his information and send it to the vice president, or someone he designated."

"A good question, but one with a simple answer. Carlos is a brilliant young man, and as suspicious as he is bright. To simply send written material to a place like Washington, DC, is not the way he operates. He wants to sit down and look into the eyes of the man in whom he places his trust. By the way, by all means bring Mrs. Smith. It would look strange if you didn't. I will take very good care of her while you and Carlos confer. Then, we can meet back at the bar in your hotel to celebrate."

Mac couldn't help but smile. "You make it sound so simple," he said.

"But it is. All you will be doing is spending a half hour with a man who one day will stand at the helm of a free and democratic Mexico. Listen closely to him, remember what he says."

"Did you know a young man named Ramon Kelly?" Mac asked.

"Oh, yes. It was through him that arrangements were made for this to happen. He and Carlos were close. Tragic what happened to him."

"You've heard, then."

"Yes. And about Ms. Flores."

"Do you know who was behind their murders?"

"We're narrowing in on that. Ah, your wife returns." Palomino got to his feet and smiled broadly as Annabel rejoined them.

"Get the loot?" Mac asked.

"Yes. We can eat."

"Senor Palomino is about to leave."

"It was a pleasure meeting you," Annabel said, shaking his hand.

"No, the pleasure was mine. Until we meet again."

They watched him go to the street, purchase an ice cream from a sidewalk vendor, turn, wave, and disappear around a corner.

"Well?" Annabel asked.

"How's your singing voice?"

"Why?"

"We're going to two parties tonight, and one is the Mexican version of Christmas caroling."

"Are we? Will your rebellious new friend be joining us?"

"Of course. He's the guest of honor. I need to fill Chris Hedras in on what the plans are. But now, let's walk, and talk. I'd like to see more of this city you're always raving about."

CHAPTER 36

That Evening

" . . . and this is Mr. and Mrs. Smith. Mac and Annabel, meet Salas, one of San Miguel's leading artists."

"A pleasure."

"Salas and I have entered into a business arrangement. I've bought virtually all his work, at a handsome discount, of course."

The rotund artist grinned. "Mrs. Dorrance strikes—what is it you say?—a hard bargain."

"And now you have enough money to live on for the next two years," Elfie said. "Come," she said to Mac and Annabel, "there are others you must meet."

As they walked away from the artist, Elfie said, "I have a dealer back in Washington salivating over Salas's paintings. I love quick profits. Ah, Viviana, my dear. Please say hello to Mac and Annabel Smith."

Viviana Diaz, Mexico's foremost femme fatale, was stunning in a low-cut cranberry sheath that hugged her voluptuous body. She broke into a smile that was all dazzling white teeth and bloodred lipstick as she acknowledged Mac and Annabel.

Annabel hadn't told Mac of her conversation with Carole Aprile about her friend's fear that the vice president might be having an affair with the former screen siren. She looked into Diaz's dark oval eyes and knew that if this supreme specimen of the female species were to make it known to a man—any man—that she wanted him, it would take the most noble of men to resist.

"Your vice president has spoken often of you, Senor Smith," she said, holding Mac's hand a little too long for Annabel's taste.

"I didn't realize you knew him," Mac said.

Annabel didn't like Diaz's expression in response to Mac's comment. It was too . . . smug.

"Have you met Mrs. Aprile?" Annabel asked.

"No, I have not had that pleasure. I'm sure she's a very nice person."

"And beautiful," Annabel said. "*Very* beautiful."

Mac looked at his wife. What was behind this edgy exchange? he wondered.

They were joined by the tycoon, Manuel Zegreda. After introductions and some small talk, Zegreda said to Mac, "I have looked forward to meeting you for some time, Mr. Smith. Perhaps later we might find an opportunity for quiet talk."

Elfie waltzed other guests over to meet the Smiths. "Some men simply were born to wear a tuxedo," she said, referring to Mac.

"Men should wear tuxedos every evening," Viviana said. "It's so elegant. And they don't all look alike, as they are not."

"And I agree," said Elfie. "Annabel, you look absolutely stunning." Annabel had purchased a black stretch wool dress with patent-leather trim especially for the trip. Standing next to Mac in his tux, they could have come from the pages of *Fashions of the Times*.

"The ambassador, poor dear, had to cancel at the last minute," Elfie said. "His wife is ill. I suggested she needed a glorious party to make her feel better, but my medical advice wasn't heeded. No matter. The governor and his wife might stop by later for a drink. The man is unbeatable, no matter what his party's fate. Come, all of you. The music is starting on the terrace."

As they accompanied her through French doors, Mac asked, "Where's Chris Hedras?"

"On the phone. He's had that damn thing glued to his ear all afternoon. Something to do with Joe's campaign, I suppose. I told him business was off-limits at my parties, but he tends to have selective hearing."

The mariachi band hired for the evening played better than others Mac had heard during his visits to Mexico. Later, that band would alternate with an American piano trio playing show tunes for dancing. The broad terrace soon filled with guests; Mac judged there to be at least thirty people.

"What do you think of Senorita Diaz?" Annabel whispered.

"She could sink ships."

"And marriages."

He looked at her quizzically. "What was that all about back there, Annie?"

"Just exercising my claws."

"Why would you want to do that?"

"A long story. Later."

The table in the dining room comfortably accommodated everyone. Two places were left vacant for the possible arrival of Guanajuato's governor, Junipero Mendez, and his wife, Corita. It was a carefully crafted guest list on which Elfie had spent considerable time. Her companion for the evening, Martin Leff, told an amusing story when they were seated, made more so by his stilted speech and practiced stentorian tones.

"I understand you've been working, Chris," Mac said to Hedras across the table as soon as soup was served.

"Yeah. There's always one crisis or another, most of them hardly qualifying as crises."

"I've been meaning to ask whether you know anything about Ramon Kelly's death in Washington."

"Just that he was killed in a street robbery. Shame what the city's coming to." He turned from Mac to speak with Viviana Diaz, seated to his left.

Much of the conversation during dinner centered on the election. Manuel Zegreda was vocal in his condemnation of the PRD's Cardenas, Mexico City's new mayor, openly labeling him a communist who would turn Mexico into a welfare state and eventually bankrupt it if he went on to become president in the next election. Mendez and Antonio Morelos readily agreed.

The discussion heated up when Salas, and two other artists, jumped in with an opposing view of the election's outcome and what it meant for Mexico's future. They were dismissed by Zegreda and other PRI supporters as bleeding-heart liberals.

Mac frequently checked his watch. Nine-fifteen.

"It'll be awkward leaving, won't it?" Annabel asked quietly.

"I've already mentioned it to Elfie. I said you insisted I take part in the sing-along. She said she understood. We struck a deal. We get to leave before eleven provided we come back for breakfast in the morning."

"No sleeping in, huh?"

"Breakfast is at noon."

"Oh, good."

They left the table at quarter of ten and went to another room, where after-dinner drinks were served, and the political debate continued.

"Ready?" Mac asked Annabel in a whisper.

"Yes, I—"

"Senor Smith," said Manuel Zegreda. "Do you find our political differences interesting?"

"Very much like our dinner-table political discussions at home."

Zegreda smiled. "I would like to show you something."

"If it won't take long. My wife and I are getting ready to leave. A previous engagement."

"Only a few minutes."

"Annie, I'll be right back."

Her eyes questioned, but she simply said, "All right. Don't be long."

Zegreda led Smith to a hallway and up a wide staircase. They followed another long corridor lined with rich Mexican art until reaching French doors leading to a broad terrace on the park side of the house. Waiting for them outside was Viviana Diaz, a vividly colored hand-painted shawl covering her naked shoulders.

"If I'd known I was coming to a party, I would have brought my wife," Mac said.

Zegreda joined Viviana at the railing. "Mr. Smith," he said flatly, "I will not take much of your time. But I felt it was important that we speak."

"I'm listening," Mac said, well aware that Zegreda was the Mexican business leader most prominently named whenever allegations surfaced about illegal Mexican contributions into the Scott-Aprile campaigns.

"You are one of Vice President Aprile's closest friends."

"We are friends, yes."

"And you are trusted by him to the extent he names you his special envoy."

Mac wondered how Zegreda knew that.

"In other words, Senor Smith, if one wanted to be certain a message was delivered to your friend, the vice president, it would be wise to send it through you."

Mac conspicuously looked at his watch.

"Show him the pictures, dear," Zegreda said.

Mac hadn't noticed that Viviana held a large manila envelope against her chest, beneath the shawl. She extended it to Mac, who stepped forward to take it.

"Go ahead, look," Zegreda said.

Mac went to where an outdoor fixture cast a pool of light on the terrace, opened the flap, and removed a dozen eight-by-ten photographs. When he was finished, he replaced them in the envelope and handed them to Zegreda.

"Nice shots of Vice President Aprile, Senor Zegreda. But there was no need to show them to me. I'm well aware of what he looks like."

"You did take notice, I trust, that Senorita Diaz is in each of the pictures."

"Of course I did." Another check of his watch. "I really must be going. My wife's waiting for me. What's the point you wish to make?"

"It would be awkward, to say the least, if the American voting public were to be informed that their vice president, considered to be—his code name is Straight Arrow, I believe—if they were informed that he finds Mexican women attractive, especially *this* Mexican woman."

"That would be a lie."

"And that he has close ties with some of our less upstanding citizens, those who owe some of their wealth and position to the drugs your people so eagerly buy and use. I assure you we have many photographs to prove that, too."

"Prove it?" Mac's guffaw was involuntary. "These pictures don't prove anything."

281

"But I will say they do, Senor Smith," Viviana said. "I have no hesitation sharing with your voters my intimate moments with the next president. Perhaps your wife, who is such a good friend of Mrs. Aprile, would like to break the news to her of our affair."

"You're talking blackmail," Mac said. "What is it you want in return?"

"That brings us to the message I wish you to carry back to Washington. Your friend, the vice president, is a foolish man, Mr. Smith. The president has the support of the Mexican people. Vice President Aprile can have that support, too."

"The support of the Mexican people? You mean people like you."

"As you wish. He has been pursuing a dangerous course of action through this so-called Mexico Initiative, attempting to build a case upon which to challenge his own president over Mexico. It would be most unfortunate if he were to become the president and carry into office his misguided views. All we ask is that he see the light and recognize that our two countries have forged an important working relationship that must not be destroyed."

"Including having drug lords paying off your leaders in return for carte blanche to run narcotics through your country into ours."

"To serve your drug users' insatiable needs, Mr. Smith. No market, no drugs. I don't know you, but you strike me as a sensible, pragmatic man. Surely you wish to see your friend become president of the United States. We would like to see that, too, provided he realizes the need to allow us to move slowly toward reform and true democracy. That will take many years. In the meantime—"

"In the meantime, I'm leaving. You picked the wrong messenger, Senor Zegreda. Some good and decent people have been killed because of the likes of you. It was a pleasure meeting you, Ms. Diaz. You're very beautiful. You're also despicable. Good night."

Mac returned to the first-floor terrace, where guests danced. Annabel stood alone, brow furrowed, lips tight.

"What was *that* all about?" she asked when Mac took her arm and headed for the door.

"It's about why meeting Carlos Unzaga and carrying back what he knows has taken on an urgency, Annie. I'll fill you in on the way."

They said good night to Elfie, Chris Hedras, and selected others, assured Elfie they'd be back for breakfast, and went to the street.

"Mac, what happened with Zegreda?"

"Blackmail is what happened." He recounted the meeting with Zegreda and Viviana as they walked quickly through the park in the direction of their hotel.

"How dreadful," Annabel said when he'd finished.

"Yeah, isn't it?"

A hundred people had gathered by the public washtubs. Students, and a smattering of American and Canadian ex-pats and tourists, were in costume. Candles carried by the students flickered in a light breeze. Mac looked for Palomino.

"Over there," Annabel said.

They went to where Palomino stood by a fountain. He was with another man with thick brown hair and a full beard, small in stature and wearing a three-piece suit. Mac and Annabel stopped a few feet from them, waiting for Palomino to make some gesture that everything was all right. His smile accomplished that. *"Buenas noches,"* he said. "This is Senor Potosi, *mi amigo."*

Unzaga nodded. Mac put out his hand. Unzaga took it, sending a chill up Mac's spine. Here he was, shaking hands with a wanted man, someone dedicated to bringing down his nation's government. How many men had he killed? To what ends would he go to satisfy his political agenda?

Mac Smith believed in order. Americans who broke the law to vent their political discontent received little sympathy from him. He fervently embraced the concept that law, based upon moral precepts—a nation of laws—was among the most precious of ideals.

But this was Mexico, a country of proud and decent people and a vibrant history, people who'd suffered for decades under leadership that lined the pockets of a few, while the majority lived lives of resigned and silent desperation.

The students began singing, and moving away from El Chorro, up Tenerias.

"Over there," Palomino said, indicating where the crowd was thickest. They joined the throng and slowly proceeded up a steep hill.

Annabel stumbled; Mac grabbed her.

"I should have brought sneakers," she said. "These cobblestones are hell on heels."

They turned right on Aldama and continued the procession, the students' voices sweet in the cool night air, their candles reflecting light off their youthful faces. People stood on the sidewalks to witness the musical march, waving hands and adding their voices to the plaintive Spanish songs. A lovely tradition, Mac thought, if it wasn't the setting this night for something far more serious.

They'd almost reached the corner of Cuadrante when Palomino subtly maneuvered them away from the crowd and to an open storefront from which the pungent aroma of cooking food reached them. Inside, men sat on a half-dozen stools at a counter. A heavy woman cooked and served platters of what came off her grill, and bottles of Mexican beer. Four small tables were also occupied. Unzaga's men, Mac surmised.

Palomino nodded at Unzaga, who stepped inside. Mac hesitated as he looked at Annabel.

"See you at the hotel bar," Palomino said, taking Annabel's elbow and herding her back toward the procession.

Mac followed Unzaga past the tables and to an older Mexican man standing by a door covered with a sheet. The man avoided their eyes as he stepped aside, allowing Unzaga to push the sheet aside. Mac followed.

They were inside a small room with a table covered in ripped yellow vinyl and two wooden chairs. A bottle of *mezcal,* with its traditional *gusano de maguey*—a small worm from the maguey plant at the bottom—stood open on the table, accompanied by two water glasses. A large, three-dimensional carving of the Virgin Mary hung precariously on one wall, her eyes trained on the table. White light from a fluorescent fixture dangling from the ceiling was harsh and unnerving.

Unzaga sat in one of the chairs: "Please, Senor Smith, join me."

In the light, Mac could see now that Unzaga wore a wig and that the small beard was false.

"You are a good man to be here under these circumstances," Unzaga said in clear English, pouring mezcal into both glasses.

"I'm here because I was asked to be by a friend."

"Vice President Aprile."

"That's right."

"Another good man."

"I think so."

He handed Smith a glass, raised his own. "To you, Mackensie Smith."

"There are more important things to toast, including the election results, but I won't argue."

The drink went down hot in Mac's throat.

Unzaga refilled his own glass, slung an arm over the back of his chair, and crossed his legs, an oddly casual pose considering the venue and circumstance.

"I don't wish to be rude, but I think it best if you tell me what it is you want me to bring back to Vice President Aprile."

"Of course. It is I who is rude. You have no reason to spend more time than necessary. This is not your fight, Senor Smith."

"No, it's not. But something happened this evening that convinces me more than ever that your fight is just. I know simply being here places you in jeopardy. What is it you wish to tell me?" He felt like a Catholic priest asking for a petitioner's confession.

"I have many things to say," Unzaga said in a low, measured voice, "beginning with murder."

"Whose murder?"

"My friend Ramon Kelly. Laura Flores. Morin Garza. Others."

Mac's heart beat faster. He hadn't expected this. "I'm listening," he said.

"There is an organization in your country called the Mexican-American Trade Alliance."

"I've heard of it. A lobbying group representing Mexican business interests."

"It is more than that, Senor Smith. It is a murderous arm of a faction within the PRI."

"Are you saying that this lobbying group was responsible for the deaths of Kelly, Laura Flores, and Morin Garza?"

"That is exactly what I am saying. Ramon and Laura had been investigating that group's ties with the PRI's old guard in Mexico City. It cost them their lives. Garza was part of the corruption but was weak, easily convinced to tell things about his union and the PRI that were damaging to them. He, too, was killed because of what he knew and was willing to say."

"Do you have proof of this?"

"Yes. I was to give it to you tonight, but thought better at the last minute of carrying it with me. It will be at your hotel when you return."

"I'm not sure that's any smarter than you carrying it around."

"I think it is, *amigo.*"

"As you wish. I have to admit I have trouble accepting that the PRI—any government, for that matter—would resort to murder to hold on to power."

Unzaga's smile was weary. "You have trouble accepting such an idea? Your own government has plotted assassinations, has it not? Castro? The Kennedy brothers."

"Castro, perhaps. The Kennedys? Not according to official investigations into those deaths. Besides, if some rogue element *had* engaged in such activities, it doesn't represent the government of the United States as a whole."

"Nor does the murder of Ramon and the others represent everyone within the PRI. Are there good people within our ruling party? Of course. But not enough to make a difference. Besides, it is dangerous for them to stand up and be counted. If there is to be significant change within our country, it will only come because those outside call for it to happen, and have the will and muscle to force it to happen."

Unzaga refilled his glass and topped off Mac's drink.

"What else?" Mac asked.

Unzaga spent the next fifteen minutes relating a litany of allegations against ranking members of the PRI—multimillion-dollar drug payoffs to elected officials and law enforcement leaders; union collaboration with the PRI in which workers who'd balked mysteriously disappeared; the arming of paramilitary forces in Chiapas loyal to the PRI whose mission it was to murder pro-Zapatista Indians; and a dozen other charges, one more shocking than the next.

When he was finished, Mac asked again, "Some of these I know of, some not. Is there proof of what you say?"

"In some cases, yes. It is included in what you will take back to Senor Aprile."

"Is there anything else?" Mac asked.

"No. I have told you what I know. Now, I can only pray that your vice president, your next president, will act upon it. There is no one here in Mexico for me to turn to, no one to right these wrongs. I place myself and the future of my people in your hands, Senor Smith."

"That's too heavy a burden to place on me, Senor Unzaga. I'm a messenger, that's all."

"And a brave one. Perhaps there is a final topic for me to raise."

"Which is?"

"Senor Hedras."

"Chris Hedras? What about him?"

"Do you trust him?"

Mac paused before saying, "Yes. Shouldn't I?"

"Chris has been very helpful with our cause, Senor Smith. It was he, on Aprile's behalf, who helped Ramon establish The Mexico Initiative. He has been a good friend to what we are trying to accomplish."

"Then why do you ask whether I trust him?"

"My questioning nature, that's all. He is close to Mrs. Dorrance. That is my understanding."

"Of course he's close to her. Chris is the vice president's campaign manager. Elfie—Mrs. Dorrance—is one of the vice president's chief supporters and fund-raisers."

"But she does not share Senor Aprile's views on Mexico, nor does Chris Hedras."

Mac thought back to the conversation he'd had with Hedras in his apartment in which Hedras had expressed dissatisfaction with Joe Aprile's stance on Mexico.

"What you say may be true, but I don't think it's reason to distrust him."

"I am sure you are right. It's just that . . ."

Mac waited.

"It's just that when I think of Ramon's death, and of Laura Flores and Morin Garza, I wonder who it was who knew what they knew and where they would be."

"Many people, I assume," Mac said.

"No. Few people, Mr. Smith. And always, Chris Hedras is around."

The sound of the student singers reached them as the procession retraced its steps down Aldama to return to El Chorro.

"A final drink?" Unzaga asked, pouring. "A drink of friendship."

They raised their glasses above the table and were about to touch rims when the chaos beyond the sheet erupted. Men shouted loudly in Spanish, followed by what sounded like tables being overturned and glasses smashing. Then, mingled with screams from the street was the unmistakable sound from the cantina of gunfire, and anguished cries.

Unzaga jumped up, pulled a handgun from his waistband, and flattened himself against the wall near the door. "Down, down," he yelled at Smith, who fell to the floor and scrambled to the rebel leader's side.

A loud male voice shouted from just the other side of the sheet: "Carlos Unzaga! Surrender! *Policía!*"

"My wife's out there," Mac said.

Unzaga tore off his wig and beard and looked at Mac with eyes glaring with anger.

"You have to give up," Mac said.

"To be slaughtered?"

"They won't kill you if you go out with your hands raised."

"They want nothing more than to kill me—and you."

"No," Mac said. "Staying here is suicide."

The commander repeated his command, louder this time.

"You don't have any choice," Mac said. "Put down your gun and follow me."

He moved past Unzaga, paused, then pushed the sheet aside and raised his hands high. Facing him was a uniformed leader of federal troops who filled the cantina and lined the street outside, automatic weapons in their hands. Bodies of young men were slumped over tables, the bar, and on the floor.

Mac walked up to the commander, stared him down, then slowly passed him. The commander shouted something in Spanish, causing his troops on the sidewalk to lower their weapons and to allow Mac to pass. He spotted Annabel in the crowd. Palomino stood partially in front of her as though acting as a shield.

As Mac stepped off the sidewalk in their direction, he was immediately surrounded by a half dozen of the costumed men who'd been part of the singing procession. But this time they weren't singing. They held weapons.

"This way, Mr. Smith," one of the men dressed in a clown costume said, leading him to Annabel and Palomino. "Come on. Let's get out of here."

They'd no sooner taken a step when gunfire again erupted inside the cantina. Mac turned to see Carlos Unzaga lurch from the back room through the bar area, his gun blazing, bullets from the troops' weapons tearing into him.

"God, no," Mac said.

"Quick," the man in a clown costume said. "Let's move."

They moved as a mass, at a run, Annabel carrying her shoes, stockings torn, down Aldama to El Chorro, and into the open-air bar and public area just outside the Sierra Nevada's four suites by the park.

"Your suite," the clown said.

Annabel opened the door and she and Mac went inside, followed by the others. It was then that Mac recognized one of the men in costume, Richard de LaHoya, who'd briefed him with Jim Ferguson at the State Department.

"This is an outrage," Mac said to LaHoya. "There was no need to gun him down like that. It was an assassination, nothing more."

"You're lucky it didn't include you," LaHoya said.

"Are you all right?" Annabel asked her husband.

"Physically, yes. This was murder—*another* murder."

"Get packed," LaHoya said.

"Why? We're not going anywhere."

"Yes, you are," the man in clown dress said. "And you're going there *now!*"

"How did they know we'd be there?" Mac growled.

"That's for later," LaHoya said. "Please, pack your bags and come with us. You'll be safe overnight. We have you on the first flight out in the morning from León to Mexico City, then to Washington."

"I can't leave. Something's being delivered to me here."

LaHoya looked at the clown. "I'll check the desk," he said. "Stay there until it arrives." To Smith: "It has to do with your meeting?"

"Yes, damn it!"

"Good job, Mr. Smith," LaHoya said, leaving.

The men stood outside the suite as Mac and Annabel packed.

"I thought you were dead," she said, jamming clothes into her suitcase and fighting back tears.

There was a knock on the door. Mac went to it.

"Whatever you were expecting already arrived," LaHoya said. "Delivered by an old man with a patch over one eye."

"Good. Give it to me."

"Someone else picked it up."

"Who?"

The night manager says it was a young gringo, maybe thirty-five, good-looking, wearing a tux."

"Chris Hedras," Mac said. "Where did he go?"

LaHoya shrugged.

"Probably back to Elfie's house," Annabel said.

"We've got to find that package," Mac said to LaHoya. "If we don't, this has all been for nothing."

LaHoya and the clown conferred. "Okay," LaHoya said. "Mrs. Dorrance's house?"

"Right," Mac said.

"Finish packing," said LaHoya.

"When we come back. Can some of your people look for the taxi with Hedras?"

"He could be anywhere."

"Start with the airport. Come on. There's no time to lose."

Elfie Dorrance's party was still going strong when they arrived. She greeted Mac at the front door, looked wide-eyed at the men surrounding him, then asked, "What in the world is going on? We heard gunfire from town. What happened to you, Mac? Your tux is dirty. The knees."

"Where's Chris?"

"That, too. He's gone."

"Gone where?"

"Mexico City. He came running in here and said he had to

leave for Washington immediately. I was shocked. It was so rude. My guests were appalled at his behavior."

"How is he getting to Mexico City?" Mac asked, noticing for the first time that Elfie's guests, drinks in hand, puzzled expressions on their faces, had gathered behind her.

"A taxi. He arrived by one, told the driver to wait a few minutes, ran to his room, came down a minute later with his suitcase and was gone."

"I need to use your phone," Mac said.

"Would you and your friends like drinks?" Elfie asked.

Mac ignored the question, went inside, and found a phone on a table in the foyer. He turned to Elfie, who'd followed him. "Get me a long-distance operator, Elfie. I need to put a call through to Washington."

It took a few minutes until the call was answered at the White House.

"The vice president's office," a young man said.

"This is Mackensie Smith. I'm a friend of the vice president and on his campaign staff. I'm calling from Mexico. It's an emergency. I must speak with the vice president immediately."

Chapter 37

Five Hours Later

Mexico City

Chris Hedras urged the driver to go faster as they approached the suburbs of Mexico City. It was still dark; the sun would not rise for another three hours.

He twisted his neck repeatedly against a dull ache that had set in soon after leaving San Miguel de Allende. It was accompanied by a blinding headache and sour stomach. He glanced down, reminding himself he was still dressed in formal wear.

They entered the city, blessedly free at that hour of its usual traffic clots. Hedras leaned over the seat back: "The train station."

After depositing the envelope he'd carried with him from San Miguel in a public locker with a combination lock—"Six-one-five, six-one-five," he repeated until confident he would remember it—he returned to the taxi and gave the driver further instructions.

"Go that way. Turn around, *idiota*! Up there. That road."

They progressed to a higher elevation, the air through the open window cooler now. Eventually, after a number of false turns while Hedras tried to find his destination, they came to a stop in front of a home surrounded by a pastel masonry wall. Hedras was asked by the driver if he wanted him to wait.

"No. Here." He handed him a wad of pesos and told him in Spanish to get lost.

He went to the wooden gate and pressed the buzzer numerous times until a voice asked through an intercom, "Who is it?"

"Chris Hedras."

The man muttered a curse. Chris repeatedly punched the buzzer again.

"Un momento."

Hedras waited until the heavy wooden gate was unlocked from inside and pulled open by a short, heavy man dressed in a gray sweatsuit. A holster containing a handgun was strung about his waist.

Chris pushed by him and fairly ran to the front door, which was open, and stepped inside. A light came on at the end of a long hallway. Oswaldo Flores, dressed in pajamas, silk robe, and leather slippers, stepped from a room, hands in the robe's pockets, cigarette dangling from his lips.

"I'm sorry to barge in at this hour," Hedras said, breathless. "But I had to come. It's urgent."

"It is fortunate my family is away," Flores said, closing the distance between them. "If you had woken them, you would not be welcome."

"Yeah, well, I'm glad they're not home, too." He glanced back at the man who'd opened the gate and who now stood a few feet away. "Where can we talk, Oswaldo?"

Flores silently led them into his home office and closed the door. He sat behind a large desk, handcrafted, and gestured to a green leather chair. A brass desk lamp cast the only light in the room.

"You look as though you've come from a party, Chris. Fun, I hope. Now, what brings you here unannounced at this ungodly hour?"

"They killed Carlos Unzaga."

Flores's face reflected no overt reaction to the news.

"He was meeting with the American, Mackensie Smith. He told Smith what he knew about things—about certain situations here."

"How do you know what they spoke of?"

"Because I was told what the meeting was about. I was the one who tipped the authorities they'd be meeting. Unzaga had a package of evidence prepared to give Smith, but I got to it first. Unzaga had an old aide deliver it. He trusts me, handed it over when I told him I'd see that Smith got it."

"Where is it?"

"Safe. But you can have it if I get what I want."

"Get what you want? And what would that be?"

"A lot more than I've been getting, Oswaldo. I need big money in case things go bad for me back in Washington. I don't know if Smith realizes it was me who ended up with the package, but that's always a possibility. I'm not worried about Joe Aprile. I'm his fair-haired boy. But I want a cushion."

"How much of a cushion, Chris? How much have you been paid so far? A million dollars? A little more?"

"Less than that."

"I see."

"I've earned every goddamn cent of it. Every penny. Now I've really put myself out on a limb. It was one thing to feed you information about the Initiative, and to help launder big money into the Scott-Aprile campaigns. Running off with evidence that could sink you and your whole game is another. I've taken a big risk for you, Oswaldo. I deserve a lot. Tonight."

Flores lighted another cigarette and offered Hedras one from a custom-made inlaid wooden box on the desk. Although Hedras hadn't smoked since he was a teenager, he readily accepted it, and the light from Flores. "You have any coke?" he asked.

Flores answered by going to a wall safe, dialing in its combination, and removing a clear plastic bag containing white powder. He then took a piece of heavy glass from his desk, along with a straw, and placed everything in front of his visitor.

Chris immediately opened the bag and poured a thin line of the cocaine on the glass. He placed the straw slightly above it and inhaled, first in one nostril, then the other. Flores watched dispassionately from behind his desk.

When Hedras was finished, he looked up and found himself staring into the business end of a loaded forty-five Flores had taken from another desk drawer.

"Hey, easy, Oswaldo. What's that for?"

"There is the matter of my daughter to discuss."

"Laura?" Hedras held up both hands, forced a laugh. "Man, I had nothing to do with that. Jose Chapas at the trade alliance set that up. Believe me. All I did was tip him to what she had come up with—which, I might add, was plenty on you and Televisa. But her dying . . . No, sir, that wasn't me. I've never killed anybody. Talk to those guys at the trade alliance."

Flores lowered the forty-five and gently placed it on the desk. "You say this evidence Unzaga delivered is safe. It would be even safer here. Where is it?"

"You give me the money, I tell you where it is."

"I'm sure I don't have in the house as much as you want."

"Bull!" Chris stood. "Look, I don't want any trouble. I never have. So I let the trade alliance and others know when certain things were going down. Garza. Ramon Kelly. Unzaga. All I did was pass along information. And I'm not here to make trouble for you." He laughed. "Hey, I'm here to keep you out of trouble. That evidence Unzaga delivered could sink a lot of people. Two million."

Flores smiled. "Two million dollars, just like that, Chris?"

"Yeah."

"I can give you half of that now, the other half in a few days."

Hedras was light-headed, his nerves on edge, thoughts flying through his mind and leaving just as fast.

"Yeah, okay. A half. What, two, three days for the rest?"

"That sounds reasonable."

"Oh, I also need your private jet to get me out of Mexico. Maybe they're looking for me at the airport. Get me to El Paso or San Antonio. I'll fly home from there."

Flores picked up the phone and dialed a number. "Oswaldo Flores," he said. "I need the plane in an hour. The passenger is named Mr. Hedras. Chris Hedras. You'll fly him to El Paso, or wherever he wishes to go."

He hung up. "Satisfied?"

"Yeah. That's good. I appreciate it. *Muchas gracias.*"

Flores returned the cocaine and apparatus for its use to the safe, returning to the desk holding two fat envelopes. He slid them to Hedras. "There should be a million in U.S. dollars there, give or take a little bit. But we won't quibble over a few dollars, will we, Chris? You've done very good work for us and it is sincerely appreciated."

Flores stood, smiled, and came around the desk, placing his hand on Chris's shoulder. "The plane will be waiting. Jasper will drive you to the airport in my car. Have a safe journey home."

Hedras stood and offered his hand. After Flores had shaken it, Hedras said, "Look, don't take this wrong, Oswaldo, but you aren't going to pull anything on me, are you? I mean, I know what Jasper's all about. He's a goon. What I'm saying is—"

"Chris, you are becoming very paranoid. It's the cocaine. It does that to people. I suggest you consider no longer using it. Jasper will take you to the airport, you will have the comfort of my private jet, and you will return home. Now, where is the envelope with the evidence?"

"The train station in the city. Locker number eleven. The combination is six-one-five. Six-one-five. Want me to write it down?"

"Not necessary. I don't wish you to take this wrong, either, Chris, but when I send someone to open that locker, the envelope will be there."

"Of course it will. You know you can trust me."

CHAPTER 38

That Afternoon

Mac and Annabel arrived back in Washington at three the next afternoon and went directly to their apartment, where they showered and changed into fresh clothes. The car that had brought them to the Watergate from the airport had moved to the parking area serving the hotel's lower entrance. It was joined by another vehicle, a plain four-door black sedan carrying Richard de LaHoya, who'd debriefed the Smiths during the flight from Mexico City, and two CIA agents assigned to that agency's Latin American division.

One of two Secret Service agents dispatched by the vice president's office to meet Mac and Annabel at the airport had accompanied them upstairs and waited in the living room. The other agent stayed with the limo driver.

"We're ready," Mac said, emerging from the bedroom.

They rode the elevator to the underground parking garage and set off at a quick pace to the hotel.

"Why was the limo moved to the hotel?" Mac asked.

"Procedure," the Secret Service agent said.

They entered the limo, and the two vehicles turned onto Virginia Avenue. Minutes later they pulled up at a seldom-used entrance to the old Executive Building at Seventeenth and Pennsylvania, in which the vice president's office was located. Former president Harry Truman had said of the mammoth, nineteenth-century, French-inspired building that consumes ten acres of floor space, "I don't want it torn down. I think it's the greatest monstrosity in America."

But its architectural shortcomings weren't on anyone's mind as they piled out of the cars and, after confirmation by phone that they were expected in Vice President Aprile's office, were escorted by two guards inside the building, across the vast main hall, and to the VP's suite of offices. They were ushered into one of the building's 566 rooms, a large, square chamber dominated by a huge teak conference table surrounded by twenty padded armchairs. The two men already there stood and introduced themselves. Mac and Annabel knew one of them, Lawrence Mayles, Washington's police commissioner. The other was MPD's Chief of Detectives Peter LaRocca. They'd no sooner taken seats when Joseph Aprile entered and took the chair left vacant for him at the head of the table. Fatigue was engraved on his face.

"I have a sense of what's happened, thanks to your phone call from Mexico, Mac. And I've been briefed on other aspects. Where do we stand?"

LaHoya spoke: "Mr. Vice President, as you know, your campaign manager, Chris Hedras, has allegedly been involved in a pattern of betrayal of you and others. We don't know the specifics of his actions, why he did it, who he was paid by, or the extent to which he participated in those actions. But evidence to be delivered to Mr. Smith by the Mexican guerrilla leader Carlos Unzaga was intercepted by Hedras. We know he went to Mexico City in the middle of the night, but have no information as to his current whereabouts. As far as we can ascertain, he didn't take a flight from either Mexico City or León."

"I can help with that," Aprile said.

He had their full attention.

"I received a call from Chris just a few minutes before you arrived."

"What did he say?" Mac asked.

"He said he was back from Mexico and that there had been a tragedy there involving this Unzaga. He said he needed some time off."

"Did he say why?" one of the CIA men asked.

"He said what happened in Mexico had taken a lot out of him, and that he had some personal things to attend to."

"Did he mention the evidence he took?" Mac asked.

"No, and I didn't say anything about the conversation you and I had last night, at your suggestion."

"Where was he calling from?" Detective LaRocca asked.

"He didn't say. I asked. He didn't answer."

Commissioner Mayles, a jowly man with a heavy beard line who'd risen through the ranks and was respected by the city's law enforcement professionals, said, "Mr. Vice President, it might be helpful if Chief LaRocca filled you in on MPD's investigation of the recent murders. Pete?"

LaRocca's unease at addressing the vice president was evident in his voice. After a false start and a clearing of his throat, he said, "Sir, two of our homicide detectives, Peterson and Jenkins, have been working the deaths of Morin Garza, Laura Flores, and the most recent, Ramon Kelly."

"And those deaths involve Chris Hedras?" Aprile asked, hoping it wasn't true.

"I'm afraid so, sir. What we've come up with . . . Let me backtrack. There's an organization in town called the Mexican-American Trade Alliance. They hosted the party that Ms. Flores attended the night she died. There's a young guy there named Jose Chapas who dated her. He was at the party but left early."

"And?" Aprile asked.

"Chapas spouted the party line when he was first questioned, but Peterson and Jenkins put on the pressure. According to Chapas, his employer does a lot more than lobby for Mexico. A unit of theirs functions as sort of a murder-for-hire team here in DC for somebody back in Mexico. Hedras, according to Chapas, funneled information to the group about people like Garza and Kelly. Ms. Flores, too. What they knew, where they'd be, what they intended to do. He knew all this stuff because he was so close with another group, The Mexico Initiative."

Aprile looked at Mac, then closed his eyes. His pain filled the room. When he opened them, he said, "Then this Chapas is a killer, a paid assassin."

"No, sir," LaRocca said. "We believe him when he says all he did was operate the communications center for the trade alliance. But he knew what was going on."

Mac Smith spoke: "Knowing now what Hedras's role was, Mr. Vice President, I'm certain he passed along details of my meeting with Carlos Unzaga. He was in a position to know everything. That act cost Unzaga his life, along with some of his followers'."

Aprile directed his next question to the commissioner. "Have you made an arrest in the murders?"

"No, sir, but we're close," Mayles replied. "This Mexican Trade Alliance was pretty good at establishing layers of detachment from the actual killers. Actually, there's one killer we've definitely identified, an American named Harry Tankowski. He worked under a contract with the Alliance. Chapas says he didn't know that Tankowski was a hired killer when Ms. Flores was thrown off the roof. He'd been told he was a consultant. But Chapas is willing to testify against Tankowski, against everyone in his organization."

"Where is Chapas?" Mac asked.

"We left him in place," LaRocca said. "Didn't want to scare anyone off until we were ready to move."

"Then he could be in danger," Annabel said.

"We intend to pull him out today, if that fits in with what everybody else is doing."

"And what about this Tankowski?" Mac asked. "Where is he?"

"In his apartment," LaRocca said. "We've had him and the south building under surveillance since Chapas told us about him."

"The south building in the Watergate?" Annabel said.

"Yes, ma'am. We're ready to go in and take him as soon as we get the word. If you say go, Mr. Vice President, we go."

Aprile said, "Mac, you look as though you have more to offer."

"I want to go back to the question asked earlier, Mr. Vice President, about where Chris Hedras might be. He said he was in Washington?"

"Right."

Smith stood. "The sooner we find Chris," he said, "the sooner we get that envelope back."

"We can put out an all-points on him," LaRocca said.

Joe Aprile said, "I had the impression from Chris that he intended to simply go on as usual, aside from wanting a few days

304

off. He didn't sound as though he was particularly upset or concerned. In fact, he said he'd drop by campaign headquarters either later today or tomorrow."

"A cool customer," Mayles said.

There were other descriptions of Hedras Mac was tempted to use, but he held his tongue.

It was agreed that the MPD would arrest Harry Tankowski, and pull Jose Chapas from the Mexican-American Trade Alliance and place him under protection.

"What about the others there?" a CIA agent asked.

"We'll need clarification on their legal status," LaHoya said.

"They're not diplomats," Aprile said. "There's no immunity."

"We'll have a legal ruling by morning," Commissioner Mayles said.

"And what about Hedras?" Mac asked.

"Let's not scare him off," Aprile said. "He didn't seem to be fully aware of what's going on."

"Can we secure the airports?" Mac asked. "He's liable to bolt."

"We'll take care of it," LaRocca said. "Buses and trains, too. And I suggest we station plainclothes officers at your campaign headquarters, Mr. Vice President, in case he does stop by."

"And his apartment," Mayles added. "Round-the-clock."

On the way out, Mac asked Commissioner Mayles what Hedras could be charged with.

"Conspiracy. Accomplice to murder."

"*If* he knew what his information was being used for," Smith said. He had his doubts.

"There's got to be money," LaRocca said, "unless he was doing it for love. Hell, there must be some federal statute against accepting payoffs from foreign governments."

"Where can we drop you?" LaHoya asked Mac and Annabel.

"Home," Annabel said. "This has been exhausting."

They pulled up in front of the south building, thanked La-Hoya and their driver, got out, and were about to enter when a commotion in the lobby stopped them.

"What's going on?" Annabel asked.

"I'll be damned," Mac muttered.

Harry Tankowski was led through the main entrance by four uniformed police, his hands secured behind him. He'd obviously been sleeping when the arrest was made. He wore a robe over pajamas; his yellow silken hair was a mess.

"That's the man who—"

Mac gripped Annabel's hand. "Yeah, that's the guy you shared your table with."

Tankowski and his police escort passed within a few feet. As they did, Tankowski smiled at them.

"When I think of how close to him we've been," Annabel said. "He's a—he was a neighbor."

"A killer, and with bad manners at that. He'll learn some manners in prison. Come on, let's get upstairs."

— — —

"I miss Rufus," Annabel said once they were back in the apartment.

"We'll pick him up in the morning. Drink?"

"Oh, yes. One of your perfect Perfect Manhattans would be, well, perfect."

"Coming up."

"I'll be on the terrace."

Mac had just put the ingredients into the glass half of the cocktail shaker and had begun to stir when the phone rang. He continued with one hand while answering with the other.

"Mac, it's Bernie Kirshbaum."

"How's my favorite dentist?"

"Good."

"I know, I'm due for a cleaning. I'll—"

"I wasn't calling about that. I thought you might know what's going on. Don says they arrested a serial killer in your building." The dental offices of Bernie Kirshbaum and Don Kruezer were in the Watergate complex.

"It's a long story, Bernie. I'll fill you in when I'm in your professional clutches. How's Mary?"

"Okay. You've been away. Vacation? Get some sun?"

Mac laughed. "There was heat. Save me a chair."

"It has your name on it. Make an appointment soon. They raised our rent again."

Mac carried the drinks to the terrace, where Annabel sat, feet propped on the railing, eyes closed.

"Your drink, madam."

She looked up, smiled, accepted the glass, and asked, "Who called?"

"Bernie Kirshbaum. He heard a rumor some serial killer had been arrested in the building. I told him he should stop using his own laughing gas."

"You didn't."

"No, I didn't." He offered the rim of his glass to hers.

"I am positively drained, Mac."

He sat next to her. "No surprise. But we're home now. Tomorrow we'll get the beast from the kennel, you'll go to the gallery, I'll don my academic robes, and everything will be back to normal. Mexico will be just a bad dream."

"Which makes me sad. I so wanted us to enjoy our few days in San Miguel. I had it all planned. It's such a shame that—"

"Is that the doorbell?"

"I didn't hear it."

"It is."

He started to get up, but she placed her hand on his arm. "I'll get rid of whoever it is."

A moment later, Annabel said, "Mac!" He immediately recognized strain in her voice, got up, and went to the foyer. Standing in the doorway was Chris Hedras.

"Hello, Mac," Hedras said, a self-conscious smirk on his lips. He was not the same self-confident, smug young achiever they were accustomed to seeing. There was bravado in his posture, but his eyes said something else. They were frightened eyes, in constant motion. A film of perspiration covered his forehead and upper lip. Although his suit, shirt, and tie were characteristically stylish, there was a wrinkled look to them; they were as wilted as the person wearing them.

"Hello, Chris," Mac said. "This is a surprise."

"Yeah, I should have called first, I suppose, but I was in the building, thought I'd take a chance. Invite me in?"

"Of course."

Mac and Annabel stepped back to allow him to enter.

Hedras laughed forcefully: "Is that humongous dog home?"

"No."

"Good. Hate to end up a meal."

He stepped inside and closed the door, looked around nervously.

"Well," Mac said, "how are you?"

"Okay. I, uh—"

"Come, sit down." They went to the living room. "A beer?"

"Sure. That'd be nice. Thanks. I could use something."

"Only be a minute."

Hedras sat on the couch. Annabel followed her husband into the kitchen.

"Domestic, if you have it," Hedras called after them. "I've had enough Mexican beer to last me for a while."

"Sure."

"What are we going to do?" Annabel whispered to Mac.

"Hear what he has to say."

"I'll go to another room. Call the—"

"You brewing it yourselves?" Hedras asked, appearing in the doorway.

Mac forced a laugh. "You took us by surprise, Chris. Annabel was just leaving."

"Oh? Why don't you stay awhile? I won't be long."

As Mac popped open a bottle of Sierra Nevada Pale Ale, he glanced at Hedras, who stood leaning against the doorjamb, one hand in his suit jacket pocket. Did he have a gun?

"I don't have to leave right away," Annabel said. Mac knew she was as apprehensive as he was but didn't want to leave him alone. He wished she felt otherwise. He reached in the fridge again and opened a second bottle, handed it to Hedras.

"Muchas gracias," Hedras said, taking a desperate swallow from the bottle. He followed Mac and Annabel back to the living room, where, once seated again, they observed him. Their unstated consensus was that he was on some drug. Mac raised his beer: *"Salud!"*

"Yeah. *Salud.*" He finished the bottle.

"So, what brings you here, Chris?" Annabel asked.

"I just wanted to apologize for the mix-up in Mexico. I had to leave on the spur of the moment—problems back here—and didn't have a chance to say good-bye to the two of you."

"No apologies needed," Mac said.

"When did you get back?" Annabel asked.

"Today. I just heard about what happened to Unzaga—and you, of course. God, that must have been frightening."

"Yes, it was."

"You know, Mac, there's bound to be some confusion about what happened in San Miguel. I thought you and I might go over it before I give my report to Straight Arrow." He laughed. "I love that nickname. Sure fits him."

"Another beer?"

"Okay."

With Mac in the kitchen, Hedras said to Annabel, "I sure was relieved to see Mac in one piece. That was nothing short of a massacre in San Miguel, an absolute massacre. I talked to Elfie. She's in shock. The whole town's in shock."

"I imagine it would be."

Mac returned, handed Hedras the fresh bottle.

"I'm anxious to hear what happened after the shoot-out," Hedras said. "I've just gotten it in dribs and drabs."

"It was chaotic," Mac said. "Unzaga had said he was having an envelope of evidence delivered to me at the hotel. I never got it."

"Really? What a shame. Any idea what happened?"

"Someone else picked it up before we got there."

Hedras drank. "Who?" he asked.

"It might have been you, Chris."

"Me?" He shook his head and laughed. "I don't know about any envelope. Evidence? Of what?"

"Some of the things Unzaga told me before he died. Actually, the envelope probably isn't that important. With what Unzaga said, coupled with independent corroboration here in Washington, the case can still be made against factions within the PRI."

"That's good to hear. An envelope? Why would you think I took it?"

"Based on the description provided by the night manager."

"He must have had too much tequila. I was so relieved to hear you escaped the assassination. I love Mexico, Mac, but it's such a violent country."

"Especially when people know where certain individuals will be."

"Sure." He paused. "What people?"

"Unzaga, for one. Those troops knew precisely where he would be, and when."

"Hard to keep those things secret. Men like Unzaga make a lot of enemies."

"The same could be said for Ramon Kelly, Laura Flores, and Morin Garza."

Hedras's eyes darted from Mac to Annabel, and he shifted position. He finished the beer and forced casualness into his voice: "Have you talked to the veep since you got back?"

"Yes. He said you'd called him. Taking a couple of days' vacation?"

"I really need it."

"Another beer, Chris?" Annabel asked.

"I've had enough."

"You were saying you needed a vacation."

"Maybe something longer than that. I never thought getting involved with Joe Aprile would end up like this. He's got this hard-nosed view of Mexico and wants to change things. He had me set up The Mexico Initiative to get him information. I did it, and what happens? Some trigger-happy bastards start killing anybody connected with it. I'm lucky I didn't get shot, too. Politics has gotten nasty, Mac, too nasty for my blood. You try to do the right thing and you end up having fingers pointed at you."

"The killing will stop now," Mac said.

"I hope so."

Mac and Annabel were thinking the same thing, that Hedras obviously thought he could bluff his way, tough it out, play the denial game.

The thinking of a sociopath, Annabel thought.

"Is someone pointing a finger at *you*, Chris?" Annabel asked.

"Not yet, but it wouldn't surprise me. You know how it is. There's always got to be a fall guy, especially in this town, with these people." He leaned back into the couch's cushions and exhaled long and loud. "I think I might pack it in. I've had a good run, all the excitement anybody my age could want. I've made a lot of contacts. Maybe it's time to call in the chips, get out of the rat race, smell those roses people are always talking about."

"Contacts?" Mac asked. "In Mexico?"

"Sure. Back in Boston, too, although Mexico appeals to me. I guess you never got to see much of San Miguel. It's a great place. I like it. You can live like a king for peanuts. Or, relative peanuts."

Smith's mind was racing. What did Hedras expect to happen as a result of his unannounced visit, that he'd be believed, that by simply denying involvement it would go away? He mentally summed up his options. Let it play out until Hedras decided to leave? Or press the issue to draw additional information from him? He took the latter route.

"Chris, Carlos Unzaga didn't trust you."

"What?"

"He didn't trust you. He told me you knew what damaging information each person who's been murdered carried with them, and where they'd be when they were killed."

"That's crazy."

"I don't think it is, Chris. And I *know* it was you who took the envelope with the evidence."

"I don't believe what I'm hearing from you, Mac."

"I know that you were the one providing information to the Mexican-American Trade Alliance. Were you paid big money, Chris, enough to justify seeing those people killed?"

"Wait a minute," Hedras said, getting to his feet. "I came here because I thought we were friends, working on the same team. I set everything up for you in Mexico—"

"And made sure Unzaga's enemies knew about it."

Mac, too, stood and braced for what might happen next. Hedras looked ready to physically lash out. Instead, he walked to the open doors to the terrace and stepped outside. Mac gestured for Annabel to leave. She shook her head. Mac went to the terrace. Annabel moved to the doors but stayed just inside.

Hedras was at the railing, hands grasping it, breathing heavily.

"It's a nice view, isn't it?" Mac said, coming to Hedras's side and looking down at the river.

"Yeah. Peaceful."

"Want to tell me about it, Chris?"

"About what?"

"Your sellout of Joe Aprile and The Mexico Initiative."

Hedras turned and faced him. He spoke rapidly. "Sellout? You aren't as savvy as I thought you were. Joe Aprile is wrong where Mexico is concerned. The PRI has kept that country on an even keel for over seventy years. Business is booming. Mexicans are working in record numbers in the plants along the border. If Joe Aprile becomes president and changes that, he'll set back U.S.-Mexico relations a hundred years."

"Or set you back? You signed on to his campaign to make sure he *didn't* become president."

"Wrong. To make sure he woke up about Mexico. I think Joe Aprile is a great guy, would make a terrific president. But—"

Smith watched as Hedras slowly sat in a chair that was behind him, his hands gripping the metal arms like an old man unsure of where his body was headed. It was as though the young presidential aide was folding into himself, a deflating rubber pool float. Mac was conflicted; anger and pity vied for position.

"Are you telling me, Chris, that everything you did came out of idealism? No money involved?"

Hedras responded without meeting Mac's eyes. "That's exactly what I'm telling you," he said. "But evidently you're no better than the rest of the bloodsuckers in Washington." Now he looked up. His words carried with them the same plea for understanding—for believing—as the beseeching expression on his face. "Look," he said, "I came to you because I trust you. You aren't part of the political mafia. You know what happened in San Miguel. Unzaga was a hunted man and they caught up with him. That's all it was. Thank God you weren't killed, too. But I didn't have anything to do with it. You've got to believe me, Mac. You can tell Straight Arrow what *really* happened."

"If I do that, Chris—and I will—you're through. You may not have pulled any triggers, pushed anyone off a roof, but you're as responsible for the deaths of Laura Flores, Morin Garza, Ramon Kelly, and Carlos Unzaga as those who did. I don't know how much money you've been paid, or who paid it to you, but your pathetic claim that you acted out of some warped sense of idealism is garbage. My dog would see through it."

Smith waited for a response. It came when Hedras pushed himself to his feet, looked out over the Potomac and the land beyond, turned to Mac and said, "If I had known how you feel, I wouldn't have bothered coming here. But you do know, Mac, that everything you're accusing me of is just speculation. If you tell it to others, including Straight Arrow, they'll laugh at you. You're a nobody, just a broken-down law professor. I work with the president and the VP. I know one thing. Joe Aprile sure screwed up when he decided to bring you in."

"Do you know Harry Tankowski?" Mac asked, keeping his voice calm.

"Never heard of him."

"The police are looking for you, Chris."

Hedras crossed the living room and stood at the door. Mac and Annabel followed. Hedras took a moment to perform what Mac considered the odd act of checking himself in a mirror and touching his hair with his fingertips. Then, he said, "Are they? I'll make it easy for them, drop by the MPD. I have nothing to hide so I have nothing to fear."

"Why don't you wait here for them? I'll call. You can have another beer and relax. You look as though you could use it."

Confusion spread over Hedras's face. He looked from Mac to

Annabel and back again. He started to speak, swallowed, looked at the floor, then up at Mac: "Won't you help me, Mac?"

"Call the police," Mac told Annabel.

Hedras straightened, glared at Smith, opened the door and was gone.

Once Annabel had notified the police that Hedras had been there, Mac placed a call to the vice president, who returned the call ten minutes later. Mac started to tell him of what had transpired but Aprile interrupted. "I've just been notified that the police have Chris in custody."

"Fast work," Mac said.

"He was taken coming out of a garage under the Watergate."

"He denied any involvement in the murders, Mr. Vice President. Not very effective in his denials. He's a sick young man."

"I wish I'd known that before I lobbied so damn hard to bring him over from the White House. You and Annabel all right?"

"Shaken, but otherwise okay."

"You know how much I appreciate what you two have gone through on my behalf, Mac."

"Of course I do. It turned out fine for us, but a tragedy for those people who died in the process."

"Fortunately, the names of Mr. and Mrs. Mackensie Smith weren't added to the list. I'll be in touch."

"Yes, sir."

"If arrogance is the worst sin," Annabel said after Mac hung up, "Chris Hedras has a one-way ticket to hell."

"Or to Mexico. There's no proof he did anything, Annie, except tell people at the Mexican-American Trade Alliance things about what others knew, in some cases where they'd be at a given time."

"That's conspiracy. And accessory."

"Not if he didn't know what use the information would be

315

put to. I know this. If I were still practicing criminal law and had him as a client, he'd walk."

"But he's through here in Washington."

"Sure, but I somehow doubt whether that will bother him much. He's right. He can go to San Miguel de Allende and live like a king, whether he received big payoffs or not. Maybe he can move into Elfie's house, add to the gardening staff."

"There's got to be *some* justice, Mac."

"Having him out of Joe Aprile's life and campaign will have to be enough."

Annabel suddenly wrapped her arms around him.

"What's this all about?" he asked.

"I almost lost you in Mexico, Mac. You could have been gunned down like Unzaga."

"I wasn't."

"But you came close to catching one, as the police say. Getting involved in politics isn't for us, Mac. You're a professor. I run an art gallery. Let's make a pledge right here and now to keep it that way."

CHAPTER 39

Two Months Later

San Miguel de Allende

Elfie Dorrance sat on the terrace of her home overlooking Parque Benito Juárez. The day had dawned unusually hot. She'd discarded her robe and wore red Chinese silk pajamas and white slippers. It was ten o'clock. Her housekeeper had served a cinnamon bun, fresh-squeezed orange juice, and strong black coffee.

A portion of the past month had been spent learning the basics of a computer system she'd had installed in her study. She found computers to be boorishly plebeian, but had decided it would be to her advantage to receive timely news over the Internet when in Mexico. She'd downloaded the major stories from *The Washington Post's* website that morning and was engrossed in reading them when the housekeeper forced a cough from a distance so as not to disturb her mistress. Elfie turned.

"Senora, Senor Hedras is here."

Elfie glanced at her watch. He wasn't due until one. "Show him up," she said.

Hedras stepped through the French doors. He wore white slacks, white loafers, and a short-sleeved yellow sport shirt. Elfie said nothing.

"Hello," Hedras said.

"Hello, Christopher. You're early."

"I caught an earlier flight out of León." When she didn't respond, he asked, "Aren't you going to ask me to join you? I haven't had breakfast. I'm hungry."

Elfie smiled. "Skipping breakfast isn't healthy. Surely your mother taught you that."

Hedras came to where she sat and stood over her. "Why are you treating me like a pariah? I expected it of the phonies back in DC, but not from you."

"I'm doing nothing of the sort, Chris. But you do understand that it's awkward to have you here."

"Why?" He pulled up a chair.

"Why?" It was a throaty laugh. "You are hardly someone a person of stature would be comfortable being with."

"Is that so? I'm now sitting with 'a person of stature'?"

"Have I offended you? Sorry. But your antics haven't landed you on anyone's A-list. You created quite a stir once they arrested you in Washington. I've been reading about it on the Internet."

"The Internet? You?"

"I've become computer-literate. But that doesn't matter. I would say you are an extremely fortunate young man."

"The past two months were hell."

"I imagine so. Chris, when you called and said you were coming to San Miguel—to live, you say?—I naturally had some soul-searching to do. You are aware that I enjoy a certain privileged position here, and elsewhere."

"Money talks."

"How typical of your age—and mentality. Say something nasty but not terribly original. You might have tried 'Your mother wears army boots.' "

"You know, Elfie, I didn't come here to be insulted. I've suffered enough insults. They accused me of damn near everything back in Washington, but they couldn't prove a thing. They had their fun, one leak after the other to the press, convicting me in the media when they couldn't do it legally."

"Which is not to say you weren't guilty. What did you do, cut a deal with someone?"

"Didn't have to. They were glad to get rid of me. Embarrassing to the political process, I was told. A stain on Straight Arrow's unblemished record. Truth was, there was nothing to charge me with. Conspiracy? Complicity? That bastard Smith worked behind the scenes to help make a case against me but he fell on his face. They got me out of town like in the Old West. On a rail, nonstop to Mexico. Straight to you, Elfie."

"Chris, I'm not in the business of bursting anyone's bubble, but I think it's time for a little candor. There's no place here for you. The little adventure you and I undertook to help the vice president modify his views on Mexico was one thing—setting up photos with some of the country's less savory people, encouraging those moments with Viviana Diaz and capturing their adoring looks at each other; she claims she never did sleep with Joe Aprile, not that that matters, but I suspect she did; I mean, if he didn't succumb to *her,* we'll end up with a eunuch in the White House—all of that was nothing more than pragmatic political hardball. But to be party to those murders, Chris. Now that was—"

He grabbed her upper arm and squeezed hard.

"Get your hands off me!"

He withdrew, sat back, and looked up into the pristine blue sky as though searching for words.

Now it was she who touched him, gently, her hand on his forearm. "I understand, Chris, I really do. The Initiative was coming up with so much that could help derail things here. Passing along what you knew about its activities was perfectly natural and normal. As you said in your many statements, you had no idea what use your information would be put to. How could you? I mean, even Laura Flores. She was on to you, wasn't she? At least that's what I hear."

"I never wanted to see anyone hurt," he said absently.

"Of course you didn't. But things turned out badly for you. That, my young friend, is the harsh reality."

He stood, went to the stone wall, and peered into the distance. When he turned to face her, he was smiling. "That's all behind me now, Elfie. Old news."

"But big news. Your picture on page one for days, alongside Mac Smith. The American press seldom makes much of the killing of some Mexican rebel leader, but when a respected law professor is almost gunned down with him, that *is* big news. *Very* big news. And there you were enjoying your sixty days of fame."

"Get to the point, Elfie."

She went to him, looked into his eyes, and kissed him on the cheek. The top button of her pajamas was undone, revealing the curve of her breasts. "The point is, Mr. Christopher Hedras, that while I am famous—you'll pardon my lack of modesty—you are infamous, and they do not blend easily together. I don't think you'd enjoy living here in San Miguel. In fact, I suggest you scrap that plan. There are other places in Mexico where you'll be able to live comfortably with whatever money you have. But not here. *Do we understand each other?*"

"You bitch!"

"Careful."

"Who the hell do you think you are? I don't need you. You latched on to me because I was close to Joe Aprile. You don't give a damn whether people died. You're probably happy they did if it helped your friends in the PRI. And you're going to treat me like I'm some lowlife, some scum to be washed out of your precious life? No, I don't need you, lady. I've been used enough by too many people and you top the list. As for money, I have plenty. If I want to live here in San Miguel, I'll do it. Maybe your adoring public would enjoy daily anecdotes over coffee about how you plotted to compromise the vice president of the United States. Should make for interesting discussion when you take your shot at ambassador."

"I've always enjoyed that about you, Christopher, your immature view of things. I *will* be ambassador to Mexico."

"You enjoyed my mature performance in bed."

"I've had better."

She returned to the table, the thin fabric of her pajama bottoms failing to conceal her body's supple movements. She pressed a button on the table. The housekeeper appeared.

"Mr. Hedras is leaving," Elfie said. "Please show him out."

He started to leave, paused at the doors, turned and said, "I've had better, too, Elfie. And younger. You're getting old and ugly. *That's* reality. Happy to have been of service."

— — —

Hedras had kept his taxi waiting. It was loaded with luggage he'd brought with him from Washington. He'd hoped to stay with Elfie for a while, until he found a suitable house. But that was no longer in the cards.

The money Oswaldo Flores had given him was deposited in a Mexico City bank, wired there from El Paso before he flew to Washington. Actually, the envelope had contained only seven hundred and thirty thousand dollars. You couldn't trust anybody.

Before flying from Mexico City to León that morning, Hedras had called Flores from the airport. He was direct; he wanted the second million. To his surprise, Flores was pleasant and accommodating. The money would be delivered to him the next day in San Miguel.

"No need for that," Hedras had said. "I can come to your house and get it, catch a later flight."

"I don't think that would be wise," Flores had said. "Things are tense here. My people in San Miguel will be happy to deliver it to you there." He gave Hedras details of where and when he would meet with his surrogate.

That night, Hedras stayed in a suite at the Santa Monica Hotel, at Baeza 22, on the eastern side of the park, a restored eighteenth-century Spanish hacienda. He drank margaritas in the outdoor restaurant to the point of drunkenness, fell asleep in his Jacuzzi, and collapsed into bed, wet.

The next day, after a large, late breakfast, he walked to San Miguel's bullfighting ring on Recreo, where he stood on the sidewalk by its main gates until an older-model green Mercedes pulled up.

"Hedras?" the man in the passenger seat said. He was middle-aged, smooth-faced, and nicely dressed in a suit and tie.

"Sí."

"Come. Get in."

Hedras approached the car. "You have the money?"

"Sí, sí. I am Senor Flores's representative in San Miguel. Por Televisa. Get in. We go get the money now. Flores told me to take you to it."

"Okay." Hedras got in the backseat and closed the door. The driver, younger than the other man, wore a large cowboy hat. He didn't turn to acknowledge Hedras, his only contact his eyes in the rearview mirror. He pulled away, the vehicle's weakened springs causing it to buck on the uneven cobblestones. They headed out of town, in the direction of the main road leading to

León. After driving for fifteen minutes, they turned off onto a narrow dirt road that twisted its way up into low-lying hills. Soon, after negotiating a particularly sharp turn, a small house with a narrow porch came into view.

"Is the money there?" Hedras asked.

"*Sí.*"

They came to a dusty stop in front of the house. The two men in the front seats got out and waited for Hedras to do the same. But he remained in the car. He'd had initial reservations about getting into the Mercedes. Now he was gripped with blinding, agonizing fear.

"Hey, Hedras, come on."

"Get out, amigo."

The men were smiling.

Hedras ordered himself to calm down. Maybe there was nothing to fear. In all probability the money was inside the house. Flores hadn't balked at the first payment, although Chris had been short-changed. Don't show them your fear.

He opened the door and got out. One of the Mexicans motioned for him to follow them inside. The house consisted of one large room with a Pullman kitchen at one end. A single interior door stood open, revealing a bathroom. Hedras had an urge to relieve himself and knew he'd have to before getting in the car for the return to San Miguel. He started for the bathroom but stopped. Get the money first.

"Well?" Hedras said. "The money. *Dinero, por favor.*"

"*Sí.*"

The well-dressed man opened a cabinet in the kitchen area and removed a large, grease-stained gray canvas bag. Relief surged through Hedras's body like a powerful chemotherapy drug. He smiled as he accepted the bag from the man.

"*Un momento,*" Hedras said. "*El retrete.*" He pointed to the bathroom and went to it, closing the door behind him. There wasn't a window; the room was dark. A gap in the wall allowed a sliver of daylight to penetrate the gloom. His urge to relieve himself had passed. He held the bag up to the light and undid the leather strap that secured its top. He reached inside and pulled out some of its paper contents, squinted to see it. It can't be, he thought. "No!" he said aloud. "Damn it, no!" He held a wad of plain paper cut the size of American paper money.

The fear was back, even worse this time. What could he do? Surely, they were waiting for him right outside the door. There was no escape. No window. Could he break through the wall? Impossible. Maybe he could talk his way out of it, offer them money. There was seven hundred and thirty thousand in the bank. How much should he offer? A thousand would be a fortune to them. He'd offer ten thousand. How do you say that in Spanish? *Diez mil? Dinero americano.* They'd listen, he told himself. If they were going to kill him, they would have done it already. Why the bag filled with phony money? A joke? That had to be it.

He pressed his ear to the door, heard nothing. He said, "Hey, amigos." Nothing.

He slowly opened the door. The large room was empty. The door to the outside was open. Good, he thought. At least I have some room to maneuver. It occurred to him that the men might have driven away, leaving him there holding the joke in his hand. That bastard Flores. He never intended to pay the second million. This was his warped way of delivering that message.

Hedras drew a series of deep breaths. The hell with the money. Seven hundred and thirty thousand dollars was more than he'd ever need to live well in Mexico. He'd use it to start a business, invest in something. He actually smiled.

He approached the front door one careful step at a time, stopping once to look through a dirt-crusted window. He didn't see the Mercedes but knew it hadn't been parked to the side of the house. He moved slightly to his left to afford a wider view of the porch. No car in sight.

More deep breaths before continuing to the door. All was silent. Outside, a breeze kicked up red dust where the car had been.

He stepped out onto the porch, feeling good. His focus now was on how to get back to town. It happened in less than a second. The taller, younger man who'd driven the car had been waiting just outside the door. His movements were swift and sure. The thin wire with wooden handles at either end came over Hedras's head and was tightened against his throat, drawing blood. The sack dropped to the porch floor, followed by Hedras, who came down hard on his knees. A sickening gurgle came from his mouth as the second man pulled his legs out straight. He was carried to a rusted oil drum cut in half to form a cistern. The younger man released one end of the wire. Hedras was dumped into the cistern, face up, eyes wide and bulging, a thin necklace of blood decorating his neck.

He tried to speak. He raised one hand in a gesture of pleading. When he saw the man in the suit reach his hand over the side of the cistern, and saw the revolver in it, he managed to say, "Please don't," accompanied by a burst of tears.

The bullet entered between his eyes. Death was instantaneous. Blood ran freely down his face, and a dark, warm, wet stain burst through the crotch of his white slacks.

The killer in the suit picked up the canvas bag from the porch while his accomplice pulled Hedras's wallet from his pocket. They closed the front door to the house and went to the Mercedes, which they'd moved while Hedras was in the bathroom. They nodded at each other, drove away, and enjoyed bottles of beer on their way back to San Miguel, laughing at having heightened their victim's anguish by including the canvas bag in the murder scheme. It was, they agreed, a good joke on the gringo.

— — —

After receiving a call from San Miguel that afternoon, Oswaldo Flores dialed a number in Mexico City and was immediately put through to Central Bank president, Antonio Morelos. After exchanging preliminary small talk, Flores said, "The depositor I mentioned to you two months ago has died today in San Miguel de Allende. Tragic."

"I am sorry to hear that, Oswaldo."

"I deliver this sad news because of the account he had opened with Banco Nacional de Mexico, the account you placed a hold on."

"*Sí.*"

"Had he ever attempted to withdraw from that account?"

"I am told he did not. As was agreed, he would be allowed to take as much as fifty thousand dollars from it, no more. But he evidently took nothing, according to the records provided me."

"*Bueno.* Those funds will be transferred as scheduled?"

"Not an official donation, of course, but into the general campaign fund."

"Exactly. As always, good to speak with you, Antonio. We must have dinner soon."

CHAPTER 40

That Same Week
The South Building–the Watergate

Mac and Annabel divided their attention between CNN and packing. They'd decided to take a long weekend away from Washington—destination, The Castle in Mount Savage, Maryland, a Scottish-style citadel on top of Mount Savage, whose previous incarnations had been as a casino and a brothel.

They took a break from packing, sat on the edge of the bed, and focused on their bedroom television. A Joe Aprile press conference was about to be joined in-progress. On the bed between Mac and Annabel was that day's *Washington Post*. The story of the murder in Mexico of former presidential deputy chief of staff and campaign manager for Vice President Joseph Aprile, Christopher Hedras, was front page, below the fold.

Aprile's press conference was being held in Detroit, coming on the heels of a political swing through the Midwest. Reporters had run the string on their questions about his political plans, and now turned to the subject of Mexico, and the death of Christopher Hedras.

"Mr. Vice President, what's your reaction to the news that your former top aide, Christopher Hedras, has been killed in Mexico?"

Aprile didn't hesitate: "I was sorry to hear of it, and my sympathy goes out to his family."

The reporter followed up: "But Hedras's role in your campaign was, to be kind, controversial. Although he was never convicted of anything, he was accused of deliberately attempting to sabotage you, especially involving Mexico."

"I'm aware of all the charges leveled at Chris Hedras, but those charges were never proved. After being subjected to our legal process, it was determined he'd not broken any laws. As for rumors that he'd tried to injure me in some way, I find that hard to believe."

Another reporter: "But he was linked to The Mexican Initiative, which he claimed was formed at your behest. Its director and head of research were murdered, and arrests have been made, including individuals from a Washington-based Mexican lobbying group."

"I was aware of the Initiative's work. However, as I've stated on numerous occasions, it was an independent, private agency with its own agenda. It would be inappropriate for me to comment further on an ongoing criminal investigation."

Question: "It's obvious that the rift between you and the president over policy toward Mexico is growing wider. Have you and he had any recent substantive discussions about it?"

Aprile smiled, shook his head. "There is no rift between the president and me concerning Mexico. Naturally, we have certain differing views on the subject. We differ on many things. But the recent elections, and widespread reforms promised by Mexico's leadership, is all positive. Excuse me. Thanks for coming. Good to see all of you."

"Just one more question," a reporter yelled as Aprile started to leave the podium. "Congressman Curtain's committee is a week away from holding its hearings into alleged illegal contributions to your previous campaigns. Curtain says he has proof of contributions from Mexican interests attempting to influence our policies toward Mexico."

Aprile leaned back to the microphone: "Congressman Curtain will hold his hearings, at great expense, and will find that the letter of campaign finance law was never violated. Have to run." Questions trailed behind him as he left.

Mac turned off the TV.

"Chris Hedras may be dead, but his shadow will follow Joe throughout the campaign, probably for the rest of his life," Annabel said, refolding a favorite sweater a third time.

"Unfortunate, but true. Have you seen my gold cuff links?"

"Top left drawer."

"The press can be so cruel," Annabel said. "Was there really any need to rehash Chris's former troubles, that he was accused of rape in high school? And that reporter from Boston claiming Chris had been a drug user? Good Lord, Mac, you'd think that when you die, all that trash should be buried with you."

"When you die," Mac said, "what your life has been follows you. You *earn* any praise you get in your obit, along with a reminder of the less sterling aspects of your life."

"Even if you've never been convicted of anything."

"Sure. With Hedras, prosecutors felt they couldn't make a case for accomplice to murder, or conspiracy, based upon what they had. Chapas from the trade alliance didn't have any direct evidence that Chris knew what they were doing with his information. Anyone else who could have testified against him was either dead or in Mexico. Besides, there's the smell of a political deal having been cut."

"Has Joe told you that?" Annabel asked.

"He's hinted at it. What I get from him, and Herman Winkler, and others, is that to put Hedras through a drawn-out and highly public trial could only hurt Joe's chances for the nomination. Get rid of him, quietly, seems to have been the operative solution. Of course, his murder will put him back in the news for a while."

"The Mexican police say it was a random killing, probably robbery. His wallet was missing."

"And Saddam Hussein is a nice guy. Chris Hedras was killed, Annie, because of who he was. No, correct that. *What* he was. He was programmed to become part of the Establishment, feed off it, suck it dry, and then laugh in its face. Add a healthy dose of greed, runaway ambition, immorality, and callousness, and you have someone ripe for a fall. I'm not pleased he was killed, but I'm not feeling any true sorrow, either. Finished with your suitcase?"

"No."

Annabel took another stab at folding the sweater to her liking. "Has Joe also hinted, as you put it, at how Chris was able to set up so many damaging photos of him in Mexico? Multimillionaire drug-money launderers. Government officials on the take—"

"Viviana Diaz," Mac added. "I wonder what she's being paid to claim she slept with Joe."

"Carole was happy when I recounted for her your meeting with Diaz and Zegreda, although I don't think she ever really distrusted Joe."

"How were so many photos with bad guys set up? Simple, I

suppose. Joe trusted Chris implicitly. So did I. Elfie paved the way with her contacts in Mexico."

"Do you think—?"

"That Elfie knew what Chris was up to and deliberately chose photo situations to compromise Joe? I choose not to think that. Everybody trusted the charming Mr. Hedras. Someone in Joe's position has to believe in the people he has around him. He can't question every person he's asked to pose with, any more than he can personally check the validity of every campaign contribution. What harm could come from some harmless photo ops? Besides, in Mexico, one never knows what lurks behind the masks people wear."

"So I've heard."

"At least the Mexican-American Trade Alliance is out of business," Mac continued. "The revelations of that young man Jose Chapas make quite a case against his boss and others. But whether it ever comes to trial is another matter. The Mexican government is raising hell over their detention."

"Finished." Annabel closed and latched her suitcase.

"Sure your sweater is folded properly?"

"Quite sure, thank you."

The intercom sounded. The lobby clerk announced that the young art student who worked part-time for Annabel at the gallery had arrived. "Send her up," Annabel said. The young student had eagerly agreed to stay in the apartment for the long weekend to avoid them having to put Rufus in the kennel again. Annabel had no sooner hung up when the phone rang. Mac answered.

"Mac, darling, it's Elfie."

"Hello, Elfie. How are you?"

"Good, although the dreadful news of Chris's murder certainly dampens one's spirits."

"Are you calling from San Miguel?"

"No. I left as soon as I heard about Chris. I'm back in Washington."

"And we're just leaving for a long weekend away from here."

"Good for you. I won't keep you, Mac. I'm calling to see whether you'd be willing to co-chair a fund-raiser for Joe next month. We're holding it in the Watergate again now that the murder rate there seems to have slowed down."

"Thanks for the offer, Elfie, but I have to pass. A very busy schedule the next few months."

"How about Annabel?"

"Up to her pretty neck."

"Oh, well, another time. Have you spoken with Joe lately?"

"Yes."

"The rumor in Mexico is that Cadwell might resign as ambassador."

"Really? I haven't heard that."

"If that happens, I've been told President Scott has me on the list of possible replacements."

"You must be pleased, Elfie."

"Just asking what I can do for my country rather than what it can do for me. What a memorable line from JFK."

"It certainly was. I have to cut this short, Elfie. Good hearing from you."

"By all means. Whisk that gorgeous wife of yours away to some secluded, romantic place."

"My intention exactly. Take care, Elfie. Good hearing from you."

— — —

Later that night, Mac and Annabel sipped cognac on the porch of their getaway weekend cottage.

"Every time I think of that hired killer living in the same

building as us, I shudder," Annabel said, rubbing Mac's leg with her bare foot.

"The only neighbors he'll have for the rest of his life are fellow cons. When Chris Hedras was at the apartment laying out the plans for meeting Unzaga, I actually thought that if I had a daughter, he'd make a good son-in-law. Some judge of character, huh?"

"He fooled a lot of people for a long time, Mac. Do you think Elfie ever will become ambassador to Mexico?"

"Sure. Ambassadors aren't chosen for their diplomatic skills. They get those jobs as rewards for loyalty."

"And generosity to a party."

"That, too. Know what I've been thinking, Annie?"

"What?"

"That I'd like to go back to San Miguel de Allende one day and enjoy it the way you said I would. Obviously, I didn't— enjoy it."

"I wonder why. I'd like that, too. Shall I call Susan and book it?"

"Sure." He took her hand. "Happy we sold the house and moved to the Watergate?"

"Yes. You?"

"Uh-huh. Nice rubbing shoulders with Washington's rich and famous."

"And infamous."

"That, too."

"Ready for bed?" Mac asked.

"Just as long as you're there with me."

ABOUT THE AUTHOR

MARGARET TRUMAN is the author of over a dozen bestselling novels of life and death amid Washington's monuments, institutions, and swirling social circles. She has also written two bestselling biographies—one of her father, the former president, and one of her mother—and a nonfiction exploration of first ladies. She lives in New York City with her husband, former *New York Times* editor Clifton Daniel.

ABOUT THE TYPE

This book was set in Bembo, a typeface based on an old-style Roman face that was used for Cardinal Bembo's tract *De Aetna* in 1495. Bembo was cut by Francisco Griffo in the early sixteenth century. The Lanston Monotype Machine Company of Philadelphia brought the well-proportioned letterforms of Bembo to the United States in the 1930s.